"Come here, Joy."

His tone indicated that his thoughts were elsewhere.

"Have you heard a word I've said?" she asked.

"Come. Here."

She heard him pat the sofa cushion next to him.

"Brad..." She allowed herself to feel how exhausted she really was.

"I'm not going to kiss you. Promise."

Why not?

She took two short steps and lowered herself onto the sofa. Brad reached for her waist and pulled her down beside him.

She could feel the heat of his body through the thickness of her terry robe. He might not want to kiss her but *she* wanted to kiss *him*. Badly.

"Lean your head against me." He wrapped his arm around her, and she put her head on his shoulder. After a few minutes she realized he was serious—this wasn't going to be a lovemaking session.

"Brad? What exactly is this about?"

Dear Reader,

First, a big thank-you for purchasing this book, the next Whidbey Island title. The success of this series is all due to your incredible support and encouragement.

Ever since Joy Alexander was briefly introduced in *Navy Christmas*, I knew she had to have her own story. Joy is a former navy JAG who picked Whidbey Island as the place to settle and begin her civilian career as an attorney after a decade in the navy. Her plans for a quiet retreat into the community are overturned when a former work colleague, Brad Iverson, shows up at her kitchen door the same morning she's starting her new job. Brad quickly becomes a big part of her life, just as he did when they worked together on a case to free a Guantánamo Bay prisoner who was wrongly accused of terrorist activity.

I like to explore how heroes and heroines react under different circumstances. For instance, Joy and Brad first met when she was an officer and he was enlisted; anything but a professional relationship wasn't allowed. When *Navy Justice* opens, they're both civilians. Nothing is keeping them from a relationship—except their inner conflicts. And, of course, a bad guy or two!

This has been the most challenging book to write in the Whidbey Island series so far, but also the most rewarding as Joy and Brad have to dig deep to find the right answers for themselves and the possibility of a life together.

For the latest on the Whidbey Island series, and my new series for Harlequin Romantic Suspense, Silver Valley PD, please sign up for my newsletter at www.gerikrotow.com. I'm also on Facebook, Twitter and Pinterest, and I blog regularly at the Harlequin Superromance authors' site, www.superauthors.com. I hope to hear from you soon!

Peace,

Geri Krotow

GERI
KROTOW

—

Navy Justice

HARLEQUIN®SUPERROMANCE®

Recycling programs
for this product may
not exist in your area.

ISBN-13: 978-0-373-60924-6

Navy Justice

Copyright © 2015 by Geri Krotow

All rights reserved. Except for use in any review, the reproduction or
utilization of this work in whole or in part in any form by any electronic,
mechanical or other means, now known or hereinafter invented, including
xerography, photocopying and recording, or in any information storage
or retrieval system, is forbidden without the written permission of the
publisher, Harlequin Enterprises Limited, 225 Duncan Mill Road,
Don Mills, Ontario M3B 3K9, Canada.

This is a work of fiction. Names, characters, places and incidents are
either the product of the author's imagination or are used fictitiously,
and any resemblance to actual persons, living or dead, business
establishments, events or locales is entirely coincidental.

This edition published by arrangement with Harlequin Books S.A.

For questions and comments about the quality of this book,
please contact us at CustomerService@Harlequin.com.

® and TM are trademarks of Harlequin Enterprises Limited or its
corporate affiliates. Trademarks indicated with ® are registered in the
United States Patent and Trademark Office, the Canadian Intellectual
Property Office and in other countries.

Printed in U.S.A.

Former naval intelligence officer and US Naval Academy graduate **Geri Krotow** draws inspiration from the global situations she's experienced. Geri loves to hear from her readers. You can email her via her website and blog, www.gerikrotow.com.

Books by Geri Krotow

HARLEQUIN SUPERROMANCE

HARLEQUIN ANTHOLOGY

HARLEQUIN EVERLASTING LOVE

*Whidbey Island books

Other titles by this author available in ebook format.

For Margaret Mitchell,
the best aunt a girl could hope for.

CHAPTER ONE

0615 Monday Morning
Whidbey Island, Washington

JOY ALEXANDER FORCED herself to ignore the clock and leisurely sip her morning coffee. She had more than an hour until her first day at the law firm—her first civilian job after a decade in the Navy. Since the law office was seven minutes away, tops, and she'd already showered, she could afford to enjoy the view a bit longer.

Five minutes. She waited for the satisfaction she usually felt when she thought about her new life, her new career. But this time she didn't feel it. Had to be first-day jitters, that was all.

The blue of the water changed to gray as the Strait of Juan de Fuca glistened in the morning light. Even though she'd planned to make the switch to civilian life for the last three years of her career as a Navy JAG, right now it felt as though it'd happened in the blink of an eye. She stretched her arms over her head, enjoying the taut feel of her muscles after last night's yoga class. She'd traded years of Navy PT tests and the sweaty gym for poses in a pristine studio, and she had no regrets.

The flutters in her stomach were purely physical reactions to her excitement at her new job.

The rumble of jet engines reached her ears a split second before two Navy F-18 Growlers shot across the sky, overflying her house, leaving the Whidbey Island airspace for the Pacific Ocean. She wondered if an aircraft carrier was waiting for them. She watched their shapes grow smaller as they gained altitude and distance. A second round of jet noise rushed over her house, but this was lower, slower. Turbojets. Sure enough, a P-8 Poseidon, followed by its predecessor, the P-3 Orion, flew by and their flight appeared slow and laborious after the showiness of the fighter jets.

The P-8 and P-3 platforms didn't land on carriers, but instead performed reconnaissance and antisubmarine missions. No doubt a Naval exercise was afoot. She'd often observed the aircraft over the past year from her home base of Naval Air Station, Whidbey Island. They always made her feel comfortable—they were that familiar to her.

She tried to ignore the pang of nostalgia; it would do nothing but increase her anxiety about starting her civilian life.

Joy had no room for anxiety in her carefully structured routine.

Scanning the horizon yielded nothing in the

way of wildlife, the real reason she loved sitting out here. Not one whale spout. A cargo ship and a smaller fishing vessel floated in the distance, and she wondered if the small boat was out there to whale watch. Maybe it belonged to an amateur photographer, hoping to get shots of the Navy's power. Aviation buffs were serious about observing Naval flight operations and referred to the loud noise of the jets as the "Sound of Freedom."

She certainly felt it was. She'd proudly been part of supporting the operators who served all over the globe in missions that ranged from humanitarian aid to the ugliest aspects of war.

Would working in a civilian firm ever be as rewarding? She doubted it. But it was time...

A single burst of bright light came out of nowhere, as if an invisible finger had lit a match against the sea. She gasped at the immediate appearance of a fireball, followed by dark smoke.

As the reality that she'd seen an explosion registered, the tiled floor of her sunroom shuddered, and a soft *boom* rolled across the beachfront.

Normally, she'd associate the blast and its vibration with one or both of the F-18s breaking the sound barrier. But she'd *seen* the explosion. Had it been an aircraft exploding?

No, the fireball was too low.

Fighting her shock she forced her gaze to remain steady on the same distant spot where she'd identified the cargo ship with a fishing boat in the foreground. Her observation could prove instrumental in helping Search and Rescue.

She blinked as the reality registered.

Only one of the two vessels remained. The smaller fishing boat was gone, vanished in the few minutes it had taken the smoke to appear.

She waited for her brain to make sense of the images. Migrating whales, inbound storms, cargo ships—those were all common sights on the ocean. But clouds of dark black smoke rising above the horizon, spewing from the flash of a fireball? Never.

It was what had preceded the explosion that made her hands shake, made her know with certainty that while she'd resigned her Navy JAG commission last month, she would never let go of her sense of duty. Something, no, *someone*, had done this on purpose, possibly as a threat to the aircraft. The timing of the blast was too close to the overflight.

You could be wrong.

Joy stood in her sunroom and ignored her internal prosecutor as easily as she denied the pain from the hot coffee that spilled on her hands. She placed her cup on the mosaic-tiled café table she'd brought back from Italy and grabbed her binoculars, a gift from her parents when she'd resigned her commission. She dialed the area into focus with the familiarity born of long watches on board a Navy ship. From her sunroom she was more accustomed to looking for whale pods or bald eagles.

She saw ominously dark smoke and snakes of bright flame reaching toward it. She adjusted the focus. Was she *sure* that had been a small vessel? It'd had a low profile; probably wasn't anything bigger than a fishing boat. The cargo ship was still there, but too far away to make out many details.

What had made that little boat explode? She rested the binoculars on her chest as she scanned the horizon, even though she knew it by heart. Her home sat on a West Beach cliff, and the only land nearer to the explosion was farther north, toward the base, where the land curved westward into the strait.

This hadn't been some kind of base exercise gone wrong. The Navy didn't drop weapons in Puget Sound.

Calm down and think.

What had she seen?

It was always the Navy's fear that a terrorist would procure a rogue weapon like a surface-to-air missile, a SAM, and take out a plane. It was a threat for anyone who flew after 9-11.

Had she just witnessed that fear come true?

She shook her head. No. If one of the aircraft had been shot out of the sky, the explosion would have been greater, the impact louder and more tangible. Plus, the explosion had occurred well after the aircraft flew by.

She'd never served downrange, never had a Patriot missile fly over her head on its way to attack an enemy missile, never had to worry about getting into bio-chem gear. Her entire Navy career had taken place in courtrooms Stateside and overseas, with one carrier tour at sea and one trip to Guantanamo Bay to serve as defense lawyer for a suspected terrorist.

Where she'd worked with an enlisted SEAL, a man she'd never forget.

She squeezed her eyes shut against the intrusive memory.

She wouldn't think about him today. She'd spent enough time obsessing over the man who'd rattled her scrupulous professional demeanor.

The last trial of her Norfolk tour that resulted from the brief time in Guantanamo Bay had almost done her in. It had convinced her that her Afghani defendant was innocent, however, and she took the case to trial in Norfolk.

That took six grueling months, but with the help of an honest SEAL and other operatives who gave their testimony, she'd been able to free an Afghan man who'd been wrongly apprehended, a true victim of circumstance. He was safely in the Witness Security Program, his life under the protection of US Marshals.

She'd also been able to help the same SEAL

keep his name free of any accusation of wrong-doing. The case had changed her in an elemental way and reminded her why the fight for justice was paramount.

The SEAL had affected her more than any other man in her life...

She opened her eyes.

Her phone lay on the kitchen counter where she'd left it. She should call the base, the police or at least her new boss and tell someone what she'd witnessed.

Her hands jerkily grabbed the pink-cased phone. Immense vibrations shook the porch screens as the *wap wap wap* of SH-60 helicopters burst through the air. Any sailor who'd spent time around a Navy base, air station or on board a ship knew the sound meant help was on the way.

She wasn't the only one who'd seen that explosion. That was the sound of the Naval Air Station's Search and Rescue team. For ejected aircrew, floating in the ocean awaiting their ride back to the aircraft carrier or nearest land, it was a lifeline. In this case, she wasn't sure who could have survived an explosion that made an entire boat disappear in a matter of seconds.

An ugly premonition raised goose bumps on her arms. She was afraid that people had been lost in the fiery blast. This far away, her binoculars too weak, she couldn't tell.

She looked for the return of the P-8 or P-3.

They were reconnaissance platforms; it was in their mission description to find mishap clues.

Today was the start of her life as a civilian. Yet one terrible act, and she was back in uniform mode, even if she wore a fancy suit and dress shoes that made her feel feminine.

She cradled the phone. The emergency and NAS operators would be inundated with calls. Would the details of what she'd seen make a meaningful difference to any aircrew at this point? SAR was on the scene. She could wait and phone in her observations after she'd finished getting ready for work…

Then she changed her mind and quickly dialed 9-1-1.

With one blast, she might be in the middle of an international terrorist event. And late for her first day of work.

FBI AGENT BRAD IVERSON didn't stop swearing the entire time he raced along the rocky shore of Whidbey's West Beach. The inflatable powerboat he'd driven back, landing within yards of the shore, was safely destroyed and lay at the bottom of Puget Sound. His clothes were wet and cold, but that wasn't anything he hadn't experienced before.

But he'd never had to take out an enemy, not since he'd left the Navy and become a civilian agent.

Getting the hell out of sight and—he hoped—to

his vehicle, where he could securely call his boss, was priority one. Because the remaining three suspects in the domestic terrorist cell he'd infiltrated during his current undercover op couldn't be allowed to find him. As soon as they suspected he'd neutralized their fourth man, they'd be after him. If they captured him, they'd throw him in a pit and keep him there, until either their deadly mission was complete or he died—preferably both.

Brad thanked God for his Navy SEAL background and, currently, his FBI training. It had saved his life. Now he had to prevent anyone else from becoming a target.

A sharp rock punched through the bottom of his running shoes and his ankle twisted too far to the right. Brad ignored the jolt of pain that flashed up the side of his leg.

He had minutes. As he took in the beach's length he could see flashing lights.

Damn it. Getting to his car wasn't happening, not now.

He couldn't afford the time it would take to explain himself to local law enforcement. He didn't even have his badge on him; it was safely locked in his desk drawer at the Bureau in Seattle, standard procedure when you were undercover.

He had to avoid being seen. The terrorists *couldn't* figure out he was still alive, not yet. An unintended camera shot of his face on the local news could prove disastrous to the Bureau's entire operation.

Past missions had seared the thin line between life and death into his soul. He'd hauled shipmates, alive and dead, off the battlefield. Brad knew death, and he knew failure. Neither were strangers.

But he wasn't about to let this op become a failure. Which left him with one option.

He'd have to break into her house. Wait until she got back from work, if she'd already gone. Otherwise, he'd face her in the next twenty minutes. The woman who had gotten under his skin like no other, yet had remained unattainable to him.

The woman he hadn't been able to get out of his mind since he last saw her, more than eighteen months ago.

"Shit."

Any plans he'd dreamed up to rekindle what he hoped had been a mutual attraction were smashed like a jungle bug against a Humvee windshield. He bent over, hands on his knees as he tried to calm his breath as it came in jagged gulps. Half crouching, half leaning against the side of a huge tree that'd been washed ashore, he knew that in his dark clothing he'd be tough to spot from the air.

She's right up above me.

He double-checked his coordinates and took in a few more deep breaths.

"Holy hell." His body wasn't that of a twenty-something anymore. Yet he had to force it to perform as it had on countless SEAL missions.

Joy Alexander's house was on a cliff directly above him. This wasn't the way he'd intended to see her again, but the entire nine-month operation, not to mention his life, was at risk.

You could expose her to the same danger.

Not if he made it up the cliff in short order.

He darted to the base of the cliff wall, where he hid behind a second pile of petrified trees, and pulled out his phone. He steadied his hands so he could pop the phone apart. Years of operational experience had taught him how to control the adrenaline surges inevitable in his line of work.

The phone's SIM card snapped out easily enough, and he put it in his pocket. The rest of the phone he smashed against the rock cliff. Not because he had to—he'd already disabled the battery—but because it felt good to smash something the rat bastard terrorists had given him.

He couldn't use this phone, and his one secure cell phone was in his vehicle. Even if he had his Bureau phone, he wouldn't use it—not until he had time to make sure the terrorists weren't looking for him, waiting for a cell phone signal to tip off his location. For now he had to stay alive and find a place to shelter while he figured things out.

He wiped his mind clear of all thoughts other than getting to the top of the two-hundred-foot wall in front of him.

The shale of the cliff cut his fingers, and blood dripped down his wrists. He wiped the sweat from his brow with his forearm. Gloves would've been smart but they lay with his destroyed inflatable on the ocean floor.

He was going to need help. It wasn't the *how* or the *where* that gave him pause. It was the *who*.

He'd done his research well. He knew exactly where she lived.

Joy.

Why was it that his only chance to untangle the vicious web that had almost destroyed him lay with the one woman he didn't want to bring into this mess? A woman who'd sacrificed six months of her life to help him and another innocent man. A woman he wanted to meet under better circumstances. He wanted to thank her properly. And yes, ask her out.

You don't have a choice. You need her help.

If there'd been anyone else, someone he wouldn't have on his conscience if things went south, he'd go to that person. He wished he could talk to Mike, his boss. FBI Agent Michael Rubio, former Navy SEAL and now Brad's boss at the Bureau. Mike had been on his SEAL team, and they'd worked together on operational missions for most of a decade. Mike had sent him to monitor Whidbey and to bring back hard Intel on the people surveilling the area for a possible terrorist attack.

He couldn't take the chance of giving his location away with a cellular communication. Plus, Mike would have too many questions. Brad didn't have time for questions.

Because this op had taken a major detour in the bright blaze of an explosion. An explosion he'd caused. Justifiably, but the local cops weren't going to wait for him to explain that part. He also had to keep the über-classified nature of this mission in mind.

His rigorous training meant his thoughts could wander as he struggled up the cliff. And that kept the enormity of the physical task he had to accomplish more manageable.

How the hell had a small-town domestic terrorist cell obtained a surface-to-air missile? If they wanted to provoke a response from Naval Air Station Whidbey, why hadn't they tried something on land? Was this to see what the Navy's local capabilities were?

No fewer than a dozen scenarios fought for priority in his overtaxed mind. The terrorist cell he'd been sent to infiltrate had seemed amateur at best, Taliban or al Qaeda wannabes.

He hadn't believed they were connected to anything on a grander scale. Until yesterday.

Channeling his frustration into the energy he

needed to climb the cliff side was another survival tactic he'd used innumerable times. He'd never had to use it in his own country, though.

Anger made the blood roar in his ears. There were terrorists running free on Whidbey Island, and they'd almost succeeded in shooting down a US Navy aircraft.

His toehold, a small ledge, crumbled as he tried to cling to it, and his ribs slammed against the rough wall. An involuntary grunt left his chest, along with his air.

Focus, breathe, reach, climb.

He'd done this kind of thing when he was in worse shape. He remembered scaling an enemy compound wall with broken ribs and a collapsed lung… The searing pain in his side didn't come close to the pain of past injuries.

The image of a beautiful woman with a voice as sexy as any he'd ever known flashed in front of him.

The same woman he hadn't been able to erase from his mind in the year and a half since he'd seen her.

Joy.

He wished it was only the pain, the shock of his predicament, that made him think of her.

Had he really thought he'd be able to wrap up this case and then go reintroduce himself? After eighteen months of no contact, except reading her Facebook page via the fake one he'd created? Not that he'd been keeping track as he faced down the devil himself and came through the hell that was his life those last six months of active duty.

He wished, too, that he had someone else, anyone other than Joy, to rely on. Anyone other than the woman who'd already done so much for him and his colleague.

Now he had to ask her to trust him again—but without the evidence he'd provided in Norfolk. He gritted his teeth. Joy Alexander deserved better than to be drawn into the reach of such evil.

But you need her intelligence, her skill...her.

His fingers ached, and he wasn't even halfway up the cliff. Worrying about Joy was just his brain's way of distracting him from his discomfort. Another operational habit.

Schedules and crises had prevented him from connecting with her sooner. Clearing his name of a murder allegation had been another stumbling block, to say the least.

If he involved her in this op, there was no longer any hope of ever having more with her than what they'd always had—business. And yet, she was the only woman who'd completely believed in him, as a Navy sailor, a SEAL, a man.

Navy Lieutenant Commander Joy Alexander.

A wisp of memory drifted through his adrenaline-soaked mind—the tall, curvy Navy JAG he'd worked with, the attorney who'd defended him. It'd been a tough case.

She'd been tougher.

They'd made a good team. For six long months in the legal offices of Naval Station Norfolk, they'd slugged it out, seeking justice for an Afghan villager anyone else might have presumed guilty. It certainly would've been easier than facing down the entire United States Justice System with what initially looked like almost zero evidence.

Joy hadn't given up from the very first minute they were introduced. In the aftermath of their trial win, his days had become bleak—for other reasons. He'd thought back to how she'd looked on that last day as she drove out of the legal building's parking lot and waved goodbye.

He'd followed her Facebook posts while she was aboard the USS *Lincoln*, and then after, when she'd moved here to Whidbey. Brad didn't post on Facebook; he lurked solely as a means of keeping in touch with the few old friends he had left. Joy had gotten out of the Navy and stayed on the West Coast to start over as a civvie.

He'd hoped to show up, take her on a date. If he got past his wariness over chasing a woman he still thought about. A woman he'd made love to in his mind countless times.

Like him, she'd been a loner. Dedicated to the pursuit of freedom and justice for all. The job was starting to wear on her; he'd seen it back then. He'd felt the same way. Dedicating your life to your country at eighteen, fresh out of high school, was noble and needed. Democracy had to be protected. Terrorists had to be stopped.

By thirty, the thrill of adrenaline rushes started to break down your body, no matter how fit you were, how dedicated. By thirty-five, you realized that the hard jobs were meant to be done by younger shipmates.

From what he'd gleaned, Joy had led a relatively charmed Navy career. Still, as they worked on the case together, he'd seen the fatigue shadowing her, too.

He knew she'd felt the attraction between them—he'd seen it in her glances, the way her hand crept to her throat in an unconscious defense mechanism. If they'd met elsewhere, some situation in which he wasn't an enlisted SEAL and she wasn't a Naval Officer JAG, their relationship might have played out very differently.

A different ending was what he'd hoped for when he saw that she'd gotten out of the Navy, too. They were both civilians now, free to take up with whomever they wanted.

And then he'd been assigned this mission.

You'll never be free.

As he pulled himself over the edge of the cliff and onto grass that felt surprisingly soft after the rough-hewn cliff side, he figured he had three more minutes to make it inside her place.

Good thing he was in her backyard.

He'd memorized her address and the surrounding locale back at the office, when he'd done a search on her, just in case.

In case he had a chance to ask her out. Instead, he had to ask her for help. Again. He vowed to get what he needed and get out before the terrorists knew he'd been here, before Joy could wind up like his ex-fiancée.

Dead.

The question he'd ignored, the question he had to disregard, nipped at his conscience.

How are you going to let her go a second time?

"WE'LL HAVE A deputy out there as soon as we can, ma'am."

"I have to report to work in an hour. Can I give you my work address and they can take my statement there?"

"No, ma'am." The emergency operator's voice was firm. Practiced in getting panicked people to tell her what she needed.

Joy wasn't panicked. But she was getting annoyed.

"I'm just trying to do my civic duty. I'm an attorney, if that helps. Former Navy JAG." It was a little bittersweet, saying *former*, but thrilling to think of her new life, too.

"Then you'll understand, ma'am, why we need you to stay put. As you can imagine, we're getting a lot of calls at the moment. Call and tell your boss you'll be late, and an officer will be at your home, either from Oak Harbor PD or the sheriff's office."

"Fine."

She disconnected and made a quick call to the firm's receptionist as she hurried to her bedroom. Maggie picked up immediately.

"I'm so sorry to do this on my first day, but it's unavoidable."

Grabbing her jewelry she went into the bathroom.

"No problem. I'll let Paul know. He's a proponent of flexible working hours, as I'm sure he told you, and you have a valid reason for coming in late." Maggie's soothing tone reflected professionalism and concern. "Are you okay, Joy?"

"Yes, yes. I'll be in as soon as possible. Thank you."

She hung up and hoped Maggie was right—that Paul wouldn't think twice about her tardiness.

Joy hated being late for anything.

After she applied her makeup in record time, despite her trembling hands, she took a minute to take in her full appearance.

And snorted.

She threw her mascara into the vanity drawer. How could she care about her appearance when she'd witnessed what could very well have been a terrorist attack?

Her stomach churned, and she regretted that last cup of coffee as it threatened to come back up. GERD and its annoying symptoms was how her body handled the stress, the overload of information and emotions; she was aware of that. It aggravated her gastrointestinal problems. But understanding her physical coping mechanisms didn't make them any less bothersome.

The beating of helicopter blades and wail of sirens had been constant. She should take the long route to the office and avoid the shore road, but she knew she wouldn't. She'd want to see what kind of crash recovery site had been set up. Of course it would be on West Beach, practically next to her house.

Back in her sunroom she couldn't take her gaze off the shoreline. Sure enough, several people were walking the rocky stretch in front of her house, two hundred feet below her vantage point. Most were in some sort of uniform, either Navy or local emergency management. A couple of the responders wore windbreakers with identifying letters like "OHPD" for Oak Harbor Police Department and "US NAVY."

The police officer or deputy sent to take her statement probably wouldn't learn anything new from her. The people who could use her eyewitness testimony were higher up on the chain of command and in Washington DC, able to make decisions that affected national defense. As a civilian, however, with no immediate access to official Navy communications systems, she had no recourse.

A sharp rap at the back door made her jump. She hadn't seen anyone walk up the side of her property, most of which was visible from the sunroom.

That couldn't be the police officer, not yet. It'd only been five minutes, and it took at least ten to drive to West Beach from downtown Oak Harbor, where the police station was located. And a sheriff's deputy would have to come from Coupeville, twenty minutes away.

Maybe the sheriff's deputy was already out this way. That was it. She forced herself to relax. And then froze.

Why hadn't the cop used her *front* door?

She crept quietly into the kitchen, wishing like hell she'd left for work before she saw the explosion.

She saw the tall silhouette through the door's window the moment she stepped onto the kitchen's hardwood floor. The cream curtains she'd hung last weekend meant she couldn't make out her visitor clearly, but based on the height and breadth of the shadow, it was a man. No evidence of a uniform hat.

Her new suit felt too tight, the tailored jacket too restrictive. What if she needed to defend herself? She tore off the peplum coat, her hands flailing as she freed her arms from the sleeves.

She didn't have a weapon.

As her jacket fell to the floor she searched under the kitchen sink for something heavy.

She really needed to get a baseball bat to keep next to the kitchen door, besides the one next to her bed. She grasped the cool neck of the small kitchen fire extinguisher.

Tiptoeing to the door, her senses on high alert, she tried to remember every self-defense move she'd ever learned. Today's events had been far from routine or normal. She wasn't going to take a chance that her visitor was a friendly one.

BRAD HEARD HER moving around the house. Joy hadn't had Spec Ops training, that was for sure—judging by the fact that she'd parked her car in the driveway, allowing any passerby to determine whether she was home. Not to mention that he'd been able to get to her side entrance so easily. She should have a tall fence around the back of her property, with a locked gate. And a more secure side door; this one wouldn't be hard to kick in.

There'd been no barking, either, so she didn't have a dog to protect her.

As he listened to her shuffle about in the kitchen, he wondered if she might be grabbing a weapon.

Unlikely. She'd never struck him as the type

to harbor a weapon, no matter how legal it might be. That was the advantage someone like Joy had over him—she'd never seen what he'd seen, never had to face down the bad guys except on paper or in a courtroom. She could still believe in the inherent goodness of humanity.

The curtains moved a fraction, enough for her to see him, make positive identification. She'd remember him—but not like this, all muddy, wet, cut up and bruised.

It'd been a rough morning.

"What do you want?"

Her voice was clear despite the door between them.

"Joy, it's me, Brad Iverson. From Norfolk."

The door opened.

"I know who you are, Brad."

He didn't give himself a chance to absorb the freshness of her beauty, or to register the wariness of her eyes as she looked at him. With moves he'd employed countless times, he wedged his foot in the door before he reached in, twisted the fire extinguisher out of her hand and clamped a hand over her mouth—her very soft mouth. Then he pushed himself inside the house and maneuvered her up against the nearest counter. It took every bit of his focus, every ounce of his strength, to make sure he treated her as gently as possible.

He had one arm wrapped around her waist, confining her arms against her torso, with her hands on his chest. His other arm was across her chest, his hand over her mouth.

As soon as he looked into her eyes, he removed his hand. If she was going to scream—and she had every right—it would be now. There were law enforcement agents, all over the area and certainly within hearing distance. It'd taken him almost half an hour to climb up the cliff.

Joy stayed silent except for the shaky *whoosh* of her breath. It smelled sweet and minty, as if she'd just brushed her teeth. His palm seemed to burn where her lips had pressed against it, and he couldn't stop looking at her full lips, her face. Her eyes were the same color he remembered. Cinnamon brown. They watched him with unnerving steadiness, missing nothing.

He lowered his arm but kept her in his embrace. This was the only time he'd ever felt her so close. Why rush it?

"I can't explain everything, but I need to know if you're willing to trust me. I'm in the middle of an undercover op, and I can't get caught by the police right now. You're my last hope before I get hauled away and blow the case."

She blinked. He felt the tension in her legs, her thigh muscles. She wanted to kick him, to knee him. He got it—and had anticipated her tactics. He held her tight and secure.

"Odd habit you have, Brad. Getting yourself into serious trouble that isn't your fault."

God, he'd missed her honesty, the unshakeable confidence that bordered on sheer nerve.

And her beauty.

"You can say no and I'll be gone. You can deny ever seeing me. I'm in a load of trouble and I need your help, Joy."

CHAPTER TWO

"I WAS SUPPOSED to report to work twenty minutes ago. It's my first day." She hadn't been able to take her gaze off Brad since he'd forced himself into the kitchen. And pressed his body against hers. She still hadn't told him that she was waiting for the police.

He groaned. "*Of course* it's your first day. It'd be too easy if you could've taken a day or two off."

"A day or two?" She clutched the granite counter at her back. It was the only way to keep her hands from shaking because of the mini-shocks of awareness coursing through her veins.

Brad stood in the middle of the kitchen, his hands bloodied. His face was scraped and his clothing had dirt and sand on it. A briar stem clung to one arm of his torn black jacket, and his dark cargo pants were nothing like his Navy fatigue uniform. These pants fit him more tightly; they had to have a lot of stretch to let him move as well as he did. She could all too easily imagine the steely muscles beneath.

"Wait. How did you get here? Were you in my backyard?"

"Something like that, yeah." He absently picked off some of the brambles.

"I never saw you. Are you hurt?"

"No. I'm fine. I'm on a tight timeline here, Joy. I don't suppose you still have base access?"

"No, I mean yes—for two more days before my ID expires. I've been on terminal leave for the past two months. I got out, Brad."

"I know. We're Facebook friends, remember?"

How could she forget? Whenever she wanted to torment herself with the whys and why nots of her love life, she looked at his profile, which he'd made under a fake name. He'd messaged her when he requested she friend him on Facebook to make sure she knew it was him. He'd only ever posted one photo—of a sunset over the view of the Atlantic from Dam Neck, Virginia. She'd imagined them there, together, in different circumstances hundreds of times since they'd wrapped up Farid's case.

Since she'd helped Brad stay out of trouble.

"What good will having my military ID do? Aren't you still in the reserves? What about your ID?"

"I don't have it. Truth is, I haven't got any ID on me."

Interesting.

"Any reason why?"

His green eyes revealed very little, but his slumped shoulders put the fear of God into her.

"Brad, what happened? Please tell me you weren't involved in the explosion."

His head snapped up.

"You know about it?"

She pushed away from the counter and crossed her arms. "I saw it. From my sunroom."

"Did you see the aircraft?"

"I saw two F-18 Growlers, followed by a P-3 and a P-8. They flew west for a minute or two before I saw the fireball. I was worried it was one of the planes at first."

"Did you see anything else that seemed suspicious?"

"No more from me, Brad. You said you needed help. If you want my help, you have to cut me in."

He rubbed his hands across the back of his head and neck, much as she'd seen countless military men do after they removed their uniform covers. It was a habitual reaction for him, a sign of his stress, perhaps. His dark hair was longer than he'd worn it as a sailor, longer than Navy regulation by far. The lustrous curls at the nape of his neck made her grip her upper arms to keep from reaching across and touching him.

He was her idea of beautiful, if the adjective could be applied to a man.

"I'm FBI now. I've been working undercover trying to break up a cell."

FBI. That was the "government job" he had. On Facebook he never got specific.

So he'd been out of the active-duty Navy this entire time. She'd thought his murky job description was because of his SEAL designation.

You could have gotten together.

No. She'd dismissed her attraction to Brad. Or rather, locked it away. Months ago.

Hadn't she?

He shook his head. "Damn, it wasn't supposed to go down like this."

His profile was achingly familiar. Yet instead of the hardened strength she remembered, he gave off an air of uncertainty. Brad, vulnerable?

"How about some coffee?" She asked for him as much as for herself. She needed an immediate task to keep her thoughts where they belonged. If she was going to help Brad she needed to listen to his story instead of thinking about how sexy he looked standing in her kitchen.

"YOU'VE GOT UNTIL the police officer shows up. You can shower after I leave for work, wash and dry your clothes, make whatever food you need." She handed him her largest mug, the one with the Navy JAG crest on it.

He raised his eyebrows in acknowledgement.

This was the man she'd come to understand first briefly in Cuba, and then Norfolk. He missed nothing; no detail was too minute to him.

"The cops?"

"I reported the explosion. They asked me to wait here until someone can take my report."

"So I'm not safe here."

"You're safe for now. Tell me what you know, Iverson."

"I'm working an undercover op. Let's just call it against the bad guys for now. My job is to infiltrate them and monitor any suspicious activity. I assumed I was bringing in the suspects today. Things didn't go according to my assumptions."

He took a long pull of his coffee. The dirt under his fingernails made her wonder if he'd had to climb up from West Beach to get here.

Was that possible? The cliff was a straight drop.

Brad was a trained SEAL and now an undercover agent for the FBI. Scaling a cliff was all in a day's work for him.

"You climbed up the cliff, didn't you?"

He ignored her and continued his explanation. "This morning I was supposed to monitor the Sound from West Beach, as instructed by the suspects. I think, and so does my team at the Bureau, that they may want to hit the Naval Air Station since they've been surveilling the area for a month. Last night one of the suspects called and told me I should watch the horizon from West Beach very closely this morning."

"And?"

"I had my team figure out what was on the docket for the squadrons on NAS Whidbey for the next several days. This morning is the start of a major West Coast Fleet exercise. When I put it together with what the suspects were feeding me, I took the initiative and decided to be out on the water instead of on the beach."

Dread seemed to wrap itself around her.

"With the Navy? On a Navy ship?"

She knew the answer before he said it. "No. I was in a small inflatable powerboat. That's all I'm going to tell you about it."

"What did you see, Brad?"

He quietly tapped the side of his mug. "One of the suspects I'm familiar with was out there in a fishing boat. I stayed as far away from him as I could, as long as I could, but then I saw what looked like a SAM in his arms."

"A surface-to-air missile?" She knew enough to realize there was always the possibility of terrorists smuggling in war weapons. The reports she'd read over the years had discussed shipments being stopped by US Customs at the border or sooner.

"Yes. I had a feeling something wasn't right about the way they'd told me to watch from the shoreline. After putting it together with the Fleet exercise—it all pointed to trouble of the biggest kind."

She had a feeling that the "something not right" was directly related to the explosion.

"Go on."

"I took him, and the weapon, out."

"Who's *him*, and what exactly do you mean by *I took him out*?"

His shifted his eyes, his expression no longer readable.

"I had to stop him from firing the SAM, Joy."

The gravity of the situation, *his* situation, hit her like a Puget Sound gale in November. "You killed a man out there today?"

"I disabled his weapon. The resulting explosion did the rest."

"Okay. So now all you have to do is call in to FBI headquarters, to your team, and report what happened." Honestly, did he *have* to play the dramatic SEAL part? Weren't those days supposed to be over?

"I can't. I blew my cover by blowing their mission. No pun intended."

"Do you think they—the terrorists, whoever they are—know you're the one who stopped the SAM?"

As she asked, she couldn't believe that Brad's cover would be compromised by anything he did or didn't do. He was a professional who'd completed umpteen missions in the most hellish places on earth. He knew how to keep his cover.

"I have to assume they do, or at the very least they'll figure it out soon enough."

She believed him.

"Let me clarify. They may suspect I'm not legit when I don't meet up with them again. They have no way of knowing which LEA I belong to. I've been playing the part of the disillusioned émigré who wanted to help quell the American Imperialists. These are all domestic terrorists. None of them speak Pashto or Dari—I threw in a few words here and there to test them. They're all homegrown wannabes. My team was alerted that they were trying to leave the country to join a terrorist group overseas."

"But they decided to get some credibility by doing one of those sleeper-type actions?"

"Yes. This is more than a sleeper cell, though. They have contacts with the bad guys overseas. That's certain now that I identified the SAM. I just don't know who that contact is yet."

Brad's wide range of skills, including his ability with more than one foreign language, was a big part of what had made him such a valuable asset to the Navy SEALs. All SEALs had intensive training in weapons identification and employment. If he said he saw a SAM about to be launched, it was true.

And the explosion left no doubt.

"The thing is, I think they're also targeting an individual here on Whidbey. They'll lie low if they have to, until the LEA presence lessens, but they're going to go after him sooner or later."

She ran her fingers through her hair. "Terrorists who are so bold they'll try to shoot down a US Navy aircraft just offshore, in US territory, don't care about the LEA all over the place, Brad. They won't wait."

His appreciation of her accurate observation gleamed in his eyes. The instant warmth that flushed her cheeks was impossible to control.

"Exactly."

THE DOORBELL RANG, and Brad saw her shoulders tense, her mouth tighten in a grim line.

"That's the OHPD or sheriff's deputy. Coming over in the respectable way." She tried to keep it light by poking fun at his entrance via her side door earlier, but her anxiety was palpable.

You've done this to her.

"OHPD?"

"Oak Harbor Police Department. Keep up, Mr. FBI."

"Are you going to tell them I'm here?"

"Why can't I? You're FBI. Don't all LEA talk to each other?"

"You know damn well they don't. I'm undercover, Joy. I can't be seen."

He knew he was asking her to trust him with little reason. He'd made no attempt to contact her since he'd been free to do so. Only now, when he was in serious trouble, had he sought her out.

"You don't have to do this, Joy. Say the word and I'll go out the back and disappear. Just give me thirty seconds lead time."

"No, don't go. I'm not going to say anything to them other than what I reported on the phone. There's no need, not legally."

He saw the inner war play out in her expression. She had a beautiful face, capable of distracting the most hardened criminal. Sometimes her face revealed what she was thinking, what she was feeling. But she was capable of hiding her emotions, too. Her poker face had let her get what they needed to set Farid free from the hell he'd been condemned to. He felt a rush of warmth.

"You trust me," he said quietly.

"That's a discussion for later. Go into my bedroom and stay there until I come and get you."

"I was standing right here, looking out through my binoculars. That's when I noticed the explosion. The vibration hit a few seconds later."

"Roger."

The Oak Harbor police officer wrote more notes, her face noncommittal.

"Have you gotten a lot of witness accounts this morning?"

Officer Katie Dade looked up and shook her head.

"Not as many as you'd think. Most of your neighbors were either in the shower or already at work, and the others heard just the explosion. You're the only one who saw it from here. But we had other witnesses who were walking their dogs farther down the beach."

By *farther down* Officer Dade meant the stretch of coastline miles from Joy's house, closer to the Naval Air Station.

"I thought they'd send a sheriff's deputy."

"Normally, yes. Your home's in the county's jurisdiction. They're swamped at the moment, so they sent me. Mind if I look through your binoculars?"

"No, go right ahead."

As Officer Dade focused the binoculars, Joy prayed they were almost done with the interview. She'd never hidden a potential fugitive before and didn't like being on the wrong side of the law, regardless of the situation or her motives. Regardless of the fact that she trusted Brad.

Motives.

Were they centered on a belief that Brad was telling her the truth, or did he still hold some kind of crazy sway over her? Or both? It would help if she knew that all her fantasies about him weren't unrequited—that he at least shared her physical attraction.

Not that it made a difference now.

"These are pretty good. You get them in the

Navy?" Officer Dade motioned at her with the binoculars.

"No. They were a gift from my parents. I got used to good binoculars when I was aboard an aircraft carrier."

"So you drove an aircraft carrier?"

"No, not really." JAGs didn't stand bridge watches, although she'd observed some of the tactical operations. Not typical for a JAG, but she'd wanted to spread her professional wings a bit.

Why was she telling a strange police officer about her Navy career? Officer Dade was nice and all, and obviously a polished professional. Still, she hadn't asked for the information.

Brad had been back in her life for less than an hour and not only was she hoping that he reciprocated her ridiculous crush, which had gone on for far too long, she was also forgetting all her legal training.

Don't say more than you need to. Ever.

"You got a pretty clear look from here. Too bad these things aren't also a camera." Officer Dade rested the binoculars against her uniform.

"Yeah, too bad."

Please leave.

"That's all you remember? You're sure you've told me everything, Ms. Alexander?"

"Yes, that's it. I'm sorry it's not more, and that I bothered the authorities with this when you already have witnesses. I know it's going to be a long day for you."

"It's fine. I mean, no one got hurt, right?"

"Did anyone? Get hurt?" Playing stupid was pushing it, but Brad needed to know what they'd found out so far.

"No, not that we're aware of. It doesn't make sense that there was an empty fishing boat out there, though. Especially one that caused such a huge explosion."

"No, it doesn't." Her tension kicked into high gear. She was a JAG, not a SEAL, and she didn't relish one second of her involvement in Brad's undercover op.

Officer Dade sighed and handed the binoculars back to her.

"Thanks for your cooperation, Ms. Alexander. If you remember anything else, give us a call."

"Will do."

Joy walked the young woman to the front door and wanted to shout with relief once the door closed and she heard the police car drive off.

That had been too close—as well as too easy.

What did it say about her that she'd lied so effortlessly? And to a police officer, yet.

"YOU DID GREAT, JOY." He leaned against the counter, his bulk making the kitchen seem tiny.

"*Great?* Lying to an officer, trying to manipulate her into telling me classified information about the investigation?" She poured coffee into his mug and took out the small bag of chamomile that was steeping in hers.

"Trust me."

That was the problem. She *did* trust Brad. It was herself she was having trouble with.

"What do you need from me, Brad?"

His stare unnerved her but she'd be damned if she'd let him see it. She met his eyes and waited for him to blink. He didn't. Instead, he glanced away and spoke as if transcribing an operational report or a court order.

"For right now, I need to stay put. I need time for things to settle. And I need to figure out why they're after a certain high-ranking military official who lives here."

"You know who they're after?" As she asked, she suddenly knew who Brad was about to name.

"Is it General Grimes?"

"General Grimes."

They said his name in unison.

General Grimes had been the Marine Corps Flag Officer in charge of the overall mission that Brad's SEAL team had completed nearly five years ago. The same mission that had depended on Farid's help. The same operation that had precipitated Farid's arrest and incarceration.

Brad put his mug down on the counter. "How did you know?"

"I didn't, but it makes sense. He's the highest-ranking military person I know of on the island. He retired here." They'd both relied on General Grimes's testimony to free Farid.

"How do *you* know he's here?"

She shrugged. "I ran into him at the commissary about two months ago. Or rather, I saw a man who looked just like him but he was in civilian clothes. I wasn't about to go up to him and remind him that I was the one who'd forced him to testify—I pissed him off enough the first time around. I read in *Navy Times* that he'd retired to much pomp and circumstance. Go figure, he ended up here, far away from the spotlight he'd still be under if he'd stayed in DC."

Brad must have heard the rancor in her reply. "He might have not appreciated you, Joy, but he respected you. He had to. You got the testimony you needed out of him, and Farid was released."

"Farid's free because he wasn't guilty of anything. Even Grimes couldn't scrape up a bad word about him without looking like an ass—or lying." The memory of running into Grimes in the commissary flashed before her. "It was weird seeing the big, bad Marine Corps General put cans of baked beans in his shopping cart like a regular mortal."

Brad snorted. "We all put our pants on the same way, Joy."

A smile nudged her lips in spite of the serious issue.

"Why do you think they're after him?" she asked. "There are plenty of active-duty admirals and generals who'd be easier to target, aren't there?"

"Maybe, but three days ago one of the cell members let it slip that they were getting closer to their 'objective.' I didn't know who they were after—I thought it was the base, or a Navy aircraft or even a random sailor. My team ran down every sailor who's been over in their neck of the woods in the last decade and now lives here. They included all retirees. Grimes was the highest-ranking person to pop up."

"You have to warn him!"

"You think?" His wit stung, and he tempered it with a quick grin. "My people have already told him. He's had extra surveillance around his property for the past two days."

"So why do you need me?"

"I need to find out who's behind the SAM and who would want to harm General Grimes and why. I suspect it's the same entity. Also, how did these local homegrown sleepers get a weapon into the country? I want to nail whoever supplied them, too. I think there's a good chance it's the same group of insurgents Grimes was fighting over there, but I can't be sure. I need you to get that information. If I could call in to my team and have them do it, I wouldn't have climbed a two-hundred-foot cliff to hide out at your place while you get the answers I need."

He held her gaze, and she was grateful he couldn't read her mind. Because a not-so-small part of her didn't regret the extra time with Brad, no matter how bad the circumstances might be.

CHAPTER THREE

"I STILL DON'T understand why you can't just borrow *my* phone and call in to your team. Wouldn't that make things a lot easier for you?"

He hated to crush her complete trust in the system. Joy was a rule-follower. It was her job; she was a lawyer. But he lived in a world where promises were valid only as long as it took for the people who'd made the promise to get what they wanted.

Where every communication was vulnerable to eavesdropping.

"First, all the comms in the area are under surveillance at this point, at least until the LEAs figure out what caused the explosion. They have to rule out terrorism, which in this case, they won't be able to do. Especially when they find out the FBI has an active antiterrorist operation in place. Second, I'm not the only undercover agent working this case—I don't know everyone from the other agencies. I can't risk calling in and having the comms intercepted. It would put the other agents at risk."

"You think the terrorists are intercepting communications, too, don't you?"

"I have no doubt, not after seeing that SAM." He couldn't tell her the classified details of covert communications and interception, but he owed her his professional opinion.

"You see the news, Joy. Very little is safe from interception with today's technology."

Joy shook her head, and he liked how her hair flowed around her shoulders, how the light reflected off her copper highlights. He'd wondered how good it would look down, out of that prim French braid she'd worn while in uniform. Now he knew.

"Why the hell go undercover if you can't communicate what you're finding out?"

"My job is to neutralize the bad guys, Joy. I have to use my judgment to determine when to come out of my covert role. With one of the most highly decorated generals in US Military history in the sights of these bastards, calling in my status isn't exactly a priority. My team will figure it all out. They probably already have."

"Won't your boss be worried that you were killed in the explosion?"

"Maybe." Her sincerity made it too easy to spill his guts, but he'd never compromised classified information before and wasn't about to start now.

"Sorry—I don't need to know any of this," she said. "Just tell me what you need from me."

"I need you to dig up whatever you can on Grimes. There has to be a reason they're after him. It's not merely that he was the lead GI over there during the most successful and intense allied operations."

"I'm not sure what I can learn that hasn't already made it into the press, but I'll try."

"That's all I'm asking, Joy. I can hold out for a day or two before I have to report in." He wasn't about to give her any more details. She needed to understand that she could trust him, but he couldn't put her at risk by knowing too much, either.

She looked at her watch, and he smiled.

"You still wear a watch, even with your smart-phone?"

"Some of us are old-school. Anyway, I've got a job to do and I'd better get moving or I'll find myself fired on the first day. Lawyers don't have the flexibility FBI agents do."

The banter was reminiscent of the joking they'd done to break up tension during the trial. Always aboveboard, always professional, never with any sexual innuendo.

The way it had to stay.

"AFTERNOON, MA'AM." THE base guard stood in front of the sentry post and saluted Joy as soon as he handed back her ID. Security was especially tight. They'd searched under her vehicle and had her open all her doors and back hatch. Not usual for someone with an active-duty ID.

"Have a good day." She saluted back and drove through the gate. The Naval Air Station Whidbey Island sign seemed to mock her, as did the sign with smaller print that stated persons coming aboard the Air Station were subject to search. She'd never had reason to feel the words were directed at her until today.

She was becoming a criminal.

Not technically, not yet. She could turn her car around and go home and tell Brad to take off, give him a fair lead time before she called the police and got herself out of the entire mess.

No one would blame her for not wanting to participate in an anti-terrorist op. Most would applaud her for doing what she could to help. The press and public would never find out about Brad—undercover agents weren't news-eligible.

She'd called the office a second time and told her boss that she had a medical appointment on base that was part of the procedure for her separation from the Navy. A bald-faced lie on her first day in the new job. It sucked lying to the person who had trusted in her enough to give her this job after her eight years as a JAG. She hoped Paul would not only understand but also support her actions.

She *was* doing the right thing, wasn't she?

You know you are.

Brad was the kind of patriot who'd inspired her to serve in the military in the first place. He was willing to risk everything—including his life—to keep his country safe and free. To preserve the national defense. This morning he could've asked her to be his lawyer, to represent him in case his fears became reality and he was charged with killing a suspected terrorist. Instead, he was seeking information to further protect General Grimes and to figure out the source of this evil.

Her tires crunched on the gravel lot in front of the base's legal offices. It took her a while to find a parking space. She was grateful that the placard with her name on it, designating her personal spot, had been removed when she'd left almost two months ago. Better that no one would be able to readily notice her car.

She'd remained dressed in her new suit and with her hair down around her shoulders instead of fastened in a French braid, the way she'd had to wear it in uniform. She hoped no one would recognize her as the former Commander Alexander. At least not immediately.

She inhaled the familiar smell of ammonia and stale coffee as she entered the executive area. Her new office in the law firm smelled like lavender and more expensive coffee.

"Commander Alexander. Bored already?" Shelly Jenkins, the receptionist who'd seen dozens of JAG officers come and go during her tenure, smiled and stood to greet her.

She wished she could spill it all to Shelly. More than a receptionist, she'd been another woman in service and a strong ally while Joy worked here.

You can't tell anyone. For their sake.

"Hi, Shelly. Nope, not bored. I'm getting ready to start my new job and wanted to stop by and see Dennis. Is he in?" She knew he was; he'd just texted her. It was paramount that her presence back on base look like nothing more than a friendly drop-in.

"Sure is. Let me tell him you're here."

Thirty seconds later, Joy sat across from Navy Commander Dennis Leighton, the JAG who'd relieved her.

"Are you in trouble, Joy?" he asked abruptly. They'd spent too many hours working together for Dennis to believe she'd stop in for a coffee chat.

"Not exactly. But someone close to me may be. I have to tell you up front that I can't give you any information, and that I'm taking advantage of the two days remaining before my ID has to be turned in." Joy had resigned her commission, and since she didn't have enough years, she wouldn't be retiring and getting a new retiree's ID. Once her terminal leave was over, she'd be a total civilian. No more shopping at the base commissary, no more cosmetic purchases at the Navy

Exchange, no more gym workouts on base. Certainly no showing up at her former command, looking for what might be classified information that she no longer had clearance for.

"I trust you implicitly, Joy. You wouldn't be here unless you believed in what you were doing." Dennis leaned back in his chair, his desk filled with files and stacks of paper.

"I know you have a heavy caseload," she said. NCIS had infiltrated a drug ring in the enlisted barracks, and the resulting arrests had given the legal department a year's worth of defense work. Now with the offshore explosion, the JAG office could be inundated with testimony and the legalities created by a possible terrorist act.

"That's also why I know you're here for a very good reason. What do you need, Joy?" Dennis looked relaxed, his head tilted slightly, his hands clasped behind his head as he tipped his chair back. Joy knew his calm demeanor was deceptive. Dennis was a gifted lawyer who would go far, whether he stayed in the Navy or got out to make his mark in the civilian courts. He was observing her closely, looking for every nuance in her expression. She'd expect no less.

"I need access to the cases I worked on almost two years ago." Three tours ago, by Navy standards. After Norfolk she'd gone on to a quick tour on the USS *Abraham Lincoln* based in

Everett, Washington, and then did her last tour here on Whidbey.

Dennis blinked. He clearly hadn't expected this. "You want me to go into the Navy JAG database and retrieve them?"

She shook her head. "No. I want the original paperwork. The archived hard copies." She needed to see for herself whether she'd missed something important that had put Brad's life, or that of General Grimes, at risk today.

Dennis lowered his arms onto the desk and leaned toward her.

"They're in a basement in DC, Joy. If they haven't been destroyed by now. Which, most likely, they have."

"You know as well as I do that those files won't be destroyed for another decade." The backlog of paperwork in the legal field was staggering. Even more so when it involved something as high-profile as terrorism.

Once she'd agreed to defend Farid based on Brad's testimony, she'd had to wrestle with the possibility that Brad had been brainwashed by the same Taliban group his SEAL team and General Grimes's command had infiltrated and taken out. She'd had to make certain that his testimony, intended to free Farid from a possible death sentence, wasn't based on a sense of guilt at having sold out Farid's village leaders. It would've been so much easier to let Brad's almost zealous drive to free his friend convince her that he was an unreliable witness and that she had no business trying to help Farid.

But she'd never been one for taking the easy road or the convenient one. She had to be able to look herself in the mirror every day, knowing she'd done her best. Brad wasn't a war-damaged SEAL—he was a good man who refused to let an innocent man take the rap for something he hadn't done. Brad's intensity had sparked the most intense legal work of her career. He demanded nothing less than her utmost ability as an attorney and as a Naval officer.

"I have to see those files, Dennis."

"I can request them, Joy, but I need to show cause."

"Tell them one of the defendants in the barracks drug ring that NCIS is investigating is former special ops, that he's claiming PTSD, and inhumane treatment during his time downrange made him snap and get involved in drugs here."

Dennis shot her a rueful grin. "You always managed to get what we needed, Joy."

"So you'll do it?"

"I can try, but no promises. Even if they've got them, you could be talking boxes and boxes of paper. How will you know which one has what you need?"

"I'll know. Can you have them FedEx the boxes to my house?"

"Hell, no. I can get them sent here if I'm lucky."

"My ID runs out—"

"In two days. I remember." His comment stoked her guilt. She'd been unable to make things work with Dennis except at work. He'd often hinted that he'd like their relationship to become more after she got out, but there'd never been any chemistry between them. Not for her, at least. She hadn't offered him the slightest encouragement. Yet he still knew her last day of active duty.

He was handsome, excellent at his job and would never think of asking *her* to break the law.

Dennis glanced at his watch. "I'll send a system request and follow it up with a phone call to a buddy of mine who's working at headquarters. If we're lucky we'll get the boxes by tomorrow. That'll give you a day to look at them. You'll have to come in to base to do it. I can't let you have access to anything after your terminal leave expires, Joy. You've already been read out."

Unspoken was the fact that Dennis was breaking the law by allowing her access to classified material after she'd been read out of her clearance.

"I'll sign a temporary clearance waiver."

Dennis nodded. "Yes, you will. I trust you, Joy, but the system could end my career over this."

"I understand. I can't thank you enough."

"Thank me when the boxes get here and you figure out who the bad guy is."

FRUSTRATION SEETHED THROUGH BRAD. As powerful as Joy's binoculars were and as advantageous as the view from her sunroom was, he couldn't make out the US platforms—boats and aircraft—at the explosion site. Had anyone realized it was a SAM that had exploded? Did the Navy think it'd been a less hostile explosion, meant as a warning to the aircraft training from the base?

Won't your boss be worried that you were killed in the explosion?

Unlikely, as Mike didn't know he was anywhere near the boat that had blown up. Plus, they'd been through the same SEAL indoctrination in San Diego years ago. Mike knew his capabilities as well as he did himself.

He thanked his handy-dandy SEAL training for having a car trunk full of survival gear that had ultimately saved his life.

The scent of Joy's laundry detergent wafted up with each step he took toward the kitchen. At least his clothes were clean, and he'd had a long, hot shower.

His stomach grumbled, and he checked the time. He'd told Joy not to call him on her house phone, not to have any communication unless they were face-to-face. She'd pick up a burner phone at Walmart sometime today, and then he could start making calls of his own.

But to whom? He didn't want to call the Bureau until he had more answers. They'd warned General Grimes and arranged for a security detail. The general was in the loop, which was a load off Brad's conscience.

Not that he'd ever been a big fan of General Grimes, USMC. The man had been such a hardass to work for in the warzone he'd been given the nickname "General Blue Balls" among the troops. Not for Grimes's ears or his staffers', of course. He'd really been a jerk with Brad during the Norfolk case, too. He'd refused to speak to him alone and ignored him when they were in the same room together. Grimes gave the impression of being a big fat egoist who'd managed to complete a successful career in the Marines but not through being open-minded. He'd especially resented it when a SEAL team who worked under him wasn't required to report directly to him.

Brad was certain that Grimes would've been content to see Farid sentenced for the crimes he'd been accused of. Crimes he didn't commit.

He picked up the remote and turned on the television, finding the news channel with ease. Military intelligence was tight with security, but some parts of the truth were bound to leak out.

As an anchor talked about the need for parents to vaccinate their children, Brad walked into

Joy's kitchen and opened the refrigerator. Fancy little yogurt containers, almond milk, a bin full of green leafy veggies. Skinny girly stuff. He looked in the freezer, hoping for some protein.

Score! The package of chicken breasts was thawing in the microwave before any sense of shame at scarfing her food could stop him. Opening cabinet doors and drawers, he found a frying pan, utensils and a plate.

"The apparent explosion happened..."

He ran into the front room and stared at the television. A live video stream of the search and rescue efforts filled the big screen, showing additional SAR units launching from NAS Whidbey.

"The cause of the explosion is unknown, but the possibility of a homemade bomb hasn't been ruled out. NCIS at NAS Whidbey reports that they are receiving many anonymous tips and that they will follow up on all of them. No body has been recovered at the scene, but officials have received indications that there was at least one victim." The reporter droned on with no further details as to why a "bomb" had gone off in the middle of the water off Whidbey Island.

With one of their colleagues missing and Brad gone, as well, what would the domestic terrorists do now? None of the cell members he'd met had struck him as overflowing with initiative.

They're just the puppets.

He knew it was always a possibility—that bigger forces were manipulating events, to make them look like simple homegrown terrorists. That was why he'd been sent in. To figure it out.

Technically, he'd failed on a basic mission. Infiltrate the enemy. Observe, collect information and report back. Instead, he'd been backed into taking one of them out and bringing the entire undercover op to a halt. He'd reviewed the timeline over and over during the past two hours, and he kept coming up with the same result. If he hadn't acted, the SAR efforts could be for Navy pilots. His hunger dissolved, and the chicken breasts suddenly seemed as appealing as cardboard. Only years of training carried him through the task of preparing a substantial protein-rich meal.

As the meat sizzled in Joy's unmarred pan in her too-clean kitchen, he forced himself to regroup.

Brad thought he'd experienced it all when he served as a SEAL for fifteen years. The fear, excitement, pride in a job well-done—all those emotions were as familiar to him as his uniform.

It was a sad day for him when he left the active-duty Navy, although he'd known it was time for him to transfer to the reserves. His body had had enough of the sleepless nights while on mission, enough of the wear and tear of hauling a hundred pounds of gear through places so remote he was sure another human being wouldn't leave a footprint there for at least a century afterward.

By the time he'd left for good, a full year after he'd finished all his spec ops, he'd been disillusioned, betrayed by his blind faith in his career and the illusion that he had a personal life.

When his ex-fiancée was brutally murdered in the suburbs of Virginia Beach while he was only twenty minutes away in Norfolk, he'd been afraid that somehow the bad guys from downrange had found him. That they'd sought out a soft spot, a way of retaliating for defending Farid. He'd been working alongside Joy Alexander at the time of Marci's death, and Joy had provided a failsafe alibi.

He wouldn't—*couldn't*—have done it differently. Farid had helped convict the man who'd betrayed not only Brad's SEAL team but also an entire village. Within hours of Farid's being freed, Marci had been murdered. Despite his paranoia, the two weren't connected, except in Brad's heart. And his suspicious, overworked, war-weary mind.

Guilt sliced into his gut whenever he thought about Marci. None of the counselors or his superiors had been able to convince him that he couldn't have prevented her death.

He'd become involved with her initially because he was still in rescue mode; it was how he'd operated as a younger man. He'd wanted to save Marci from the shitty family she'd grown up in, but when her prescription drug habit had gone beyond the recreational phase, he lost any sense of control over her addiction. He'd found her passed out countless times from her favorite cocktail—Xanax and Pinot Grigio—and after a wrenching soul search, he'd had to end the relationship.

As painful as it'd been to tell her he was leaving and why, she'd shown no remorse.

In fact, within weeks Marci connected with someone else—a man who could be there every night for her and love her without the drama and strain Brad's lifestyle inevitably brought to their relationship. Turned out her new boyfriend was also an addict and got her hooked on what led to her murder.

Heroin.

The death had been ruled a homicide by stabbing. In fact, Marci's throat had been slit with one of Brad's deadliest knives. He hadn't realized she'd stolen the weapon until it was too late. She'd probably taken it to trade for more drugs.

The killer had almost certainly been her drug dealer. Because of the knife, Brad could easily have been implicated in the murder, but since he was with Joy at the time, he was cleared. He'd had a solid alibi—Joy Alexander and her entire staff. They'd shared dinner with the JAG team the night after they'd closed both cases successfully.

If he'd ended it earlier with Marci, and if Marci had lived, would he have sought out Joy sooner?

He'd never know.

He flipped the chicken and watched it sizzle as he told himself he needed to eat, but his hunger had disappeared. He told himself that he wouldn't lead Joy into any deadly traps if he could help it.

Joy's home phone rang and he stilled, listening to see if he could tell where it was coming from. He noticed the caller ID the minute he found the phone on the far kitchen counter. It was a local number, the name unfamiliar to him. He waited for it to go to voice mail.

"It's me. Don't pick up, and don't stress. I'm using a friend's cell phone. Just make sure you delete this right away. I got onto the base, and I should have the files we need by tomorrow, or the day after at the latest. We're putting other people at risk here, and we'll have to work fast once we have the data. I'll be home by six if my new job goes as I expect it to."

Joy hung up and the machine immediately blinked that she had a new message. Brad played it once more before he deleted it.

He wished it was that easy to wipe out his feelings for her. He couldn't go through another relationship that went nowhere. Joy was in nesting mode; she'd gotten out, bought a place and made it hers. The furniture, the plants, all the art on the walls…

His work would never allow him to settle down, much less include a partner in his life. It was too risky.

Joy deserved better.

CHAPTER FOUR

"THAT WAS QUICK." Serena Delgado, the firm's most recent hire before Joy, spoke from her desk, which was positioned across from Joy's. They shared a spacious office set off by rich wood trim and a startling view of the Cascade Mountains.

"It was a simple last-minute crossing of t's and dotting of i's. You know, medical stuff." Joy held back a grimace at her clumsy cliché. "They'll probably call me in again over the next day or so. The Navy moves at its own pace."

Serena typed on her keyboard before replying. "My experience was more with the Army, but from what I've seen on base when my son or I go to the clinic for our medical care, the Navy is pretty efficient."

Was that a tone of disbelief? A glance at Serena allayed Joy's paranoia. Serena had a large stack of files at her elbow, eyes glued to her computer screen. She was just making small talk to help Joy feel welcome.

Joy hated lying, and Serena's generosity made her guilt that much worse.

I'm going to hell for this.

"I agree with you about their efficiency, but separating from the Navy is an administrative function with a lot of hoops to jump through. Just when I think I'm done, I get another phone call to come in and take care of yet another piece of paperwork."

"I know all about military red tape and paperwork, trust me." Serena's attention was entirely on Joy.

"Oh?"

"My husband was killed on active duty. In the war. The Army was wonderful to us, but the process was long. If I hadn't had such a good CACO, Pepé and I would still be waiting for our benefits to kick in." Serena referred to the Casualty Assistance Calls Officer, the military person who took the surviving family of a deceased active duty member through the complexities of survivor benefits.

"I'm so sorry for your loss, Serena. I trained as a CACO when I was on board the *Abraham Lincoln.*" And she'd been grateful she'd never had to serve the duty of being a surviving family member's sole link to the military during a time of such grief. Many of her friends had been CACOs and had found it emotionally taxing.

"It was a while ago, and Pepé and I have a good life here."

"You said you were Army. Where were you stationed? What brought you to Whidbey?"

"The short version is that I'm originally from Texas. I had a long-lost relative here, and she and I reconnected. I inherited her home when she passed away. But initially I'd learned about Whidbey when Pepé and I attended a resort for Gold Star families on San Juan Island. You might have heard of it—Beyond the Stars. I fell in love with the area and started to research the feasibility of staying. And then, of course, there was Aunt Dottie… Anyway, I was looking for a new life for Pepé and me, and this proved to be it." Serena restacked a pile of papers on her desk. "How about you, Joy? Are you planning to stay on Whidbey?"

"Yes. I've bought a house out on West Beach with just about all my life's savings. My last tour was here. I requested it after coming up to Whidbey for a weekend break from the carrier."

"Is there someone special here? Someone who gave you a reason to stay?"

The flush that was heating her face was impossible to stop. Until this morning, she would've answered with an unequivocal "no."

Before Brad pushed open her kitchen door and pressed his body against hers…

"Um, no. No one special here. I made the move on my own."

"That's brave."

"No braver than moving here after such a huge loss—with a child."

"Touché."

They shared a moment of quiet commiseration before Serena's gaze went back to her screen. A few seconds later she spoke again. "Believe it or not, we almost met last year. I'm involved with someone you know."

"Oh? I thought you looked kind of familiar."

"We didn't exactly meet but we were both at the Fords' Christmas party. Winnie pointed you out, but I never got the chance to talk to you."

Recognition dawned. "You're with Jonas, aren't you?"

It was Serena's turn to blush. "Yes. We're engaged and getting married at Thanksgiving. He told me you and he had briefly dated, and I didn't want it hanging between us. He thinks the world of you."

Stunned at the revelation, Joy stared at Serena. They were complete opposites physically. Joy had a boyish figure, and Serena was all curves. Serena's hair shone black and straight, while Joy's was strawberry blond and curly.

If Serena was Jonas's type, Joy had never stood a chance.

Her laughter surprised her as much as it did Serena. At the wariness on Serena's face, Joy said, "Please don't take this the wrong way—but I'm relieved! I blamed myself for not being able to make it work with Jonas. We never got past the dating part, you know." A kiss on the cheek was all she could give Jonas without reminding herself he wasn't Brad.

Because, even then, thoughts of Brad were still with her, months after the last time she'd seen him.

"I didn't even bother to ask him to recommend me to Paul." Paul, her boss, was Jonas's older brother.

"Jonas didn't give me details about you two, and I'm not fishing for any. I just thought you should know." Serena looked so happy, Joy knew it was the truth.

"There aren't any details to tell you. We went out a few times. That was it. He's a good man. You've got a keeper there."

"Yes, I do."

"I promise I won't be such a chatterbox every day, Serena. Don't let me interrupt your work."

"It's nice having you here, Joy."

"Thanks."

Joy settled into her chair and braced herself, trying to focus on her new cases without letting her mind wander back to Brad.

"Don't worry about Paul, by the way. He's the most easygoing boss I've ever had. As long as the work gets done and we satisfy our clients."

Serena's fingers were on her keyboard and her eyes on her screen as she spoke. Joy liked a woman who could multitask.

"Have you ever *not* done that?"

Serena's luminous brown eyes blinked before her attention rested on Joy again.

"No, not yet. But there'll be a first. There has to be. There's always something waiting to go wrong."

Serena had no idea how astute her observation was. In Joy's case, something very large had gone wrong, or at least thrown her off her game. Possibly on an international scale. Involving terrorism.

Joy dove gratefully into her work. She felt a flash of regret that she couldn't appreciate this day in its entirety, but she kept going. There'd be time to enjoy her new job later. After she'd helped Brad and his worries were behind him. Behind both of them.

Would that be it? Would Brad go back into the netherworld of her fantasy life, only a memory?

More likely she'd find herself in a deeper emotional pit than the one she'd been in after Norfolk.

As tears threatened to spill, she blinked and opened the top file on her stack. Usually she had no problem dredging up enthusiasm for her cases, no matter how menial. But she'd been a fool to think she could become invested in anything with the worry of Brad's predicament looming.

But Brad's problems were just that. His. She'd help him and then he'd leave. He wasn't the settling-down type. And Joy was done with moving, as much as she was done with men whose work took them around the world.

She'd had enough of it as a child with all the State Department moves her Foreign Service parents had made. They were currently posted to France for the second time.

"Oh, Joy, I forgot to mention there's a fresh pot of coffee in the break room. I've been making it every day after lunch, but now that you're the most junior staff member, perhaps you'd like to take over?"

"Sure."

Only someone as nice as Serena could point out so sweetly that Joy was the current low man on the totem pole.

Concentrating on something as mundane as coffee would keep her from drowning in the chaos that Brad had brought into her life mere hours ago.

JOY KEPT HER trip to the grocery store after work as short as possible, but she couldn't skip it. Not with Brad needing to eat. She hurried through the crowded aisles, wondering what to feed a trained killer. Did that make her an accomplice to murder? He'd had to "take out" the man in the boat. The SAM shooter. Would he have to kill anyone else on this particular undercover mission?

Stop it.

He'd be hungry after a day at her place. She'd

planned to get Indian takeout tonight, to celebrate her first day back at work. Instead, she was harboring a probable fugitive and wondering if she should stock up on canned goods in case they had to hunker down.

"Excuse me." She pushed her cart through the pasta aisle, throwing boxes of elbow macaroni into the basket. From the dairy cooler she took a half gallon of milk and some cheese, then made her way to the meat case, where she picked out the leanest ground beef she could find. She hadn't eaten red meat regularly in years, but she suspected Brad would wolf it down.

And she could freeze the leftovers for hearty meals later.

Later?

Her life had gone from controlled and serene to preparing for the apocalypse with the explosion of a small fishing boat. Only because she'd witnessed it.

Oh, and because Brad had scaled the West Beach cliff to her house.

"Credit or debit?"

"What?" She looked at the empty belt where she'd placed her groceries.

"Credit or debit?"

"Debit. I mean cash." Digging in her wallet for the extra cash she'd withdrawn while she was on base, she sent up a silent prayer of thanks.

The withdrawal from the ATM had been a last-minute decision, just in case.

Just in case she had to go off the grid with Brad. She shook her head. Her imagination was getting the best of her.

A gust slammed into her as she pushed her cart through the parking lot and to her car. Good thing Brad had made his climb *before* the winds picked up.

She almost laughed aloud as she loaded the groceries into her trunk. She'd never done anything remotely illegal before today, which was in direct contrast with going back on base and requesting files she had no official business having. She was the lowest of the low in the eyes of the military justice system. A traitor, even.

The drive home seemed unusually long as sheer exhaustion washed over her.

Cold dread at her decision to allow Brad respite in her home didn't help. Sweat broke out on her forehead, and she tightened her hands on the steering wheel.

She had no desire to dig deeper into her own psyche, to examine whether her fear was simply the result of her situation. Or was it because the man of her dreams was finally in her life again, in her home? Unlike real life, dreams were safe. Maybe she should ask him to leave…

No, no, no! She'd made her decision and besides, this wasn't permanent. These circumstances

had to be more straightforward than either she or
Brad thought; the most seemingly complicated
scenarios were often far simpler than panic or
anxiety blew them up to be. Case in point—Farid.
He'd been a kid who'd wanted to save his village and gotten caught in a firestorm of political
and military brass. His stint in prison had ended,
rightfully so.

If she had anything to do with it, the files
would help her put Brad's problems behind both
of them within forty-eight hours.

Once inside her garage she killed the engine
and hit the button to lower the garage door. Only
after the door was firmly closed did she get out of
the car and grab the groceries from the back hatch.

"Hello?" She walked into the kitchen and
stopped, listening for any indication that Brad
was still there.

"Over here." He walked in from the sun porch
wearing a USS *Abraham Lincoln* baseball cap she
recognized as hers.

"Is that all my clothes you're interested in, or
am I going to find you've been through my un-
derwear drawers? Please tell me you aren't wearing my Wonder Woman panties, too."

Brad's eyes narrowed but his reply was calm,
unruffled.

"I make it a policy never to cross-dress while
on mission."

His humor made her smile, but she noticed that his eyes remained wary. She'd missed him, missed his joking. Their banter.

"Just as well. Cross-dressing could complicate things at the moment." She took in the papers strewn on the sofa and his boots next to the end table.

"I thought you were going to lie low. Aren't you worried about someone seeing you from the sun porch?"

"With this hat on and sitting between your two potted palms? No chance. Everyone's focused on the area of the explosion, trying to determine if it was a terrorist action."

"What have they been saying on the news?" She put the perishables in the fridge and pulled out a baking dish, saucepan and frying pan. It might be bland and predictable, but her home-made macaroni and cheese spiked with the ground meat was an easy dish to make, and she suspected Brad would appreciate something that resembled comfort food. She could use a warm meal, too.

"Nothing much."

He maintained eye contact with her.

"I couldn't check the news at work, and I didn't want to ask anyone while I was running errands. I figure the less I comment, the better. No need to draw any unwanted attention to myself."

At least until Brad was out of her house and

off on his next FBI adventure. Because he would leave. She wanted him to leave.

Sure you do.

She set the cheese grater on the counter and wrestled her measuring cups out of the gadget drawer.

"Well, there's nothing new. The media's dropped hints that base officials think it could be at worst a domestic terrorist, or possibly a disenfranchised vet. The reports say that NCIS, FBI and local authorities are looking into the backgrounds of several suspects."

"You still believe you're going to get nailed for this, don't you?" She melted butter in a saucepan and stirred flour into it then slowly added milk.

"I have no doubt I would if I came forward now. I'd be cleared in short order, but meanwhile, the press might leak my name or photo, and the terrorists would gain the upper hand. I have to wait. If you get me the information I'm hoping for, by the time I make contact again I'll have the case wrapped up. Here, let me help."

Brad made short work of grating the Gruyere and cheddar.

Trying to appear casual, she quickly added the cheese to the simmering milk. The water she'd put on for the pasta started to boil, and the meat was browned.

"I know I'm just a lawyer, even if I'm a former JAG. My job in the Navy was to support you and other operators. Admittedly, I haven't experienced anything close to what you have. But do you think you might be a little paranoid after your time as a SEAL? After going through the trial and then… Marci's death?"

There—she'd dragged the ugly, wrinkled, stinking elephant into the room.

"That's in the past."

She dumped the entire box of elbow noodles into the roiling water. Brad needed his carbs. Maybe, right now, she did, too.

"It's not in the past if it's still haunting you today."

"What do you want from me, Joy?"

How about your hands on me, your lips on me, your undying affection…

"I want you to look at this objectively. You're hiding out in my house because you had to shoot a terrorist before he could launch a SAM at one of our aircraft. And you're undercover, which makes it even more interesting. You found out that they're targeting General Grimes. You don't want to blow your cover or let it out that the Bureau infiltrated the cell. I get that. But you could've had me call your boss, for heaven's sake. I mean, really, Brad, what's with all the drama?"

His eyes widened an instant before they narrowed, and he pushed back from the counter he'd been leaning against. His body vibrated with anger.

The man *did* have feelings.

"You think this is *drama*? That I'm making this up? I'll grant you, I've seen more than the average GI or SEAL, and I'm more messed up for it. I've lost more, too, including any chance at a normal life. But I'm in this for the greater good, Joy, not for myself. I haven't turned this into some blown-out-of-proportion video game. Real lives are at stake, and I'm not going to stop until I take these bastards down."

He stood inches from her and she reached out, placing her hand on his chest. His heart thumped under her fingertips, and she longed to embrace him, to hug away the hurt.

"I do believe you, Brad. I just wanted you to say it out loud."

His expression softened as anger gave way to incredulity and then relief. "You never doubted me."

"I worked with you for six months. I saw you risk everything for a man you barely knew. I was there when you were accused of your ex-fiancée's murder when you had nothing to do with it."

He reached out and traced her cheek with a shaky finger. "You never doubted me," he said again.

She drew in a shaky breath. "Oh, I had my share of doubts. I wasn't downrange with you and Farid. I had to double-check everything you told me—for your sake as well as his. And for my own sake. We all had everything to lose, and one man's freedom to gain. I'm not a saint, Brad. There were times I wanted you to be less of a man than you were. Than you *are*. It would've been easier, that's for sure."

She needed all her effort to keep her gaze on his chest, away from his eyes. When his finger moved from her cheek to her chin and tilted her face up, she tried to will her emotions away.

When their eyes locked, Joy felt a jolt of awareness travel from her lips to her most intimate places. Abruptly, she dropped her hand from his arm.

What did he see in her eyes? Had he realized she'd harbored a deep attraction to him? Still did? That the proper JAG had always had the hots for her enlisted defendant?

You're both civilians now.

His eyes burned with intent but nowhere did she see disdain or pity. Maybe Brad felt some of the same attraction, the same feelings she struggled to contain.

"Don't you think I was attracted to you when we worked together, Joy? Do you think you were the only one who felt it? Felt—" he stroked the side of her neck "—this?"

His breath was warm on her face and she burned for him. It was as if every hour she'd spent fantasizing about him, about being together, was concentrated in this single moment.

CHAPTER FIVE

BRAD HAD DREAMED of kissing Joy since the minute he'd realized they could have more than a lawyer-client relationship. They'd needed each other in Norfolk. He'd needed her to help him free Farid. She'd needed him to help get her client released from an unjust incarceration.

"We're both out of the Navy now, Joy. No more 'ma'am' and 'Chief.' It's just you and me, plain Brad and Joy."

Back in Norfolk he'd counted on her to do her job and to make sure he didn't implicate himself in any wrongdoing by defending a man who'd associated with known terrorists, albeit for the right reasons.

She'd been an officer, he an enlisted man. A relationship was off-limits even if the case hadn't been an obstacle between them. And he'd had to end his engagement to Marci; he wouldn't have gotten involved with any other woman until he took care of that.

But she'd tempted him. Joy's strength of character, her intelligence and her beauty—*Joy*—

called to him each and every damned day they'd worked together. At first he'd blamed it on months of not getting laid. Then he told himself it was because she was the only woman he was with on a consistent basis. At the end of a particularly grueling day, he'd almost leaned against a concrete wall and pulled her toward him for a kiss. He'd blamed it on not having access to regular workouts, but he knew, deep down, that wasn't the reason.

He'd fought his attraction to Joy for too long.

And now she stood here in front of him, her dark eyes reflecting her desire. He couldn't take his gaze from her crimson lips, lips that emphasized the translucent ivory of her skin.

He kissed her.

He had to keep this gentle. Easy, simple. A kiss, no more. Curiosity playing out between former colleagues who shared an extraordinary chemistry.

Joy moaned, and his good intentions went to hell.

He pressed her against the counter with his hips and had his tongue in her mouth before he could give himself a chance to second-guess any of it. She reacted in the most womanly fashion as she pushed back into him. Soft, smooth, hot.

They fit together so damned well. It was more than he'd imagined. It was more than lust. It was an attraction born of mutual respect and understanding of the other person and what they both stood for.

The temptation to take that kiss to the conclusion he'd fantasized countless times was just about overwhelming.

A *hissing* sound invaded the cloud of lust surrounding him, and he felt Joy's hands on his chest but he kept kissing her. The side of her neck was softer than any silk.

"Brad." She choked out his name, her voice rising in pitch.

"Kiss me, Joy," he muttered. "Just kiss me."

There was that *hiss* again.

"Brad." A firmer shove.

"What?"

"The noodles. They're boiling over."

He let her go and she turned, still in his arms, and shut off the flame under the overflowing pot. The starchy smell of burned pasta filled the kitchen, and he fought coming back to the reality of where they were, what was ahead of them.

Because all he wanted to do was keep kissing Joy.

JOY PUSHED HER hair out of her face with shaky hands, but she knew her knees were even shakier. When Brad's tongue had licked her lips, it was as though the ground she stood on had been shaken by one of those earthquakes that occasionally hit the West Coast.

All from one kiss. A kiss that was far more potent than any in her dreams.

She grabbed the sides of the pasta pot and squealed.

"Ouch!"

"Pot holders would be good."

Just like that, Brad was back to being the stalwart guy. He could act unperturbed but he'd felt what had passed between them as much as she had. She'd felt his heartbeat increase and felt the unmistakable erection under those too-sexy cargo pants.

"This is going to be mush." She poured the over-done noodles in the colander and placed the pot back on the stove to cool.

"It'll be great." He sounded…relaxed. As if he felt as comfortable being here as she did having him. As if no time had passed…

"You've been out of the active duty Navy for almost a year," she said. "Did it ever occur to you to call me?"

"Yes."

Don't ask the question if you're not ready for the answer.

For once she listened to her mother's wisdom.

SO HE DIDN'T want to discuss why he'd never called, never did more than "friend" her on Facebook.

She was an adult, no stranger to relationships

that had no future. Take Jonas. They should've been able to maintain a casual, Navy friends-with-benefits relationship. A lot of her female colleagues enjoyed the opportunity to date without expectations.

She hadn't lied to Serena. She and Jonas had never gotten past a few dates, very casual ones, at that—a meetup at the gym for a workout or at a local coffee spot. No romance involved. Her heart hadn't been in it. Neither had Jonas's, apparently, as he'd come back from the last of several career deployments to get engaged to Serena. Another work colleague, Dennis, was her perfect match on paper. He was a JAG, too, a lawyer who understood the demands of the job. But again, she'd never felt as much as a tiny sizzle with him.

Brad was different. Her attraction to him was something she'd never experienced before—not this elemental, damn the torpedoes, full-speed-ahead kind of desire. The frightening part for her was that it had started when they worked together, when a relationship was against Navy regs.

He'd never given any indication that he wanted anything from her but her legal expertise.

Except for that searing kiss five minutes ago.

So why did she feel this niggling sense of rejection?

As she sprinkled the remaining Gruyere and cheddar on top of the noodles, meat and sauce in the greased baking dish, she glanced at Brad.

Zip. Nada. His expression was back to the one she'd lived with for six months, working alongside him. Professional, detached, uncompromising.

"It strikes me as odd that an FBI agent has no one in his organization he can trust when his back's against the wall. Don't you have a partner?" she asked.

"My partner's on family leave. His wife just had twins, and he's taking several weeks off. I'll be provided with a temporary partner once I get back to my regular routine. Right now my boss and the higher-ups wanted someone with war experience in this part of the Pacific Northwest. We've had reports for months that suggest a homegrown terrorist group's been targeting either NAS Whidbey or Port Everett, or both. With my background I was the obvious pick to go undercover."

"And you wouldn't necessarily do that with a partner, anyhow."

"Right."

The casserole was in the oven, so she began to prepare steamed veggies in her pressure cooker. If they were going to enjoy a carb fest, she needed to include some greens. She had brownie mix in the pantry, and frozen yogurt in the freezer. Did they need dessert, though? Normally her mouth would be watering at the thought.

Instead, she picked up her glass of ice water to

moisten her dry mouth. She took several gulps before she grasped what Brad had said. The glass almost slipped out of her hand before she clunked it onto the counter.

"You think it's the same group Farid helped you take out in Afghanistan, don't you?"

Brad shrugged. "That's what headquarters and the Intel analysts were telling me. These guys fit the pattern. We had indications that they might try to interrupt the Naval exercise that's going on this week in Puget Sound and the Strait of Juan de Fuca. I was supposed to be halfway between the shore and the *Abraham Lincoln*. You know Old Abe is the flagship for the exercise."

"As expected." She didn't know a lot about Navy Special Operations or practice scenarios, but Brad was probably familiar with all the possible circumstances under which the Navy trained.

"I was at the boat rental place two days ago, ready to get my own little powerboat to take me out to the prearranged area, when it occurred to me that I'd be better off using my own equipment. If anything was going to happen at sea, I wouldn't be able to prevent it, but I trust the ability of the aircraft carrier and her ship's company to do their jobs. I certainly couldn't protect them."

"What are you most worried about?"

"That's classified."

Joy shook the bottle into which she'd mixed oil, vinegar, lemon juice and salt. When she finished, she poured a generous amount over the ready-made salad she'd bought.

"Save the classified routine for someone else, Brad. I'm the one risking my neck getting classified information for you, remember? What about your boss? Can you contact him now?"

"I could use your phone, as you suggested. But I'd rather not. I'm pretty damn sure that everyone's calls on this side of the island are being monitored. So if a call went into the Bureau from either your landline or your cell, it would immediately pop up. I don't want to bring anyone into this, no matter how legit they are."

"Maybe you should calm down and be a little more trusting of the process."

"I trust no one."

Joy washed her hands and looked out her kitchen window at the windswept coastline. The emergency vehicles of this morning were gone, but she knew Brad was correct. Several lookouts had been assigned to keep an eye on the beach for whatever—or whoever—washed up in the next few days. She didn't have to see them to know it.

They were looking for the domestic terrorists whose group Brad had infiltrated.

She shuddered. The thought of American citizens willingly working for such an evil cause gave her the creeps.

Brad was a solid military man who now worked for the FBI. He wasn't going to emerge from his undercover role until he had the answers he needed. That they *all* needed to ensure the safety of the base and surrounding area.

"I'm going to get into more comfortable clothes," she told him. "Please help yourself to some of this and I'll be right back. We have to come up with an action plan." She pointed to the dish of crudités and hummus she'd prepared and left on the dining room table.

"I've kept myself occupied all day. I think I can manage another five minutes." He walked over to the table. "Wow, you've fixed us a regular feast."

"It's the least I can do to support my local counter-terrorist undercover FBI agent."

"Well, not the *least*."

Joy didn't react to his comment—she wasn't sure he realized he'd said it so loudly.

Brad's tone was steady, the same level voice she remembered from Norfolk. But his expression was worrying. It wasn't the five o'clock shadow or the rumpled hair. They'd worked long hours together with few breaks and had seen each other at their worst.

It was the faraway look in his eyes. As if he was there physically, talking to her, but his mind was preoccupied with figuring out a puzzle.

She'd have to help him get to the bottom of it. Especially since she preferred her yoga pants and T-shirt to an orange jumpsuit.

THEY SAT WITH half a bottle of wine unfinished between them as she took notes and Brad leaned forward with his elbows on his thighs. She'd left the dinner plates in the sink for later, much as that pained her. What they were doing was more important.

"You must know something or you saw something downrange that's incriminating to whoever wants General Grimes, and maybe you, dead. Let's list all your missions and detachments. Anything you think was suspicious about them."

Brad actually laughed, a rumble from deep in his chest. It seemed to echo in her dining room.

"The real question is what mission *wasn't* suspicious or fraught with shady characters. Hell, Joy, do you think they send former SEALs and FBI agents to deal with the 'aboveboard' terrorists? Do you think there's such a thing?"

The skin around his eyes crinkled, and she noticed his even white teeth. He'd always been attractive, but as an enlisted man he wasn't available to her, even with his engagement on the rocks. He'd acted on his beliefs and on what he knew was right; she respected him for that. His behavior was typical of most Navy personnel she'd known, but she'd met a few officers as well as enlisted who'd crossed the line into fraternization. Brad had never so much as tried.

His good looks and their chemistry tempted her nonetheless.

"Cut me some slack, Iverson. I don't have the battle scars you do."

"I'm sorry, Joy. I guess I needed to blow off some steam with a good laugh."

"Glad I could help. Now that it's out of your system, how about refocusing and going over what you know?"

The thought of a bomb or a missile hitting either of the bases on Whidbey and injuring innocent civilians as well as Navy personnel stoked the fire that'd fueled the most fundamental reasons Joy had joined the military. She'd wanted to serve her country, protect its citizens and help defeat the bad guy wherever and whenever possible.

"Joy, you know I can't tell you any of that."

"You can't tell me details, fine. But you can list who you've been targeting. No names—just call them persons A, B, C, whatever. I just need a timeline."

"I realize now it was a cell of four, three since this morning's events. I think one of them is a veteran, unfortunately. Army."

"I hadn't even thought of it being another vet." She should have, though. The horrors of war were enough to make the most stable, honest human being turn to alcohol, drugs and worse. Mental illness rates among war vets were skyrocketing, and the VA Hospitals overflowed with PTSD patients.

"It's not anyone I ever worked with, not former Navy or Marine. The guy was in the Army and saw several people in his unit killed or injured by an IED. Based on what I've seen of him, he probably has TBI."

Traumatic Brain Injury. "That's rough."

"I've met all three players in this local cell face-to-face. The shooter is the first one I didn't know. The cell's small, and they're not the type who have the months of training by al Qaeda or ISIL behind them. They're homegrown terrorists who want some kind of vengeance because they feel the US Military wronged them—or the cause they've been associated with online."

"Only one of the three you know personally is a veteran?"

"Yes. There's one guy who acts like he has ties to another suspect, but I don't have anything solid there. Look, you have to trust me. I know my job, Joy."

"If you know it so well, why are you here asking me for help? Asking me to put my honorable discharge on the line, not to mention my new civilian job? A job, by the way, that wasn't easy to land?"

"Because I *need* your help. I can't say it any more clearly. I can't do this alone. If these lowlifes have somehow hooked up with the worst of the bad guys from overseas, they have to be stopped more than ever. I promise you, you'll come out a hero when all's said and done."

"I'm no hero, Brad, nor am I interested in being one. I'm a lawyer. A civilian lawyer. Maybe you just should've taken them out with your SEAL methods."

He grunted. "Trust me, it crossed my mind. But a SEAL's trained to take out the enemy on foreign soil. Not civilians in American territory. As an FBI agent, I have to play by the rules, too. And there's more—don't ask me for details here. The longer I track them, the more Intel we get, and the better our odds of finding how and what they're communicating with the overseas operatives. How they got hold of a surface-to-air missile, for instance. Plus, the likelihood that they're going to slip up increases with each hour I remain undercover. These seemingly loner operatives could help us blow open a much larger network."

She leaned back in her chair. It was mind-boggling to consider how much the FBI and other LEAs did to keep the country safe on a daily basis.

Her task was much simpler.

"Tell me about your boss."

"Mike Rubio. You met him briefly during the Norfolk trial. He was the officer in charge of my SEAL team. We've worked together for almost two decades."

"And yet you have no way to contact him other

than through official channels? I'm not getting this, Brad. You have to have someone to reach out to. And won't he be worried about you?"

"He might be, but we've been through worse. I already told you. I can't make a move until I know where the cell is and what they're up to. Or if my team's narrowed in on them or even taken them out by now. That might not show up in the press right away."

"Yeah, I know." So many Navy cases had initially attracted media attention, but after it was determined that it would be in the nation's best interests to keep the facts classified, reporters had been notified and the cases left to die a quiet media death.

"Do you think Mike's looking for you?"

"I'm sure he is."

She knew that Mike was like family to Brad. It was the SEAL bond.

"I understand, but you don't have to be a SEAL to understand that you share deep bonds with your teammates."

His teammates. Afghanistan.

He nodded.

"The *overseas operatives* you mentioned, the terrorists—you had something to do with targeting them downrange, didn't you?"

Admiration flashed in his eyes a second before his expression returned to its battle-hardened mode. "That's classified. But yes, I may have a connection, or a personal interest if you will, with the bad guys driving these domestics to commit terrorism."

She wanted to push him on this, to find out more. If he'd been on a witness stand, she would have. But he was in her living room, and she knew he'd shut down completely if she got too close to the truth.

He thought he was protecting her, no doubt.

"It must be hard to have left the Navy, only to find the same bad guys are wreaking havoc in your own country."

"Yeah, it's not pleasant. But at least I know who I'm dealing with." He stared down at his clasped hands.

A moment later he looked up at her again. "It's a kick in the gonads that we didn't take care of them all during the war. I thought we had, on several occasions, but this particular group is like a hydra."

"That's their basic structure, isn't it? The sleeper cells exist to become operative and go live just when they seem to be eradicated."

"Yup."

He stood up and started to pace. "I feel bad telling you all this, but since it'll help you find the information I need…" He turned to her, his gaze searching for something she didn't understand.

Or didn't want to.

"If I'd overlooked anything during our debriefs,

one of the other guys would have spoken up. Same goes for Mike. I've often seen things he missed. That's the point of the debrief and operations report. Everything of consequence, and a lot of extra stuff no one ever uses again, is in those reports. I'm telling you, Joy, any leads from our contacts downrange have been thoroughly exhausted by now."

"Hmm." She'd read some of the reports from the raids on Farid's village. Even with her need-to-know status as a JAG, she'd come across several places in the reports that had been sanitized for the legal proceedings. The lines blacked out by a Sharpie had troubled her then and troubled her now. Was the answer to the cell's motives in those lines?

"Spit it out, Joy." She loved the way they'd slipped back into their easy working relationship. They'd worked well together and shared similar views on world events. And Navy justice.

She'd left her sexual fantasies about him to her imagination, however. But after being kissed by Brad tonight, she couldn't control her desires anymore. His touch had broken her carefully constructed dam against unwanted emotions.

Leave it alone.

She couldn't relive that kiss, not now.

"I hate to say this, but unless you can come up with something more specific, we're going to have to wait on the files. Once I get a good look at them, I might be able to piece together some kind of scenario. I don't suppose we can go talk to Grimes in person?"

He shook his head. "Not yet. I'm not ruling it out, but it's better if we lie low for now."

Joy sat up straight.

He'd said *we*.

CHAPTER SIX

"I'M NOT ONE for drinking during the workweek but today feels like it's been three weeks in twelve hours."

She refilled their wineglasses and pushed Brad's toward him. Thankfully, he seemed a little more relaxed.

"Believe me, this isn't the way I planned to meet you again."

"Really? You planned to meet me again?" Intrigued, she sat back down across the table from him. Ignored the flip-flop of her stomach at his admission. He didn't mean it the way she wanted him to. Did he?

He turned his glass between very capable fingers, swirling the wine. It'd been such a brief moment, that kiss earlier. Yet she'd stored away the memory of how wonderful his fingers had felt as he caressed her face, ran them through her hair, stroked the nape of her neck.

"I resisted looking you up for a long time, Joy. In case you haven't figured it out, I'm a damned mess. Before Marci, I'd never had a relationship that lasted more than six months. Marci and I lasted longer and even got engaged only because I was out of the country for three quarters of our time together. I'm not a good roommate."

"Oh?"

"I've been on my own for too many years. I'm trained to be a nomad, rootless." His eyes sparkled in the candlelight. She was glad she'd lit the table votive as the blue glass sent a soothing reflection across the burnished oak. Like the water of Puget Sound in the morning.

Before she'd witnessed the explosion.

"All of us in the Navy feel like nomads. There's no crime in wanting to keep moving around." It had grown old for her, but she'd done it as a kid, too.

"Did you move when you were a kid?" she asked.

He looked surprised at the question. "No. I grew up in a big rambling suburban house with four siblings. They've all become doctors like my parents. I'm the only exception. You?"

"We moved a lot. I have one brother, who's a diplomat like my parents. Mom and Dad are in Paris, Tommy and his wife, Elaine, are in Djibouti." She took a sip of her wine and choked on it. Coughing, she put the glass down.

"Don't feel obligated to drink with me." There was humor in his tone.

"It's just that I'm more of a hot tea girl this late."

He nodded. "So you moved a lot when you were young?"

"Yes. All over the world. Going to the Naval Academy seemed a natural fit for me, since I didn't want to do the exact same thing my parents had, but I wanted to serve. I went to law school after my first tour and I never looked back. Until…"

"Until?"

"Farid. That case was the hardest I've ever had. If you hadn't been so solid in your testimony, Farid might have faced the death penalty for something he didn't do." She shuddered.

"He's innocent, Joy. You still believe it, don't you?"

"I do. But you have to admit, it would've been easy to think he wasn't. And now, with this incident, it'd be handy for the international terrorists if they had an agent already in-country. To a lot of people, it might seem reasonable to think Farid's the one calling the shots. Or if not him, someone he's connected to. If these local terrorists were at all suspicious of you, they could've shared your photo with their contacts. Farid would recognize you anywhere. How do you know, in fact, that they don't have their aim on you?"

"It's too convenient. Of course, the bad guys would use him, or me, as a fall guy if they could. But Farid's not even 'Farid' any longer. He's in WSP, as you undoubtedly remember. And no one, other than my colleagues and SEAL team, knows I went FBI." Farid had been placed in the Witness Security Program and lived quietly somewhere as an American citizen.

"I'm sure you're right. But I have to cover all the angles."

His sigh reached out across the table and she wanted to comfort him, hold him, reassure him.

But she couldn't even reassure herself that this would all turn out okay.

"The war trials put you off the Navy life, then."

She shook her head. "No, no, not the Navy life, per se. I just had a come-to-Jesus moment where I had to face certain facts. I'd been dreaming of settling down for years. I didn't have anyone to settle down with, so I had to find a place I could call home."

"Weren't you ever afraid you'd be sorry after you got out? That you'd have regrets? Do you?"

"Not at all. I can always go into the Foreign Service as a counselor, or work for a firm overseas if I'm so inclined. We never know what the future holds, but I've been the happiest and most at ease since I bought this house and started a new life for myself here. It might sound fanciful, but Whidbey Island has woven its magic around me."

"And that includes knitting. I noticed some projects and yarn in a basket by the fireplace. I don't recall you showing a crafty side when we worked together, though."

"I don't just knit. I'm interested in community theater, too, but there wasn't any opportunity for acting in the Navy. Knitting can travel with me anywhere. I even knitted in Gitmo and on the carrier—in my room with the door closed. I wasn't about to share my creative escape with the other officers."

"I don't blame you." He leaned forward on the table and took her hands in his. She trembled at how quickly the warmth ran up her arms and made her face feel hot. Her nipples tightened in arousal, and she was completely focused on Brad. "Listen to me, Joy." As if he knew she was fantasizing about him.

"I'm all ears."

"I wanted to come and find you, ask you out. It's something I thought long and hard about. When I got transferred to the Seattle office, I looked you up and saw that you were still assigned to Whidbey. I'd hoped to wrap this case up on Monday or by the end of this week at the latest, and then..."

"Then what?"

"I would've called you, asked how you were, asked if you were involved with anyone." He took a deep breath. "Then I'd have invited you out, picked you up and taken you to a waterfront restaurant. Talked for hours. Caught up, allowed you to see the side of me you never got to know."

"What held you back? Marci's death?"

"Isn't that enough, Joy? I couldn't try to start a new relationship with so much baggage. I didn't think I was still in anyone's crosshairs. Apparently, I may be."

He released her hands and sat back in his chair.

"Brad?"

"Yeah?"

"The answers are no and yes."

It was her turn to show him *her* other side.

THE SPARK IN Joy's eyes scared Brad more than any inbound missile or bullet ever had. He had to make sure Joy didn't take anything he'd said the wrong way.

"I told you this so you'd know I didn't forget you, Joy. But I'm a lousy bet for a relationship. I could never bring you into the mess that's my personal life. And I never took you for the casual dating type."

The spark died a quick death.

"Apparently, FBI agents get trained in playing God. Anything else you want to tell me about myself?"

"You're right. I'm an ass."

"That's about you, not me."

Her strength of character was what had drawn him to her on a deeper level than her sexy looks.

She'd never been afraid of him, or afraid of challenging his convictions. Joy's trust cracked open a door in his heart he'd thought forever sealed by years of ops and a nomadic existence.

"Joy, why have you trusted me? I didn't seek you out sooner, I busted my way in here and now I'm screwing up your first week at your new job."

"*Shouldn't* I trust you?"

"Touché."

She broke eye contact with him and looked away. "Timing's everything. It's pretty clear to me that we're not meant to be more than friends or colleagues. I'm grateful I'm still in a position, of sorts, to help you with your mission. On the personal front, well, let's just say I'm in the market for stability. No offense, but former SEAL current FBI agent doesn't fit the job description."

He couldn't keep from laughing and, after a pause, she joined in. Her eyes sparkled as her face relaxed into a wide smile. This was how it would be if they'd met as two normal people. No missions or cases preventing them from enjoying their time together.

He made another silent vow that he wouldn't let any harm come to her.

"I'm not expecting this to get drastic, Joy. In a few days I'll have these bastards under lock and key, and the system will take care of the rest. But if there's even a hint that it's going south, I might have to ask you to come with me. To take off."

"Please. You're being dramatic again."

He heard the sadness in her voice. If he didn't have to worry about innocent civilians being put at risk, he'd turn himself in now to get her out of potential trouble and leave her to the life she'd worked so hard to achieve.

"Maybe I am."

"How much do you trust your boss?"

"With my life. Mike's not the bad guy here, Joy."

"But you said you can't trust *anyone*."

"What are you suggesting? It's not him, Joy."

"How do you know that? How close have you been since you started working for him at the Bureau?"

Her questions were spot-on, and the pounding in his temples began again. No amount of alcohol was going to dull the pain of the thought of betrayal, no matter how ludicrous.

"It's not him," he insisted.

"If you're sure, then I accept that." But she didn't look convinced.

"You know what I think, Joy? I think you watch too many damn TV shows. Not everyone's a bad guy. I'm as aware as you are that some of our people have turned. But no one I've worked with has."

"We need a break. Our brains need a chance to process all this." She stood up and stretched. He let himself stare at her body as she reached above her head, her snug yoga pants and T-shirt leaving little to the imagination.

"I'll take the sofa." He wasn't planning to be anywhere but right by the front door, and within earshot of the kitchen side door.

"You'll never be able to rest."

"One of us needs to stand watch."

"I'll do it. You can sleep in my room and I'll stay out here."

"Like hell you will."

"Are you pulling your macho card on me now, Brad? Because it's been a long day and I'd love three or four hours of solid z's. I can do guard duty until four or five, then you do it so I can get some sleep before work."

He heard her words, her logic. Did the woman ever relax and just let it go?

"Go to bed, Joy. Like I said, I'll take the sofa."

His request was met with silence. He felt her uncertainty across the kitchen.

"See you in the morning, then. You'll come and wake me if you need me?"

"Yes."

Her soft sigh and the sound of her bare feet on the wooden floor underscored what he longed for, but would never have.

Joy.

CHAPTER SEVEN

JOY DIDN'T KNOW if it was her anxiety or an unfamiliar sound that abruptly woke her at three-
thirty in the morning. She waited, her pulse
pounding in her ears.

The doorbell.

She scrambled out of bed and stumbled over
to the bedroom door. She'd left it ajar. Still in her
yoga pants and hoodie, she slid her feet into her
slippers.

Feeling her way along the darkened hallway,
she heard the doorbell again, this time followed
by a sharp pounding.

"Police! Open up."

Her focus on getting to the front door quickly
shattered as she ran into Brad.

"What are you going to tell them?" His whisper was urgent.

Didn't he get it that she was in, she was committed full throttle to helping him? If her kiss
hadn't told him that, didn't the fact that she'd let
him sleep over give him a clue?

"Nothing. I'm telling them nothing. Shouldn't

you be hiding in the basement or something?"
She shoved at his chest. It was harder, and he was
more solidly built than she'd realized.

The door.

"You can tell them whatever you need to, Joy.
I'll be out of here."

"Stop it. I don't have to let them in, remember?"

"Unless they have a warrant."

"Now who sounds like a lawyer? Go and hide.
I've got this."

She did. She had to.

Perspiration dripped between her breasts. It
was one thing to manipulate the truth to obtain
files that might contain information that would
help Brad nab some serious bad guys, especially
when Whidbey and its civilians were being targeted.

Lying to the police, however...

She opened the front door to a group of three
men, all in OHPD uniforms.

The officer closest to her had his hand in midair, ready to hit the door again—with a final
warning before they forced themselves into her
home? Was that a battering ram in the hands of
the four additional men who stood in her driveway? Undercover, perhaps, since they weren't
in uniform?

"Can I help you?"

"Joy Alexander?"

"That's me."

"Captain Mark Cross, Oak Harbor PD. We need to ask you some questions."

"With a battering ram?"

He shrugged, and she saw no sign of sheepish awareness that their tactics were overkill for a house that held a single citizen. As she looked more closely at him and his partner, she noted that their uniforms didn't quite match. And they didn't have the usual OHPD insignia she was familiar with. As a JAG she'd worked with all levels of LEAs, and these dudes weren't cops. She'd bet her house on it.

There weren't any vehicles in her driveway or right in front of her yard, so she had no way of knowing how they'd gotten here. They could be walking from house to house, but...

You're the one they're after. They know you have a connection with Brad. Don't be the weak link.

She shivered. The door had to stay open to indicate that she wasn't hiding anything or anyone, but she wasn't letting them into her home. She couldn't.

"You know about the explosion off the west shore earlier, I assume?" "Officer" Cross was an attractive man with steely eyes and short, silvergray hair that glinted under her porch light. He was stunning.

His fake uniform and "cop" demeanor, not so much.

"I gave my report earlier to Officer Jones. I've seen the news on TV. Is there anything else I need to know?" She purposely used a false name for the officer who'd interviewed her.

None of them reacted to the name. They nodded and acted as if they agreed with her, as if they knew about her report.

As if they knew the fictitious Officer Jones.

"We have reason to believe a suspect is hiding in the area. We're assigned to check each house on West Beach Road."

"And your warrant?"

His eyes narrowed, and she saw one of the other men shift his feet. Whoever these "cops" were, they knew at some level that they were overstepping the bounds.

"None of your neighbors has asked for a warrant, Ms. Alexander."

"I'm thinking none of my neighbors are licensed attorneys, *Officer* Cross."

His head went back, a slight movement that she could easily have missed. But after years of working with criminal defendants and military prosecution, she knew how to read body language. Prided herself on it, actually.

"Officer" Mark Cross was a phony of the highest order, and yet he hadn't expected her response.

He broke into a wide grin, his teeth glinting in the dim porch light.

If he thought she was an innocent Little Red Riding Hood, he was in for a surprise. She had poison in her basket.

"You're in the Navy, Ms. Alexander. You of all people should understand the importance of timely investigation."

"I *was* in the Navy. I'm out, working for attorney Paul Scott. And I don't know anything about the explosion, other than what I've already reported to the police. I called it in minutes after it happened, before I left for work today—yesterday. You must have seen my report. I have nothing to add." He didn't need to know she still had one more day on active duty. She could point out that she knew damn well he wasn't really a cop, but she refrained. Let him think he had her fooled.

Joy stood her ground, allowing her body language to inform Cross—or whoever he was—and his cohort that she wasn't stepping aside. There'd be no search of her home, not without a warrant.

"Do you have an ID, Officer Cross? For documentation purposes?"

His face reddened.

Got you!

"I don't carry my wallet or ID on missions of this nature."

"I understand, truly I do. And I need you to understand that because of my law background,

I'm not going to let you into my home without a warrant."

She shut down her fear, shoving it to the farthest corner of her mind. She'd deal with it later. The fact was, these men could easily overpower her and ransack her place, finding Brad in seconds. She was betting they wouldn't.

Hoping, no—*praying* they'd leave.

She stared at Cross with complete audacity, matching his arrogance with her own. When he looked away, she knew she'd won this round. His police persona was back in place, his expression neutral.

"Sorry to bother you, ma'am. We just need to make sure you're safe."

"I am. You're the only person who's knocked on my door besides Officer Jones." Still no reaction to the false name. Lying was getting easier; she'd have to address the question of moral integrity later.

"Well, if you have any problems, don't hesitate to let us know. Be advised that we may get orders to return." *With a warrant.* He didn't have to say it.

"Thank you, *Officer.*"

She watched them turn around and walk back toward the road. It was too dark, and the high fir trees obscured her view, so she couldn't see what kind of vehicles they'd used.

Only after they were out of sight did she close the front door and collapse against it.

"How come you're so sure they weren't really Oak Harbor Police?" Brad asked as they sat at the kitchen table, sipping coffee she'd brewed once she'd acknowledged she'd never get back to sleep.

"Remember, I'm not in OHPD jurisdiction. If the authorities needed to search the homes in this area, they'd send in the sheriff's department. But, okay, they might use OHPD if they're as busy as they were earlier, when they sent out the *real* officer. Which is why I made up a name for the officer who came by yesterday morning. They didn't even react."

"With a case like this, the Feds will use all the locals, no matter who they are."

"True. But these weren't locals."

"What did the guy who did the talking look like?"

She poured more sugar into her mug. There wasn't enough sugar in the world to take the bitterness off being awakened by pseudo-cops in the middle of the night. Especially after a long day of wondering how deep she wanted to get into what was turning out to be an international terrorist plot.

With the man seated across from her as the focal point...

She described "Officer" Cross.

"You thought he was attractive, didn't you?"

She felt a flush creep up her neck and wanted to blame it on the hot coffee.

"Uh, I was a little too distracted to notice. I was busy trying to keep them out of the house."

She couldn't see his eyes, couldn't read his response. He hadn't flinched at the threat of half a dozen men breaking into her home and presumably dragging him out of it. And yet he cared whether or not she'd found this Cross guy attractive?

His stillness forced her hand. "Yeah, okay, he was a good-looking dude."

At Brad's continued silence she let out a long breath.

"You know him, don't you?" she asked.

"Probably."

"Good guy or bad?"

"Depends. But he's not someone I'm concerned about." He sipped his coffee and she wanted to throttle him. His mind was no doubt way ahead of hers, his ability to hide his reactions unnerving.

"You have to find a new place to hide, don't you?"

"It's not about hiding, Joy. It's about learning who's behind the cell, what they plan to do next. It's possible they've figured out I'm still alive, and they may have made the connection between us. If I'm in their sights, you could be, as well."

"That was my choice. Helping you, I mean."

Her hands shook and she wrapped them more tightly around her mug. It was the adrenaline, the caffeine—and a little fear.

The warmth of his hands around hers was as startling as it was welcome. His palms were bigger than her mug and encased hers. She closed her eyes and reveled in the security they promised, if only for this brief time before he left.

Because he would leave.

"No, I think I had something to do with convincing you, Joy."

"Stop it. This has nothing to do with our… our kiss."

"I shouldn't have done that. I'm sorry."

"As much as I want to enjoy having the fearless Brad Iverson apologizing to me, why don't we call it what it is? I kissed you as much as you kissed me."

"You did."

"We're both messed up."

"No doubt."

"So let me help you, Brad. I can. We just need some answers."

She felt him shaking his head.

"No. I can't live with the threat of another person I care about being taken out by the bad guys."

"Brad, Marci had other problems…" They'd never discussed it. She'd signed an affidavit supporting his alibi when she'd received it from the court system in Norfolk, Virginia. The need to reach out to him after they'd finished Farid's case had been strong. But she'd respected his privacy. And accepted that if they were ever going to become more than colleagues, he'd have to be the one to reach out first.

But she'd never expected him to, no matter how much she'd hoped for it.

"You're fierce, and you never back down when you believe that what you're doing is right. It's one of the reasons I love working with you, Joy."

He released her hands, and she immediately missed the intimacy of his touch. And felt like slapping him for not seeing her as more than a shipmate.

He'd taken the possibility of more kisses off the table. It was for the best.

Wasn't it?

"You don't deserve to live like this, Brad, even for a couple of days. Life on the run is for rookies. We're getting too old to play these games. Let me drive you onto the base later this morning and get you into the legal office. Or I can take you to my new office. As my client, you'll be safe, and you can call the Bureau from there."

"I'm not involving you or your workplace. Besides, I have a feeling my boss knows I'm okay now—those were our guys at your door. Even with my evasion tactics, he knows I'm here. He wouldn't have sent them otherwise."

"Why didn't you tell me? And why didn't they push me aside and come in and get you?"

He didn't answer her first question. "Too messy, and not necessary. You're a witness, they have no idea what I've told or not told you and they don't want you to disappear, too."

"Who says I'd disappear?"

"Because if I do, I could take you with me. That's looking at it from their perspective. From my point of view, however, I don't want to upset your life any more than I already have, but you may have to come with me for a few days. I'm hoping it won't need to happen, of course."

Disappear with Brad.

Her skin crawled, and she wanted to be in her sunroom sipping coffee with a Brad who wasn't haunted by the demons of his past, real or fabricated. Even when it was the good guys tracking you for all the right reasons, things could go wrong.

Stay in the present.

"I believe in you, Brad. I believe you're innocent of any terrorist plot, that goes without saying, and that you had no choice but to take out that missile and its handler. I also believe you'd better figure out whatever you need to figure out quickly. If our side knows you're still breathing, it won't take the bad guys long to figure it out, too. And they'll be after you."

And her. She was now as much at risk as he was.

The terrorists would see her as an obstacle, someone who'd gotten in their way.

She set her mug on the polished surface of the table she'd found at an antiques fair in France when she'd visited her parents in Paris earlier this year. For years she'd been collecting pieces of furniture, pottery, exotic fabrics—all with the goal of having her own place and never moving again.

The thought of having to pack up and go, even temporarily, left her cold. Would she really have to leave, get out of sight, as Brad was suggesting?

BRAD'S SKIN STRETCHED over his knuckles as he clenched his fist on the table. He needed every bit of self-control not to pound it on the wood until it was bloody. Or slam it through a wall. Or better yet, smack himself in the face.

"I've made a huge mistake, Joy. I never should've involved you in this. It seemed like a decent shot, getting the information I knew you'd be able to find in the court records. It's snowballed too quickly, and I need to get the hell out of here. All I ask is that once you've got the files and have gone through them, please take the information to General Grimes. He'll be able to fill in any blanks."

"You're the one who needs to meet with him, Brad. Now, not later."

"It's too risky."

"Did you ever talk to him about what you saw out in the field? Whatever it was."

"Yes."

"Yes?" He heard her incredulity. After a heartbeat or two, he could feel her anger simmering.

"The entire time we worked together on Farid's case, you never mentioned that you'd spoken to him."

"It was a private conversation and wasn't relevant at the time. It had nothing to do with proving Farid's innocence."

"I disagree. The officer in charge of operations in the field had everything to do with it—if you told him about your mission!"

"First of all, he gave you a deposition early on, which you yourself said was less than helpful. He had the big picture in mind. He was a successful leader because he knew how to delegate. Second, I had no idea that some of what I'd shared with him might eventually prove to be relevant. Like you, I thought that once we got Farid released and into Witness Protection, the bad guys would call off their witch hunt."

"Obviously, they've still got some eye of newt to toss into the pot." How did she manage to retain a sense of humor, not to mention a hopeful, almost upbeat temperament when her life had been put in danger—by a man who could never give her what she deserved?

And why was his body responding to her nearness when his only focus should be on keeping her off the terrorists' radar and protecting her from the unforgiving mess that was his life?

"Grimes is living on the southern part of Whidbey," she said. "In the middle of the woods."

"How do you know that? Do you keep a dossier on everyone you've ever taken a deposition from?" He imagined her recoiling in the darkness. He hadn't meant to sound so snarky.

"I have a good memory." She laughed. "It's the one thing that's gotten me where I am. What's saved me and my career is that I remember anything I've ever seen in writing."

"A photographic memory?"

"Yes, except with all the information we have available now, compared to when you and I were in school, I don't hang on to the pictures in my mind like I used to."

"I think I was in school a while before you were."

"No, we're the same age, actually."

"You know my date of birth," he said with a laugh. "Of course."

"It's close to mine or I'm sure I wouldn't. We're both September babies."

They'd never shared that kind of personal information before. She didn't include her birthday on Facebook, so he'd had no way of knowing her age. She'd taken his deposition and had access to his entire military file—the part that was unclassified.

If he was smart, he'd leave now and get as far away from her as possible. Leave her to the life she'd created for herself.

The thought occurred to him as light peeked through her darkened windows. The edge of dawn was starting to creep in.

"How quickly can we get to Grimes?"

"He's forty minutes away, tops." After a brief pause, she added, "I'll drive you there."

"Like I said, I shouldn't involve you. I can't have you on my conscience, too." Dread pooled deep inside him. It might be too late for him to disappear and hide out. Worse, it might be too late for Joy, too.

CHAPTER EIGHT

JOY'S HAND FROZE as she lifted her coffee. "Are you talking about Marci? Your ex-fiancée—she was a drug addict, Brad. They arrested her murderer. I saw the same reports you did when I signed the affidavit that you were with me and our team." She'd looked up the media reports, too.

The silence they shared left her fears unsaid. He believed he'd failed at the most important mission he'd had—to save a loved one from her life of drug addiction.

"Some people are truly beyond saving, Brad, no matter what you do. You're one of the country's top FBI agents. But addiction—it's hard to fight, hard to defeat. Unless the addict genuinely wants help."

"You sound more like a counselor than a lawyer." His derision and his anguish cut through her, but she had to at least try to convey her belief in him.

"I've worked with a lot of people over the years. Just being in the Navy is like a primer in addiction training, don't you think?"

He grunted.

"The Navy's a microcosm of society. You know that, Brad. Except you get squeezed together with hundreds of your best buddies in a tin can in the middle of an endless ocean. It brings a whole new meaning to Psych 101. You can't tell me you haven't seen your share of alcoholics on deployment. If you ask me, it's worse when they get back home—finally able to drink as much as they want, and no missions to keep them dry long enough to see that what they're doing is crazy."

Her sermon was met with a stony silence.

"I think you'll feel better after you meet with Grimes. We'll go as soon as the sun comes up, before I have to be at work. We should get the files later today, too. They'll tell us something."

"*If* they tell us anything, you can fill me in later. You're right—I need to see the general. I don't feel safe just sitting here anymore, Joy."

"You think I have to get out of here, too?"

"You might."

The weight of that reality made her want to weep, to rage at him for messing up what had become her first taste of "normal" in all her years since college. Go on the run? Where?

This was complete insanity.

"If you're convinced I need to, I can wait it out on base, take a room in the Bachelor Officers' Quarters…" Her resistance conflicted with Brad's concern. She saw his gaze take in her expression, and he leaned toward her.

"You don't have to do that. Not yet. Let's focus on getting me to General Grimes and you getting hold of the case files."

"Okay."

"You're my only hope at this point, Joy." His sigh distressed her with its exhaustion, its obvious frustration and was that…surrender?

"I'll go to work today. I can't just skip out on a new job and besides, it'll look more natural and less suspicious. As I said earlier, let me drive you to General Grimes's place. If you need to, hide in the backseat and pop out once we're there and past any security. We should leave within the next thirty minutes so I can be back in time to get ready for work. I'll go in to the office as if nothing's different." And she'd be able to get the files from Dennis the minute they came in.

The early-morning light revealed the lines of his face, and she wanted to reach across the table and brush the lock of sable hair from his forehead. She liked how his longer hair made him both more approachable and wilder-looking—in a sexy way. The FBI had standards, and he'd have to cut it again once he was no longer undercover.

"You've got a good plan as far as the files go, Joy. But General Grimes probably doesn't have any answers. If he did, I'd know what they were, since I'm the one who spoke to him."

"You had a lot going on, Brad, and bullets were flying. Your adrenaline rush and then later, the decompression, could have wiped some things out of your mind, for better or worse."

He shook his head, and his stubbornness infuriated her. "Don't you think I've already scoured my memory raw looking for details I might have forgotten? Do you think I like walking around knowing there's a chance I missed some detail, and that's allowed terrorists to continue their campaign against the US? Against innocent civilians?"

She reached out her hand and covered one of his clenched fists. His skin was smooth and dry, and his hand seemed huge on her table. His hand stiffened, but he didn't pull it away.

"We all do what we can in the moment," she said. "That's especially true in combat. There's nothing you can change about a mission that took place years ago. You have to accept that or you'll never move forward."

"I didn't have any problem moving forward when I was in your kitchen yesterday."

She felt the heat on her face, but he wasn't going to scare her away with his sniping.

"I realize you've gone over the events hundreds of times. That doesn't mean there isn't something left, some dark corner you've missed. You've got to figure this out, or you're going to beat yourself up about it for the rest of your life, even after you catch these bastards."

Brad knew that he—no, *they*—were dealing with a terrorist organization that sent out tentacles who knew where? A group of individuals linked by a web of zeal and belief in the power and rightness of their cause.

"My biggest fear is finding out that whoever's behind this has been tracking me all along. That I've put everyone in my life in danger."

She nodded. "That's not necessarily paranoid in this day and age. What you're worried about is improbable, but not impossible. There's no doubt that you might have to run. I might have to, as well, but let's keep the focus on your meeting with the general. I'll get the information from the files this morning. Then I'll meet you back at General Grimes's. Let's hope this resolves itself quickly and simply—with the apprehension of the cell you've been surveilling. Then the suits can go after the international connections."

He stared at her until she wondered if he was having some kind of mini-stroke. Stymied, she waved her hand in front of his face.

What she didn't expect was Brad's reaction as he grabbed her wrist.

"You can drop all of this now, Joy. I'll disappear, and your life can go on the way you've planned. I'll find another way to get the information in the files."

"No."

She endured his stare for a moment, noting how his intensity made his green eyes glow almost aquamarine.

He let go of her wrists and stood up straight. "Then let's get moving. I'll go shower."

Her confidence ebbed with each step he took toward the guest bathroom. The sinking sensation in her middle, combined with the cold sweat clinging to her skin, wasn't unfamiliar. It was like an old friend, her anxiety. A big reason she wanted to avoid moving again. Avoid change.

Helping Brad meant changing in a difficult and fundamental way. By going with whatever played out, no planning allowed. No planning possible.

In fact, planning didn't matter when you were faced with something as dynamic as a terrorist threat.

Or when you encountered feelings. Your own. And someone else's.

Deep breaths. Focus on something tangible now.

She looked at the mugs in the sink. They needed to be rinsed, loaded in the dishwasher. She should run it now so she wouldn't come home to dirty dishes.

Would she come home? When?

Stay in the present.

The mugs clattered as she pushed them together and turned on the hot water.

"I rely too much on schedules and itineraries, anyway," she muttered to herself.

REMORSE MADE BRAD'S shoulders painfully tight, even under the steaming shower.

He turned off the shower. Joy's towels were huge and fluffy compared to the old ones he'd unpacked in his new place in Seattle. Despite his intention to settle down, once again, his career had his life careening into chaos.

Something had to give, but right now he couldn't afford the introspection it would take to figure that out.

A soft knock startled him out of his thoughts. "Come in."

As she pushed open the door, he remembered he had a towel wrapped around his waist. Nothing else.

"Joy, wait—I need to get dressed." He reached for his pants.

"It's okay. You're decent enough, and I'm not coming in any farther."

It wasn't *her* reaction he was concerned about. He turned and faced her. "Make it quick."

"I only wanted to tell you that I'm sorry if I've come across as though I think you're an inconvenience. As if I don't want to help you with every bit of this."

Her face was in shadow, and he didn't dare

get any closer. Even his self-control had limits, SEAL training or no.

"Joy, if I could turn back the clock, gone somewhere else yesterday, I would. You have every right to be pissed off at me, at the situation. This is scary stuff."

"I'm not scared. And I'm up for whatever you need." The break in her voice betrayed her, but he had to give her points for balls. She had enough courage for both of them.

"Of course you are. I wouldn't expect any less from the same woman who...who helped free Farid."

He bit his tongue, hard. Hell, he'd almost blurted out that he cared about her. As in, had feelings for her.

Deep feelings.

Not just the kind that made him want to drop his towel and close the gap between them, either.

"I'm ready whenever you are." She meant "ready to leave." But he heard the other meaning, the one he wanted to hear.

"I know you are, Joy. That's what's scaring me."

"Nothing scares you, Ivy."

She used the nickname she'd given him in Norfolk because she said his hair made him look more like an Ivy League student than a SEAL. He'd been letting it grow out after months downrange...

"FALSE. I'M SCARED of lots of things. Pretty screwed up, in fact. I've already admitted that."

She ignored him. "You know why I called you *Ivy*? I told you it was your haircut, but that was only part of it. I saw in your records how much education you have. You never even mentioned that you have two master's degrees. One in criminology, the other in psychology. And if you ever finish that dissertation, you'll have a doctorate in criminal psychology."

"I get bored on shore duty."

"No, you're a genius, Ivy. A bona fide genius." She sounded as if she was talking to a rock-and-roll star, or a favorite athlete.

"This is no-shit serious, Joy. I am messed up, I believe my life and now yours may be in danger and I'll do everything in my power to keep you safe. We don't have time for this kind of chitchat. Is there anything else?"

"Oh, I'd say I understand how no-kidding serious this mess is, and I told you, I'm in. Do you think I'd make an illegal request for files I no longer have clearance for, lie to law enforcement, let you stay in my house if I wasn't?"

"No. But I've seen things you haven't. This could get very ugly."

"I'm not some newbie ensign, Agent Iverson. Get dressed, will you?" She spun around, and he gave her credit; she could make an exit.

Until a dull *thud*, followed by her cry, echoed in the hallway.

He acted without thought and was beside her, wet towel and all. Her back was hunched, and he slid his hand over her shoulders. "Are you all right?"

"Yes, I just stubbed my toe, that's all."

She stood up quickly as if she was trying to get away from his touch. He pulled his arm back reflexively then reached out to steady her.

Protecting Joy was instinctive.

When she spoke and her breath caressed his cheek, he realized her face was closer than he'd noticed.

"This is awkward, isn't it?" Her strained voice hinted at the same turmoil he was wrestling with.

"It's never awkward with you."

His lips missed hers in the dark, and his kiss landed to the left of her mouth. He took the opportunity to adjust his stance, wrapping his arms around her and pulling her tight as he reached his mark on the second try.

Her breath mingled with his. He wasted no time on sweet kisses or tender nips. He needed to feel the inside of her mouth with his tongue. Apparently, Joy had the same need, and her tongue eagerly met his.

Brad knew kissing Joy would be incredible— how could it not be after he'd imagined it for so long? Months of wondering, of wanting, of fighting his desire. That kiss in the kitchen had satisfied nothing; it had only stoked the craving he'd been forced to ignore. The craving to go after her, find her, explore this connection between them.

See if it might lead to more...

Now he'd placed her in harm's way and instead of making her safety—and the mission—his number one concerns, he was allowing himself to feel something he hadn't felt in forever.

Contentment.

Immediately followed by an emotion he thought he was an expert at managing.

Fear.

He lifted his head and released her as quickly as he'd embraced her.

"I'm sorry, Joy. This is the last thing I need to be doing right now. I've broken my promise to you that it wouldn't happen again."

"We're in a tense situation. It's natural that we need a way to vent."

"I've been in a lot of tense scenarios, Joy. Trust me when I tell you that I've never felt a need to decompress like *this* before."

The house rattled and she gasped. "The wind." She took a shallow breath. "It gusts in from the strait and shakes the rafters."

Her voice revealed her trepidation, her anxiety.

"Let's get out of here, Joy."

CHAPTER NINE

PULLING OUT OF the driveway on her own was anticlimactic. Brad had left the house on foot fifteen minutes ahead of her after instructing her to drive toward her new office as if this was any other workday. He cautioned her to watch for anyone following her.

Joy gripped the steering wheel as she drove down West Beach Road. "I'm a lawyer, damn it, not some special agent."

Her words seemed to hang in the car as she tried to process the fact that her new job wasn't the priority at the moment. First step was to find Brad and get him in the car. Then they'd drive to General Grimes's without any drama, or so she hoped. And prayed.

After that she could still get to work in time for a normal day.

She continued along the smoothly paved surface of West Beach Road. On any other occasion she'd appreciate the beautiful drive. Through the fir trees lining the road, she caught brief glimpses of the cliff views off the Strait of Juan de Fuca, its waters glistening in the bright sunlight. Driving through the forested part of the road onto the cleared highway that led into town, she forced a smile onto her lips. Brad had said that she needed to look "normal." That she was being watched, no question. She wouldn't be able to tell whether or not the authorities wanted her to *know* she was being tailed.

No sooner had she pasted a smile on her face than she noticed a dark car in her rearview mirror.

"Crap!"

Brad had said to forget picking him up at their predetermined point—near the long drive that led up to a dog kennel, an obscure area—if she even suspected she was being tailed. He'd wait for an hour before striking out on his own.

She didn't have the training Brad did, but she'd represented enough clients who'd been followed, or who'd had the training themselves. She knew that the first way to determine if she was being followed was to take a few unexpected turns.

Blowing past the place where she was supposed to pick Brad up, she headed into the island's main city, Oak Harbor. Let the bastard follow her into Starbucks during morning rush hour.

To her distress and anxiety, he did. The driver of the dark vehicle, which had stayed behind her the entire trip, walked into Starbucks two minutes after she did.

Keep cool.

She gripped her purse, steeling herself to make a quick exit if need be.

"Joy?"

To say she jumped out of her skin was an understatement. She swallowed a scream that would have pierced the eardrums of the barista.

A display of large mugs stood to her right. If she needed to, she could grab one and deliver a blow to someone's head.

She turned around and stared at her "tail."

"Paul!"

Paul Scott, her new boss. Great.

"I thought that was you. What, isn't the coffee at the office good enough for you?" He flashed a warm smile at her.

"Were you just on West Beach Road?" she asked.

He gestured at his running attire. Certainly not what he'd worn when she'd seen him at the office.

"Yes, I go over there for a run once or twice a week before work. It's convenient to have a shower room in the office. You know the showers at work are for everyone, right?"

"Of course." She tried to allow relief to flow through her, relax muscles that were bunched in a fight-or-flight response. "I, um, hope to use them myself, once I'm more settled."

He looked her up and down, obviously taking in her more casual clothing.

"I just left a yoga class."

He nodded. Totally believing her.

"You can try out the new sauna I had installed last summer."

"I'm used to driving to the base gym for my shower and sauna. I haven't found a place in town yet. It'll be pure luxury to have it in the office."

"It might be a little over-the-top, but I do want to keep everyone who works for me happy." Paul seemed pleased with her observation. She'd never been an ass-kisser, a "smack" in Navy parlance, and hated to start now. But if it kept him unaware of her actions of the moment, she'd take the hit. There'd be time to explain herself later, after she got the information Brad needed to close his operation.

Crap! She couldn't tell Paul she wasn't coming in today. Her plan had been to call in, but Brad had insisted she leave her phone at home. One less thing anyone could track her with.

Usually the coffee line went quickly, as the early-morning baristas were the best; today, of course, it crawled. She tried to discourage further conversation by staring at the menu that was posted above the counter area.

"How are you feeling on your second day of work? How did yesterday go?"

"Great! I loved it." She ignored her guilt over taking a longer lunch on her very first day to go to the base and arrange for files to be delivered that had nothing to do with her new employment.

"Everyone's been so nice and welcoming. I can't thank you enough, Paul. My initial cases are very doable." Did she just say *doable*? She couldn't help flinching.

"Glad to hear it. I know the transition from active duty to civilian can be rough at first. My brother is Navy, and getting ready to become a full-time civilian. You've met his fiancée—Serena."

She nodded, willing the line to go faster.

"They met in unusual circumstances having to do with a family house. Have her tell you about it sometime. At any rate, take all the time you need to adjust and get settled in. I like to think I run a family business, and you're part of our family now."

"Thanks, Paul."

She was grateful that he didn't know she'd briefly dated his brother. Or if he did, he saw no reason to bring it up. And she wasn't going to tell him what she and Serena had discussed yesterday. She was just getting to know Serena and didn't want to betray her trust.

Serena was right; Paul was the perfect boss.

"Are you glad you went into law?" she asked.

"Yes. It's afforded me a life here on Whidbey, which works well for my family." She could tell that Paul was starting to get tired of their small talk, too, judging by how he pointedly studied the menu.

Would the damn floor open up and swallow her, please? Her legal training and Navy experience had taught her to interpret facts in all kinds of ways, but outright lying would never be natural to her.

It's for the right reason. Lives are at stake. It might involve national security.

"Can I help you?"

Finally. Reprieve in the form of a coffee cashier.

"Cappuccino. Whole milk, please."

"Anything else?"

"Bagel with everything, toasted."

She wasn't hungry but had to keep up the ruse that she was on her way into her second day of work with no other plans. Dressed as if she was coming from a yoga class she'd never attended.

"I've got it." Paul's hand reached around her, and he gave the cashier a credit card. "It's on the office. I'll take a large morning blend, please."

Joy smiled at him. "Thanks, Paul. I appreciate it. You don't usually come in here, do you?"

She would've noticed him before; he was too distinguished-looking not to attract attention, and she'd frequented the shop often when she worked on base.

"No, I prefer the little mom-and-pop drive-through, but my run went longer today. I need to get in early for a conference call with Seattle and New York, so this was closer."

Of course he had a conference call. Paul was an accomplished, busy lawyer.

And he'd just hired a lying, law-breaking woman who'd probably be on the lam before the week was out.

IT FELT LIKE FOREVER, waiting for Joy to turn around and come back for him. Fifteen more minutes, and he'd hike it down to General Grimes's place on his own. Thirty-two miles on foot—it would take him the entire day to get there, especially with his need to remain hidden.

He heard barking, and the bushes around him rustled. He knew the yelps were from the dogs in the nearby kennel, but the rustling had him on alert. Suddenly, with no fanfare at all, a large possum rambled out from under an overgrown rhododendron. He stepped aside to let it pass by, grateful it hadn't been anything to worry about. Like a terrorist.

Or a skunk.

His respiration rate was up, and sweat beaded his forehead even in the cool morning. He sat down in the tall grass, closed his eyes and forced himself to calm down.

Images of yesterday's events flashed across his mind. The SAM apparatus in the small fishing vessel. The enemy agent lifting it, preparing to fire. The crisp blue of the sky as he fired his own weapon. The subsequent fireball.

Joy's lips.

Joy. He didn't deserve her belief in him. The sheer determination on her face as she told him she'd get the answers he needed had allowed a tiny flicker to ignite in his cold, dark heart.

Hope.

He opened his eyes.

He had to talk to Grimes.

JOY WAS NEVER more grateful to be leaving the coffee shop for the parking lot. The diversion from her route had cost her fifteen minutes. Running into her new boss, almost literally, had made her wonder if she was really the right person to help Brad. Lying, hiding an undercover FBI agent and sneaking him to a secret meeting while she foraged through classified government documents that she had a mere thirty-six hours to access—she hadn't been trained for any of this.

Not intentionally.

She smiled to herself as she thought of how scarily qualified she actually was to do all those things. She might not think of herself as a liar, but the ease with which she came up with blatant falsehoods had to be credited to years of piecing together seemingly random facts to create a defense or prosecution. The cappuccino was hot but worth the immediate lift it gave her. As if she and Brad hadn't consumed enough coffee over the past twenty-four hours!

Her usual confidence reappeared in the form of knowing she'd find the answers he needed. Brad had stumbled across something significant when he was in the middle of a difficult mission overseas. She was sure of it. They just needed the case documents to figure out what and to whom it was so damned important.

She could do this.

"Joy!"

She spun around and faced her good friend and knitting partner, Emily Bowman. She and Emily had met at the base gym during a Pilates class over a year ago.

"I don't usually see you out and about in the mornings!" Emily's brunette bob fluttered in the wind, her corkscrew curls wild, her cheeks flushed from exertion.

"Hey, Emily. Are you on your way to or from the gym?"

Emily laughed. "You know me too well. When I got off duty at the hospital, I hit the 0530 spin class they've started. You should come and join me."

"Yeah, well, with the new job and all…" Lying to protect Brad's innocence was one thing. But now she was putting on a false front with a close friend. Emily had helped her through a rough period when she'd been weighed down by cases on base and had just broken off with another man she'd dated. It all seemed like such a waste of time. All that effort trying to find a man she could be with. When all she really wanted…

Was an irrevocably unavailable man.

"Oh, no worries. I understand. You know how crazy I've been since my book came out!"

Emily's book. Crap. Joy had forgotten—the signing was last night.

"Oh, my goodness, Emily, I missed the signing! I'm an awful excuse for a friend. Please tell me there's another one?"

"There is. Tonight, in the yarn shop in Coupeville."

"Oh, um…"

Emily's face clouded for an instant before she smiled and patted Joy's forearm.

"Joy, it's no big deal. It's a knitting pattern book, not some big juicy novel or Pulitzer Prize contender."

"It's *your* book, Em. You used my rosewood needles to create the sweater pattern!"

"Yes, I did." They'd been on a two-day jaunt to a fiber festival in Oregon. Emily had forgotten her complete needle set in the midst of designing a lovely tweed pullover for her pattern book. Joy had her circular set with her, including the size Emily needed. It was a small thing as far as Joy was concerned. But Emily had been so grateful she'd knitted Joy an intricate lace scarf with the leftover yarn from the sweater. Joy cherished the scarf, which was the first gift she'd received from anyone on Whidbey, and it had made her feel she belonged somewhere besides an aircraft carrier, courtroom or Navy base. It made her feel that Whidbey was *home*.

"Do you think you can make it tonight? Maybe we could do dinner before the event."

Joy faltered. This was getting harder.

"Oh, I wish I could, but I have a meeting with my new colleagues that's going to take all afternoon. I'll probably have to grab something from a drive through for dinner."

Emily shrugged as though it was no big deal.

But it was. Emily was her friend, and Joy prided herself on being there for the people she cared about.

Wasn't that why she was slinking around like some kind of a black ops wannabe for Brad?

"I'll see if I can get out of it early, Em." She sent up a silent prayer that she didn't have to go on the run with Brad before the signing.

"I know you do—stop stressing out. We can go to dinner another time. And if you make it to the signing, great. If not…"

A tall, slender man walked past them, so engrossed in his cell phone that he accidentally bumped into Emily.

"Whoa. Sorry." The man paused and stiffened as if he'd been hit by a two-by-four. It was impossible to miss the look of annoyance in Emily's eyes.

"Must be a really important text." Emily's grim tone surprised Joy. Her friend was usually upbeat, although she'd had her own sad times, losing her husband, Peter, to cancer while they were still newlyweds. But that had been more than a decade ago, and Emily seemed happy with her life. She was a talented Labor and Delivery nurse, and all the new mothers adored her.

She and Joy didn't talk much about Emily's dating, but judging by the way Emily glared at the inconsiderate texter, Joy realized that maybe she and Emily suffered from the same thing.

They didn't know how handle it when a man showed interest in them.

"Emily." The man put his phone in his jacket pocket and stared at her. "Good morning."

Emily didn't repeat the greeting. Wow, this guy—whom she obviously knew—must have really pissed her off somehow.

Joy glanced around. She had to get to Brad ASAP or he'd start hiking to General Grimes's, and she'd be out of touch with him until he showed up there tonight.

"I've got to go. Emily, I'll see you later, okay? Bye!" She smiled at Emily and was stricken by the shock on her friend's face. Emily raised her hand.

"Later, Joy."

Joy told herself she deserved to go to hell. Not just for lying so blatantly to Emily, but for leaving her to contend with a dude she obviously wasn't pleased with. It broke girlfriend etiquette.

But Joy didn't have time for manners.

"CAN I BUY you a cup of coffee?" Dr. Ben Franklin, US Navy Commander and Pediatrician, showed no sign of the exhaustion Emily felt to her bones. Blast the man.

"No, thanks." She made a show of smoothing her fleece jacket over her bike pants and headed to the shop door.

"You can't keep avoiding me, Em." He fell into step beside her, and she wanted to scream.

"It's *Emily*. And I'm not avoiding you." She refused to look at him. That had been her undoing. His expression. His knowing eyes. His mouth—she couldn't let herself think about his mouth.

"You are." He reached around her and opened the coffee shop door.

Of course he was a gentleman. As well as a Navy Commander. Oh, and a highly respected doctor.

"Thank you."

The immediate warmth of the shop and the hum of voices calmed her reaction to him. A bit.

"I see you worked out after our shift."

"Yes."

"I was in the gym, too, but mostly I ran the

path. A good workout after a hard shift is the best 'sleeping pill' I've ever known." He referred to Naval Air Station Whidbey's running path, which had magnificent views of the water.

"I go to the spin class on Tuesdays. When I'm getting off the night shift, it's perfect."

"Do you like it?"

"I wouldn't do it if I didn't." She fixed him with her death stare, developed during years of working with sometimes-arrogant doctors who were a little too sure of their ability and not so good at listening to mothers in labor.

All it got her was a flurry of awareness as he met her stare with a steady gaze that made no attempt to disguise his interest in her.

He grasped her wrist, his hand gentle. "Please, Emily. Let me buy you coffee, and breakfast if you haven't had it. I need to talk to you."

If he'd said "we need to talk" or "you need to hear me out" or "let's be adults about this," she would've walked away and found solace in a bowl of Cheerios and the stale store-bought coffee nestled in her refrigerator door.

She was trained to take care of others, trained to assess, to listen to a patient's needs.

Ben wasn't a patient, but his request was genuine.

"Okay. But it's not a date, Ben. I mean it."

"Who's putting labels on anything?"

CHAPTER TEN

SHARP PAINS SEARED Joy's chest, and she briefly wondered if she was having a heart attack.

It was the damned coffee. She was more of a tea drinker, and having so much coffee on an empty stomach—no, make that a *nervous* empty stomach—had kicked up her GERD. Gastro-esophageal Reflux Disorder, the bane of over-achievers worldwide.

She'd been diagnosed with it after her tour in Norfolk. During the long months when she'd told herself she was crazy to fall for a man she'd never kissed, a man who was off-limits to her.

It wasn't a cardiac event. It was her GERD.

She rummaged in her purse for the bagel and took a bite, chewing as she drove back toward their rendezvous point. Brad had said he'd see her and come out of the woods and onto the road. Under no circumstances was she to park her car or get out to look for him. He said it was a stan-dard precaution and made her promise to follow it.

Her hands were shaking again. What was she

so damned afraid of? Death—that was a good thing to be afraid of.

You're afraid you're doing this because you've fallen for Brad, not because it's the right decision.

Maybe.

Her GERD could be attributed to fear, too. She'd never faced the possibility of running for her life before. The circumstances with Brad had put this fear in her belly. Definitely Brad.

She was putting her entire life on the line for him. Everything she'd worked for over the past several years and especially this last year. It wasn't only her new job or her hope for a satisfying civilian career and a local community to call home that were at risk. If she blew this, she'd also find herself dishonorably discharged from the Navy and disbarred from the legal profession.

Finding employment with a dishonorable discharge was problematic, to say the least.

She threw the bagel back in her bag. Nothing was going to taste good until Brad's situation was resolved. Worst case? She'd end up dead alongside him. Someone, or several someones, had their sights on him, and if her hunch was correct, this had been going on for a long time. Since the op in which he'd met Farid...

As she approached West Beach, she slowed near the road they'd chosen as their rendezvous point. There was no sign of Brad in the tall grasses and weeds that grew from the shoulder up onto the slight rise and the fields. She looked between the trunks of fir and cedar trees that lined the wooded areas. No luck. Movement in the shadows caught her eye, and hope flared. Until she identified it as a small Whidbey Island doe, staring thoughtfully at Joy's vehicle while she chewed brush.

Awareness of needing to blend in with local traffic, while slowing down enough not to miss Brad, increased her nausea, and she turned the AC on full blast.

She was seven minutes late. Not bad considering she'd had to deal with both Paul and Emily. But in Brad's world, seven seconds could mean the difference between life and death, and to make it seven *minutes*, well...

"Don't lose it now." She forced her spine straight and lowered the windows to let in the fresh morning air. The warmth of September was in the scent of the pine needles that had roasted in the sun all month long. August had been lovely, but September was almost always the warmest and sunniest month on Whidbey.

"Hey!"

The shout reached her just as she was about to turn around and go back past the kennels. She looked in the rear-and side-view mirrors; thankfully, no one was on the road with her, not even a bicyclist.

She brought the car to a quick stop on the shoulder, and she waited, prepared to make a U-turn if necessary. Seemingly out of nowhere, a figure lunged at the passenger side of the vehicle.

"Unlock it!"

Brad's voice jolted her from her momentary shock, and she unlocked the doors with the button on her left armrest. She felt a rush of air as he opened the back passenger door, heard a slam, and then he disappeared from her rearview mirror.

She turned, straining, to see him in the well between the back and front seats.

The car immediately filled with the scent of pine and cedar he'd brought with him. His profile against the lower part of the backseat was stark, and he looked as if he hadn't eaten in days instead of having a substantial breakfast with her a couple of hours ago.

Before the sun came up.

"Go, go!" Brad gestured at her, urging her to turn around and drive.

"I'm going!"

"What the hell took you so long?"

"I had company."

"What kind of company?"

"I thought I was being followed. Well, I *was* being followed—so I drove to Starbucks instead of coming to get you, just like you told me. It turned out to be my boss. And then after I got rid of him, I ran into a good friend who, by the way, I'm supposed to meet tonight at her book signing in Coupeville."

"Forget that."

"It's not that easy." She breathed out a sigh of frustration. "I think we made the right decision. It's probably better if I keep up the appearance of sticking to my usual routine. Even if I'm questioned, no one can *prove* you were in my house, and I won't have anything to tell them."

"You know I'll be at General Grimes's."

"No, I won't. The only thing I'll know is that I dropped you off somewhere south of Coupeville, along the Old Farm Road. I won't have any idea *exactly* where you are."

"Unless you're right, and he does know something about the big guns behind the cell I've infiltrated."

"Yes." She kept driving.

BRAD HAD BEEN in worse getaway situations than on the back floor of Joy Alexander's crossover vehicle. The most damnable piece of this whole mess was that each moment he spent with Joy drew her deeper into the possibility of getting hurt.

Risk was part of the life he'd chosen. And it was the same for the other team members, no matter what service or agency.

Joy was different. Sure, she'd worn a uniform,

had been a JAG. She'd taken the same oath of office he had, and since she'd signed up during wartime, she knew her life could be at risk, like that of any other sailor.

She hadn't signed up for this mission, though. He'd dragged her into it. After keeping her out of the worst of his disaster of a life after Norfolk, he'd shown up on her doorstep yesterday and all but forced her to help him.

His hope that there'd ever be a right time for them was crushed by the knowledge that he'd been so selfish in going to her.

Although there was no other JAG, no other person, he trusted as much as Joy.

Shit. He was in deeper than he'd realized.

"You okay back there?"

Her voice had a catch in it that he remembered from Virginia. Whenever the case had her stymied or he hadn't given her the answer she'd expected, her voice started to quaver the tiniest bit. He didn't think anyone else noticed it, but he had.

He'd noticed an awful lot about Joy.

"I'm fine," he replied. "Are you sure you know where Grimes lives?"

"Well, sort of. I'm fairly certain it's between two different developments, off the beaten path. I've been down here for parties with my knitting group."

He grunted to himself. The thought of lawyerly Joy Alexander looking all domestic as she held two needles and a piece of yarn contrasted with the woman who'd defended Farid with her entire legal arsenal.

"I heard that." Of course she had.

"Knitting group is the new cocktail hour, you know."

"Make mine on the rocks."

"Very funny. Which brings me back to the book signing. I have to show up there, Brad. Too many questions are going to come up if I don't. I never miss knitting group unless I'm sick—or when I had watch. Now I have a new job, so I was able to explain why I missed Emily's signing in Oak Harbor last night. But the other gals will wonder what's happened to me if I don't show for her signing tonight."

He knew she was right, but he didn't like the idea of—of what?

Being away from her. Not having her nearby, within view.

"Okay. After you drop me at Grimes's, go to work. Go through the day as you normally would."

And forget you ever saw me.

"I will. I should get the files by this afternoon."

"If General Grimes doesn't have what we need, they'll be my only chance. You still checking to see if anyone out there is watching you? Following us?"

He studied her profile as she looked in her

rearview and side mirrors before returning her focus to the road. Joy wasn't classically beautiful; she was stunning. Her straight, uncompromising nose was balanced by her full lips. Lips that had been so soft under his.

"Not that I can tell."

He half sat up and rested his head against the side of the passenger seat. He could see her profile, but he was still out of sight.

"You've done enough for me, Joy. If you get what we need from the files, just report your findings to the base NCIS. They'll be able to get the truth to the right people."

"Do you really believe that, Brad?" She turned to send him a no-nonsense glare, and his heart stopped as he saw tears glimmering in her eyes.

"Watch the road, Joy." He couldn't allow himself to care for this beautiful woman, no matter how he felt about her. These were emotions he'd never experienced before. There was something intense between them, all right. That intensity was what had him on edge, even more than the fact that his cover might've been blown.

Because the moment he let any emotion get in the way of a mission was the moment it went to hell.

"Your fiancée, Brad—what happened there?"

"She was killed. You read the reports before you signed my alibi."

"I did. I'm not asking how she died. What I

mean is, why did you fall in love with her?" Only Joy would be asking him about his deep dark secrets while he crouched on the floor of her backseat.

"I thought it was time for me to start the family life. I'd hit thirty, and I was the last single guy on my team."

"Fair enough, but what really attracted you to her?"

"She needed me."

"Was she using before you met her?"

"Yes. Look, Joy, I'm from a family of doctors. We've all got the caretaking gene, if you want to call it that. It's a characteristic that's ingrained in us. I went overboard with Marci, trying to heal someone who didn't want to be healed. It was a relationship that never had a chance."

At his silence, she shook her head and he could feel her incredulity before she spoke again. "Did you tell her that?"

"No. There was no point. I broke it off. I'd just realized that I'd agreed to marry her out of compassion or, rather, what I thought was compassion."

"But?"

He flicked his thumb against the leather of her seat cushion several times.

"*But* is the crux of it. My caring was really my attempt at playing God, thinking I could fix her, control her intake of drugs and booze."

"Why didn't you mention any of this in Norfolk, Brad?"

"It's not that complicated. You were an officer."

And he'd been enlisted. Now that they were both free to pursue a relationship with each other, it didn't matter. His life was too chaotic, and Joy's was too...neat. Controlled.

Bile rose in his throat at the reminder of his pain at finding out Marci was dead. And then to find out she'd been brutally murdered for less than fifty bucks worth of heroin...

"Sorry for bringing it up again."

"No, I'm sorry, Joy. Getting you involved in my life is a big mistake."

"We've already had this conversation. Several times. Now, be quiet while I find the general's house."

He couldn't help Joy navigate, so he settled back onto the floor of the car, feeling his own self-loathing in every bone.

JOY KNEW OF four or five homes nestled in the backwoods area where she drove along a winding road. She was fairly certain one of them was General Grimes's. He'd taken all the measures needed to keep his location private, avoiding social media and not appearing on any websites or internet lists. She hadn't been able to find his address in various searches on her personal laptop, and didn't want to use her work computer yesterday to look up any information related to the case.

Thankfully, Whidbey had a small-town air, and she remembered hearing one or two of her knitting-group buddies mention a newly retired military bachelor who'd recently moved in.

Not that she thought of General Grimes as a *bachelor*. The man was pure military leadership, the stuff history was made of.

Having Brad so near, even on the floor of her car, was distracting. She'd never questioned her driving skills before today.

She braked in front of one driveway that looked promising, only to see the name "Farley" on the mailbox.

"Are we there?" Brad's voice rumbled up from the car floor.

"Not yet. Sorry about the quick stop."

"No problem. My head's battle-hardened, didn't you know?"

"I have no doubt."

She smiled but kept her gaze on the shoulder of the road, looking for the next mailbox. Feeling a sense of relief, she drew closer to a bright red and yellow mailbox with the unmistakable emblem of the US Marine Corps on its side. Even the reclusive General Grimes wasn't above showing his pride.

"I think I've found it."

"You're not sure?"

"As sure as I can be at the moment." The homes on this stretch were all in a price range the average military pension could never afford. The pension of a retired flag officer, however, fit the bill. She swung onto the graveled road and concentrated on not hitting any of the potholes.

Her initial exuberance deflated when she came grill-to-bar with a closed gate.

"Where are we?"

"Nowhere. We're at the gate to the property—and it's locked. I think I should get you past this point instead of what we planned." She saw a call box and lowered her window. "Be quiet."

"Yes?" A gruff, familiar voice boomed through the tiny speakers.

Pushing the red button, she spoke slowly and clearly.

"General Grimes? This is Commander Joy Alexander. We worked together in Norfolk."

"What can I do for you?" It was him. She'd recognize the surly tone anywhere, even through a cheap intercom system.

"I need to speak to—"

"It's Senior Chief Petty Officer Iverson, General. We served together in—"

"I know who the hell you are. Come on up."

As the gate swung open, Joy turned in her seat to face Brad.

"I thought you were keeping a low profile?"

"We're out of range of the road. No one can see

me. Do you think he's going to call the police or the TV stations?" Brad's eyes glinted in the light that cut through the tree canopy. Once again Joy felt the deepest longing for him—and regret that they hadn't met at some other time. But doing right by Brad was more important than her unshakable need for him.

"No, of course not. Remember his disparaging remarks about the media when he was on the witness stand? I don't know many officers who like the media, but his feelings toward reporters made me feel almost bad for them, even the obnoxious ones."

Brad laughed. "Yeah, he isn't one to mince words. Joy?"

"Yes?"

Did he want to kiss her again? Because she wanted to kiss him. She only had to lean in, twist a little more in her seat...

"Drive."

THEY WERE STOPPED within a few yards by a man in full camouflage gear with a rifle in his hands.

"Oh, my G—"

"Roll the back window down, Joy."

"Are you kidding me?"

"I know these guys. I've worked with them before."

Of course. One of the guards. She hit the button with her left index finger.

"Ray, how you doing, man?"

"That you, Brad?"

Joy rolled her eyes as the men did a brothers-in-arms kind of greeting. She ignored the little twinge of envy at their natural understanding and camaraderie. She'd left that life behind, set sail on a different course.

She knew she'd made the right decision.

"We're going up to see the general," Brad said.

"No problem." The guard's deep brown eyes assessed her, and Joy offered him a smile. She'd lowered the front passenger window, too. She counted two other guards walking around the area, all suited up similarly to Roy.

"I'm Joy Alexander."

Roy nodded. "Nice to meet you. Stay safe."

"Will do." She checked her rearview mirror to make sure Brad was done talking. His eyes met hers, and she was powerless against the attraction that unfurled deep within her.

"Won't they tell your boss they saw you here?"

"Drive, Joy." For the second time in five minutes she stopped thinking and trusted Brad's direction.

CHAPTER ELEVEN

THE FAMILIAR TALL, lanky form of General Jeremiah Grimes, United States Marine Corps, Retired, stood at the bottom of a wraparound porch. He wore a bright, almost garish orange flannel shirt, and Joy wondered if he wasn't hot in the September sun that slanted through the tall firs surrounding his A-frame. Even this early in the morning, the day was warming up.

"General." Brad shook the bald man's hand as Joy took her time walking around the front of her car. She wanted to get out of here as soon as possible. Away from the energy these two men exuded.

What was it with General Grimes? She'd had to interview him before he took the stand in Farid's trial. General Grimes was a straight arrow; his career record revealed nothing but a stellar history as an infantry officer who'd dedicated his life to his nation. He'd never mentioned a family. She only knew these facts about him from reading his official biography. When he'd testified in Farid's trial he'd disclosed no more than he'd had to.

He'd been a pain in the ass to work with.

On paper, and even in person, General Grimes represented the best of the US Marine Corps. The epitome of a military careerist.

Yet he'd unnerved her with his tone, his air of patronizing tolerance. She'd thought he hated lawyers or women or both. She hadn't cared; what she'd needed from him, she'd gained, and Farid had been freed.

After a while she'd realized Grimes treated everyone the same way.

His narrowed gaze landed on her, and she steeled herself to meet his eyes with the same cool expression. He didn't corner the market on professional posturing.

"General Grimes."

"You're the JAG from Second Fleet in Norfolk, right?"

"Yes, sir."

"Never figured I'd have to deal with you again."

Tough.

"No reason to think you would."

"Actually, I'm the one who needs to talk to you, General," Brad put in. "Commander Alexander has to leave for work."

"It's Ms. Alexander as of noon tomorrow. I'm on the last of my terminal leave, and I started my civilian job this week. And I think it's a good idea for me to stick around for a while, until I need to report in." She shot Brad what she hoped was a look he'd understand.

Shut up and let me be an extra set of ears for you.

"Why don't you both come in and grab a cup of coffee? We're not going to solve anything standing out here."

When Brad threw her a "what the hell are you doing?" frown behind the general's back, Joy ignored him. He wasn't the only one who could adapt to changing circumstances.

They climbed the steps and entered the cabin. Walking on the polished pine floor, Joy looked around, taking in the high ceiling and Marine Corps memorabilia dotted throughout the great room. A sword and scabbard hung in an X over the mantel of a giant fireplace, the holder emblazoned with the US Marine Corps' symbol—the world encircled by a snake.

"You take it black?" The general's question sounded more like an order, and Joy wasn't about to refuse, GERD or not.

"Thank you." She lifted the chipped mug with *Quantico* stamped on it to her lips. The coffee smelled strong and delicious.

Brad helped himself to the second mug, also well-worn, with a map of Okinawa, Japan, on it. Joy ignored the urge to smile. General Grimes had commanded thousands of Marines, led them through hell and back throughout his career, and had a respectable pension, plus any personal savings he'd squirreled away. Yet he used nostalgic cracked pottery, surrounding himself with the bits and pieces of the life he'd left behind.

"Thanks for letting us in, General. I really appreciate it."

"Why wouldn't I? From what the security detail tells me, you have a lot to do with my safety. It's unbelievable, isn't it? The bastards can't keep the war on their own turf. They're trying to bring it here."

"Not if I can help it."

"That's the spirit. Now, what can I do for you two?"

"Do you remember when we spoke after that first operational push in Afghanistan?" Brad leaned against the kitchen counter, as did the general. With their casual demeanor, they could've been discussing the Whidbey weather and not a mission that had changed the course of so many lives.

"Yeah." The general took a sip.

"Can you remember any of the debrief—anything my teammates and I told you about what we experienced?"

"That was a long time ago." Grimes set his mug down.

"We need to know whatever you remember, General." Joy wondered if Grimes thought she was afraid of him. She wasn't. He was simply a product of his training and came off as a tough guy. There had to be a real human being in there somewhere.

He awed her, to be truthful. Not that she'd ever admit it.

"We've already done this, right? During the trial in Norfolk?"

She shook her head. "No, this isn't about Farid. He's still free, in the Witness Security Program. Are you aware of anyone he would have known who'd still want to hurt you? Or Brad?" She gestured toward Brad, in case General Grimes only knew him as Chief Iverson.

The general nodded and took in a deep breath. "Have a seat." He pointed to his kitchen table. Once they were seated, he looked each of them in the eye for several seconds.

"I was afraid it would come to this," he said in a stage whisper. "If not with that campaign, then with another one. The world's gotten smaller."

It was all she could do not to roll her eyes. The general had a serious case of retired flag officer syndrome with these theatrics.

"Of course I know who'd want to get even with you. So do you, if you think about it."

"Who is it, General?" Brad's question was a demand. Spots of color lit up his cheeks, and Joy wondered if he was clenching his hands to keep from strangling Grimes. Why hadn't he mentioned any of this during the trial?

"The one from Gitmo. The guy the two of you set loose. His village had a lot of angry men in it. They don't see him as a hero—he's a traitor to them. You have to remember that the Taliban brainwashes them to believe that we, the Americans and our allies, are to blame for all the death and destruction."

"So you're saying he's indirectly responsible because the people from his former village are angry with him? Why would they come out here, though?"

"My guess is they want to get on the news somehow—maybe to let that one you got released see they're still viable. It's their way to ferret him out, if you ask me."

Joy shuddered at the thought of Farid coming to harm after everything he'd already been through.

"You've done a lot of thinking about that case, General." This remark earned her a glance from Grimes. Maybe he wasn't such a Marine Machine.

"You have a boss at the Bureau, Iverson?"

"Yes, it's Mike Rubio—former Navy Lieutenant Rubio."

"Same guy who was lead on that SEAL team with you, right?"

"Yes, and my closest friend. We're lucky to be working together again. What does he have to do with this?"

"You sure he hasn't set you up? That maybe he wants you out of the picture?"

Shock hit her as General Grimes said the same thing she had. She looked over at Brad and saw the way he was staring at Grimes. He seemed as surprised as she was.

Brad shook his head before he responded.

"You know how ridiculous that is, General. You don't like SEALs, fine, but Mike's the best our country has. The best of the best. You saw that firsthand when we were downrange."

Grimes took a swig of his joe. "Never hurts to turn over every rock."

"Any other rocks you think we may be over-looking?" Joy ignored General's pinched expression. As if she was irritating him.

"The explosion was all over the news this morning." Grimes motioned with his hand toward the big-screen television that sat in the corner of the room. "It's a punch to the gut to see that all our work, all the young men and women sacrificed—and the terrorists are still out there. Trying to come here."

He leveled a stern glance at Joy and then focused on Brad. "I'll do whatever it takes to keep us all safe. I don't have the same confidence in the Bureau you work for."

At their stunned silence, he strode over to the table that held the TV and picked up the remote. Seconds later the room reverberated with the sound of a news anchor's voice. A map of Whidbey Island was projected behind her, with a photo of a Growler jet superimposed on it.

"It's believed that the explosion near Whidbey Island yesterday morning was set off by a former Naval Officer who's suffering from post-traumatic stress disorder. Officials are not releasing the name of the suspect until he is safely in the custody of the US Government."

Air *whooshed* out of Joy's lungs, and she propped her elbows on Grimes's table, proper military manners be damned.

Brad didn't budge. He sat stone-faced with his fists resting on the table in front of him. As though he were ready to do battle with Godzilla.

Didn't anything shake the man?

"I know it's not unheard of for an agent to be used as a temporary scapegoat. I don't have a problem with it if that's what the mission calls for." He said nothing else. Joy's lawyerly opinion told her it was to protect Grimes, too.

"Looks to me like either your boss sold you out, or the authorities don't want to alarm the public. By the way, how do I know it's not you who blew up that boat?" Grimes fired off.

Joy mentally braced herself for whatever Brad said next.

"You don't. And does it really matter at this point? I doubt you would've let us in the door if you thought I was playing on the wrong side. And you still haven't answered the question, General. What was it about the mission four years ago that's got someone after me?"

Grimes stared at Brad, and Joy admired the way Brad returned his stare with no hint of backing down. She also appreciated that Brad wasn't giving Grimes any information he couldn't glean from the news reports.

"Sounds to me like you got yourself in a world of hurt, son."

Son? From Grimes? To Brad, the Navy chief he'd treated like absolute dirt during the proceedings for Farid?

"Brad didn't do anything wrong, sir. You know him. You worked with his team on a number of missions. We're here to see if you recall anything that can help us get to the bottom of who's really responsible for this plot against you, and possibly the Naval base."

Joy was surprised at how steady her voice sounded, considering that her insides were quaking.

"I've worked with a lot of officers and troops over the past decade. Any one of them could be considered stellar. And just like that, any one of them could turn on a dime, too." The general snapped his fingers in midair. The crack seemed loud in the silence left by the powered-off television.

"Brad's not one of them."

Brad sent her a look of sincere…annoyance.

"I'm not talking about you. I'm talking about your boss at the Bureau." Grimes acted as if Joy wasn't there. She could handle that, provided they got what they needed from Grimes.

"I'm with you on that, General. You can't trust me any more than you can trust the next guy. That's why we're not staying long—just long enough to see what you remember about our debriefs. To see if there's something we missed."

"I told both of you everything I knew during the trial. But let me give you a quick refresher. Your team, Iverson, was assigned to secure the three villages on the western edge of the territory we were responsible for. Two of the three went like clockwork. The third village was problematic. We had civilian casualties as a result—all caused by the Taliban, but everyone blamed us. The terrorists who are after you now are probably related to the suspect you let out of jail. With the aid of my testimony in Norfolk." He didn't hide his disgust.

"General, I'd say you're missing a few key points about the op. And the terrorists I've been monitoring are domestic." Brad's jaw was tight, and a vein throbbed on his forehead.

"What I remembered was enough to free a man you both believed to be innocent." Was he still bitter over the fact that Joy had curtailed his desire to opine on the stand about how no Afghan villager who'd had any contact with the Taliban could ever be trusted? She'd respected the fact that he'd had to send in thousands of young men and women to face down the enemy, but she wasn't going to allow prejudice of any kind in her courtroom.

Well, the US Military's courtroom.

"Farid was innocent." Brad spoke quietly yet with fierceness.

"Really? So where is he now?"

Joy spoke up. "Witness Protection."

Brad answered simultaneously, their voices in unison. "You know that, General."

Grimes shook his head, his thin lips curled in a frown full of derision. "Let's play it my way. Pretend Farid wasn't innocent. That he's still connected to the terrorists. If you were him, and you were freed by the enemy and placed in a 'safe' community, aka Anywhere, USA, what would you do?"

"Farid *was* innocent, General," Joy insisted. "A court of law declared him so."

Brad flung her a "shut up" glance.

Anger made her skin prickle, and she wished she could kick his leg under the table. Or better yet, take her chipped coffee mug and throw it through the mirror that hung on the wall.

"There was no evidence to keep him incarcerated, Commander Alexander. That's a far cry from being *innocent*."

"I worked with him for over seven months, General. I know his character." She'd met Farid's family, too, and celebrated with them when he'd been freed. Brad had been there as well, and had worked as hard if not harder to free the man who'd been in the wrong place for all the right reasons.

Just like Brad yesterday.

She suddenly felt a germ of doubt. They couldn't have been wrong, could they? Her case had been airtight once it went before the court.

"General, let me get your opinion straight out. The bad guys wanted me dead, and now Mike's in cahoots with them?" Brad's voice, incredulous verging on sarcastic, cut through the fear that was trying to grab hold of her logic.

"Do we need to go over everything again?" Joy looked at the microwave clock. "I have to get to work. General, can Brad use your phone to call me when you two are done here?"

Grimes shrugged. "Leave him here all day. It's as safe a place as any for now."

"I'LL WALK YOU OUT." Brad was beside her in a flash. She suspected he didn't want to give Grimes the chance to prevent their private conversation.

Back on the gravel driveway, Brad reached over and took her hand. "Thank you for what you're doing."

"No thanks needed. It's the right thing to do. I have to admit I'm not thrilled about leaving you here with General Tough Guy."

Brad chuckled. "He's a badass, isn't he? But there's nothing to worry about. He's wrong about Mike, you know. It's his way of feeling involved when he's not part of it anymore. I understand how he feels."

"We both do. It's never easy leaving the military, whether it's after a few years or a lifetime."

They stood in silence, gazing out over the wooded area around General's deck.

Brad squeezed her hand. "Go. He's more apt to say something useful with just me here."

"I don't disagree with that. He doesn't like me."

"He's just as tough on me, Joy. He's a ball-buster."

"Maybe. Promise you'll call me at the office if you need anything." Her voice broke, and she blinked. Where were these emotions coming from?

She looked at the lines that radiated from the corners of his eyes, his sun-darkened skin, his rough beard. His placed his fingers under her chin, and she raised her head. She didn't want him to see her tears but needed the eye contact.

"You're the only person who's ever done so much for me, Joy."

"It's my job."

"Not now, it isn't." His gaze shifted to her lips.

"Brad, not here…"

He gave her a quick, firm kiss.

"I can damn well kiss you if that's what we both want. We're equals in this."

JOY DROVE TO the office with the taste of Brad on her lips, grateful that she'd only be thirty minutes later than her start time of nine o'clock. Paul had given her a lot of leeway as a newbie and she was willing to take advantage of it. She used the showers allocated to the attorneys, since she didn't want to waste time going back home to get ready. Fortunately, the small shower room was empty, and she was able to enjoy the hot water for a good ten minutes.

As she sat in front of her computer and worked on the firm's caseload, her mind kept drifting back to the conversation with Grimes. The man had never been one of her favorites, but Brad was right. Grimes's assessment of the situation was most likely correct.

She immediately picked up her desk phone when it rang two hours later. "Joy Alexander."

"Joy, it's Dennis. Your package arrived a few minutes ago. Do you want me to bring it to you?" Dennis's voice was as steady as if he was talking about a book order and not classified information that she wasn't privy to anymore. Well, only for the next few hours.

"No, I can come back to base."

"I don't think that's the smartest course of action."

"Oh?"

"We're basically in lockdown until they find out who was responsible for the explosion. It'd take you an hour to get past the initial check at the gate."

She put her hands in her lap and leaned back from her keyboard. Yesterday's base security had already been tight. She couldn't wait that long.

"Okay, I'll have to meet you somewhere. What's convenient for you?"

A brief pause. Odd, because Dennis had never been the type to hesitate.

"How about the parking lot near Deception Pass, right off the highway?"

Joy looked at her computer's clock. "I can be there. What time?"

"Noon."

Dennis ended the connection, and Joy replaced her phone. In less than an hour she might be able to crack open this case for Brad.

"I'VE COPIED AND pasted the pertinent parts. I didn't want you to have anything that could get you in trouble, like the date and time stamps."

They stood outside her car in the small lot for

Deception Pass Park. Cars pulled in and out as other workers took advantage of the beautiful day to have impromptu picnics and walks.

Dennis was in running gear, no doubt using his lunchtime workout to bring her the case notes. He looked strong and fit, his fresh-faced attractiveness unmarred except for the small worry line between his brows.

She'd worked with Dennis long enough to know when he was stressed.

"Thank you so much, Dennis." She reached through the car window, took the large envelope and placed it on her passenger seat.

"I just hope he's worth it, Joy." Sincerity reflected in the depths of his eyes and for about the hundredth time, Joy wished they'd had some kind of chemistry between them.

"I'm sorry it didn't work out for us, Dennis. You're a true friend."

"Aw, that seems to be my role in life. The male friend." There wasn't any self-pity in his comment. Only a self-deprecating smirk that revealed his own regret.

"You're a good man. There's a lucky woman out there who's going to find you."

They'd had so many discussions when they worked together—about life after the Navy, whether they wanted to have families, what their favorite pastimes were. In the end, Joy had resigned her commission, and Dennis had received the promotion she'd dreamed of getting when she'd started out.

"How's the new job going so far?"

"I can't say I'm, uh, completely immersed in it, not yet."

Dennis nodded. "Understood. Promise me one thing, Joy."

"Anything."

"Let me know when you find whatever you're searching for. And if it doesn't work out with this guy, let me take you to dinner."

"That's two things, Dennis."

"I mean it, Joy."

"I know you do." Impulsively she reached up on tiptoe and kissed his cheek. "I'll call you when all's said and done."

She walked around her car and slid into the driver's side, looking back only once to see that Dennis was watching her car pull out.

Why couldn't the nice, safe, steady guy be the one she had all that chemistry with? She turned onto Highway 20 and headed south toward Oak Harbor.

As a sailor she'd give her life for any of her shipmates, hands down. But as a civilian, as a woman with her heart on the line, there was only one man she'd consider risking it all for.

Brad.

CHAPTER TWELVE

HALFWAY THROUGH THE AFTERNOON, Joy slipped out to her car for her coffee break. She smiled at a couple of other office personnel who were out enjoying the day. Serena, too, was outside, seated on one of the patio chairs arranged on a side deck of their building. Built like a home, the legal office looked inviting, and yet it maintained an air of professionalism and quiet authority.

Leaving her windows down to enjoy the warm breeze, she thumbed through her old case notes, looking for her personal commentaries on Farid's, Brad's and Grimes's statements. If she located her personal observations first, she'd be better able to compare them with their testimonies.

She wondered if the authorities were monitoring Dennis. It'd be a stretch, but with the explosion and the focus on terrorists, and his request for the files on another terrorist trial, it was possible he'd set off some sort of communications security trip wire. And it would be her fault.

He'd been smart by copying only what she needed and leaving his official copies on base.

He could record the destruction of the files he had and send the report to headquarters. It wouldn't be the first time a JAG had looked into a past case to double-check the facts. If necessary he could claim he'd asked for the wrong case numbers.

It didn't take her long to reread her entries. At first glance, she didn't think she had anything she could use.

"Secure the villages…"

Grimes's words from this morning reverberated in her memory.

She scanned the court documents for Grimes's statements on the witness stand. He'd kept his answers short and succinct, just as he had when she'd interviewed him beforehand. The mark of a flag officer—he was used to his subordinates hanging on his every word.

The hours talking to him, feeling as though she was talking to a brick wall, came rushing back. He'd been monosyllabic in his responses wherever possible. He'd never given her one damn personal insight into what had really gone on when his Marines had entered the villages shortly after Brad's SEAL team had secured them and declared them safe.

Any GI who saw his buddy shot down by the enemy was bound to have a problem with local nationals. At least until that GI was away from the battle and able to sort out the difference between extremists and ordinary, law-abiding citizens.

GERI KROTOW   181

And while Grimes had led troops into battle with a nearly perfect record, not all his troops were pristine examples of the United States Marine Corps. War crimes against civilians had, regrettably, been committed by both sides. Grimes was famous for routing out any Marine who didn't live up to the highest moral standards expected by the Corps. Any illegal incidents had never touched Grimes's career. They shouldn't have; although he was accountable for all the actions of those under him, he couldn't be held responsible for the behavior of a few rogue Marines. Surely he carried the weight of those disreputable actions in his heart, though.

As she continued to reread her notes, she realized that Brad, General Grimes and Mike had all replied with the same answer to any questions that concerned Farid's village. Brad and Mike's SEAL team had been instrumental in securing the village, but there was a lapse that evening, between the time they'd secured it and a full Marine force had come in and fortified what they'd accomplished. During those few hours, the Taliban had plundered the village.

"They told the villagers that if they were even suspected of talking to the Americans, their entire families would be tortured and killed."—Lieutenant Michael J. Rubio, USN

"It was heartbreaking to see Farid's entire extended family harmed in one fashion or another

by the Taliban after we'd promised them they were safe."—Senior Chief Petty Officer Bradley Iverson, USN

"It's a peril of war. We can't always protect those who need it most."—Major General Jeremiah Grimes, USMC

Hands shaking, she highlighted her own written reactions. After the trial, she'd found out that the members of Farid's family who'd survived had been given political refugee status and allowed entry to the US. Like Farid, they were offered safety under the WSP, but whether they'd accepted it or not she didn't know.

She'd have to call Dennis and thank him profusely. He didn't realize it, but by copying what he knew was pertinent, he'd helped her focus on an area that would've taken her hours to get to otherwise.

A chill of premonition raised goose bumps on her arms, despite the warmth of the car. Cracking the mystery of the international terrorist who was—presumably—behind this domestic cell wasn't a job for sissies.

She longed for Brad to be here. She needed his expertise, wanted to bounce her thoughts off him. There was no one else she could trust to discuss this with...except for a former boss and mentor, Helen Bolling. But she hadn't contacted Helen since she'd decided to resign her commission.

Besides, this wasn't anything she felt comfortable discussing over the phone.

"Great place for a break, isn't it?" Paul's voice yanked her from her disturbing thoughts, and she discovered him leaning into her open window. She smiled and tried to act nonchalant as she shoved her case notes into a plain canvas grocery tote.

"It's fabulous. I didn't know there was a place like this to eat lunch and work." She jerked her thumb toward the deck as she raised her windows and opened her door.

Paul straightened as she got out of the car. "We had that put on this spring. Since so much of what we do is on laptops, I thought it'd be nice. Next year I'd like to add an awning, maybe screen it in, so we can use it when it rains, too."

She managed a laugh.

"I'd love that at my house, too. I do have a sunroom, but I'm not planning to put screens in—too windy."

"You're on the shore, right?"

"Yes. I lucked out, that's for sure. Found a smaller place that fit my budget." Even so, it had taken most of her savings.

"It's all in the timing." They walked back to the building, and Joy felt like the lowest worm. Paul was the most gracious man, and he was her boss. She felt blessed. And how did she repay him?

By sneaking around and lying during her first couple of days on the job.

Back inside and sitting at her desk, she vowed to make a dent in her newly assigned caseload. Serena was still outside on the deck, and the office was blissfully quiet, unlike her mind. Joy became immersed in her civilian work, which was a welcome break after reliving the Norfolk case.

"Joy?" Serena called her from the office door, keeping her voice low.

"Hi, Serena. What's up?"

"There are three men here to talk to you." Serena took a half step into Joy's office. "They're some kind of law enforcement. FBI or maybe NCIS. They didn't say."

"Really? Okay." Doing her best to look surprised, she got to her feet and smiled. "Probably about what happened offshore yesterday."

Serena nodded. "You have a view of West Beach and the water, don't you?"

"Yes. It's usually a beautiful scene, but yesterday it was a little more exciting than usual."

"They don't seem to have learned anything new, at least according to CNN."

"Are the agents in the conference room?"

"Yes." Serena sat down at her desk. Joy wished she could explain it all to her; she seemed levelheaded and didn't have any of the emotional involvement that could be skewing Joy's own judgment. She sighed. There'd be plenty of time for explanations later, after she and Brad had figured out the who and why of his predicament.

As she walked down the short hallway, she braced herself, trying to appear as noncommittal and professional as possible. There was a good chance one of the men in the conference room was Mike Rubio, whom she'd met in Norfolk, during the trial. Until she had more answers, everyone was a suspect.

She entered the firm's meeting room. "Joy Alexander?" A tall blond man with dark eyes flashed his badge at her. Joy leaned in far enough to see that he was FBI.

"I'm Agent Barrett, and these are Agents Cruise and Gordon. We'd like to ask you a few questions."

"Sure. Have a seat." She sat in one of the leather-cushioned chairs, forcing them to sit, too. Reminding them that they were on her turf. Or her boss's, at any rate.

"What is your relationship with Bradley Iverson?"

She blinked, tilted her head. Thank God for her interest in theater. She'd started to brush up on her skills lately, hoping for a role in one of the community performances once she was more settled. Otherwise she would've started to sweat.

"Do you mean Chief Iverson? The SEAL?"

Agent Barrett's eyes narrowed, and she saw

his nostrils flare. Not stupid, this one. He didn't appreciate her playing stupid, either.

"Yes."

Hoping to score points with the other two agents, she looked at each of them and smiled. "Is he always this warm and hospitable?"

Agent Cruise didn't flinch, but she caught the twitch at the corner of Agent Gordon's mouth.

Score!

"Answer the question, Ms. Alexander."

She made a point of glancing at her watch. "Drawing on my Navy experience, shouldn't you be asking these questions on base? Wouldn't the base or persons related to the base be the obvious targets of a terrorist act?"

Agent Barrett didn't move, but she had the distinct impression that he wished he could reach across the table and force her to focus on his questions.

She sighed audibly. "Yes, of course I know Brad. We worked together on the Farid case almost two years ago. He was getting out, wasn't he? Said something about wanting to start his own business."

It was scary, how easily the lies came once she started.

"A business?"

"Yes, he talked about a used bookstore that specialized in military history and fiction."

"When was the last time you saw him, Ms.

Alexander?" Agent Cruise's jovial tone validated her guess that he was the "good cop."

"Let's see, we finished the case and I left Norfolk the next day. That was last year—maybe thirteen months ago."

"We have reason to believe Iverson was near your property within the last twenty-four hours. Have you seen him?"

Agent Garrett wasn't screwing around.

Neither was she. Not with Brad's life. Or this op, which had undeniably become her op, too.

"Why would I see him? We've had no contact since the trial."

"Did you witness anything out of the ordinary on the beach yesterday morning?"

"Besides two Growlers, a P-8 and a P-3 overflying my house, followed shortly after by an explosion that could be terrorist related? No."

"Did you report what you saw, Ms. Alexander?" Agent Barrett's method was familiar to her but no less annoying. She had the distinct impression that he suspected Brad had been in her home. But he had no evidence. The fake OHPD officers who'd shown up at her door had not seen Brad. Even a heat signature wasn't proof that Brad had been the person staying at her place.

"Yes. I spoke to an officer from the Oak Harbor PD yesterday, right after I saw the explosion. Officer Katie Dade, if memory serves." She looked at them as if that should end the conversation. Agent Barrett kept staring at her.

"Then I saw the media reports and realized I didn't have anything to add to the observations—it seems we all saw the same thing." Thank God General Grimes had flicked on his TV. She'd recognized several of her neighbors speaking to reporters.

"Did you notice anything unusual last night? Any attempt by anyone to enter your home?"

"No, except for the Oak Harbor Police Department showing up in the middle of the night, claiming they had reports of an assailant in the area. I told them I'd had no problems."

At least that was truthful.

"OHPD?" Agent Cruise's comment received a sharp look from Agent Barrett, while Agent Gordon's face remained stoic.

Judging by their reactions, her assumption about the OHPD "team" who'd shown up at her door last night was correct. Moreover, they must've been FBI if these agents knew about it. Agencies didn't always share information when it came to undercover ops. Hadn't Brad said as much?

"Yes." She kept still, playing the part of innocent bystander to the best of her ability.

Agent Barrett flipped a business card in front of her. "Call me if you remember anything else."

"Will do."

They all rose, and Joy smiled. "I'm sorry I couldn't be more helpful, gentlemen."

"Are you?" Agent Barrett's eyes missed nothing. She wondered if he saw the route she'd already worked out in her mind to reach Brad. Hopefully before these guys got to him. Her concern over their taking Brad into custody, if only to get him back to his office in Seattle, remained paramount. She was determined to help him find his answers and close out this case before he had to go back to his desk job. She wanted him to be *able* to close out the case properly.

With the bad guys behind bars.

"Yes, Agent Barrett, I am."

She held his gaze until he turned and left the room. Agent Cruise followed. Agent Gordon paused at the threshold and winked at her.

"It's been a long two days," he said.

Joy nodded and gave him an understanding smile.

Only after she was sure they were gone did she make a beeline for her desk. Her fingers burned to call Brad.

A memory of her and Brad hunched over Farid's printed testimony flickered in her mind, and she found herself yearning for the synchronicity they'd experienced during the case. The two of them had been a solid team, and against all evidence to the contrary, they'd freed Farid. It was a shared history that would bind them forever, regardless of what happened over the next few hours and days.

But if Grimes was correct and Farid turned out to be a double agent, they'd both been duped. And they could both be dead before they had a chance to rectify their misjudgment.

CHAPTER THIRTEEN

AS THE WORKDAY came to a close, lawyers and administrative staff left the building with a quick "See you in the morning!" or "Don't work too hard!"

Joy stayed. She needed the quiet and the solitude to finish going over her notes from the Farid case. Taking them home didn't feel right. At least here she was on neutral territory and not likely to be bothered.

And when she was done with them she could use the state-of-the-art shredder in the supply room.

She gripped the edge of the desk as she stared at her notes. She hadn't read another word since she'd found what she'd suspected was here. Proof that Brad might have been targeted by some unknown person from Farid's village since the very start of this horrible, horrible mess.

The office seemed to close in around her, reminding her to breathe in the confined space. How could she have missed this?

Right there, in the transcript of the testimony

Farid had given them. Farid's innocence was un-mistakable; he'd done what he could to save his family's village, to protect the only way of life he knew.

She'd forgotten how decisively Farid's family had disowned him once he spoke to the US Marines. He'd told her that, told the court, but she'd been so focused on clearing him, on making sure his few brief conversations with one Taliban insurgent didn't affect his status. Farid had passed the correct intelligence to Brad's SEAL team so the Taliban could be driven from the village.

She still wanted to do some sleuthing on Grimes, just in case something had happened on his watch in Afghanistan, something that was his fault. She doubted it at this point but couldn't afford to leave anything unexamined.

"THERE ARE THINGS—people, places, causes, forces—bigger than we are, Iverson." General Grimes sat in one of the crude chairs that surrounded the equally primitive dining table in the center of the great room. Brad had no doubt that Grimes had built the place himself. They'd shared a simple lunch of canned tuna, mayo and white bread that reminded Brad of the meals his grandparents had served when he'd spent weekends with them. Unlike his grandparents, though, Grimes was all business, no warmth.

Brad hadn't come here to grip and grin. "You

retired to the middle of nowhere, General. Why didn't you stay in DC as a consultant or part of a think tank?"

"You're joking, Iverson, aren't you?" Grimes's mouth bent into an inverted U.

Brad shrugged. "You could be making a nice paycheck after all the years of serving Uncle Sam and risking your life."

"I didn't get into the Marines to make money. You obviously didn't, either, if you traded in your uniform for a shiny badge. You could be a consultant, too."

Brad made a point of glancing around the house. "You look like you're living lean, General."

"Simple's how I like it."

"Didn't you ever want to have a family, kids?"

"I have a daughter."

Brad studied the older man's face for any sign of emotion. Just when he'd concluded that Grimes was carved from granite, the General spoke.

"I was married to a beautiful woman for the first ten years of my career. We were blessed with a lovely daughter. She's in her twenties, an adult on her own. My wife—she died."

"I'm sorry."

General's jaw muscles tightened, and his posture made him once again resemble a statue.

"She got cancer. Ovarian. By the time they caught it, there weren't any treatments she was eligible for. Back then they didn't have good diagnostics. From what I read, it hasn't improved much. It was a tough time."

His lips barely moved.

Brad cleared his throat. Words were superfluous.

Grimes toyed with the corner of the table. "I made it back from a training exercise in time to hold her hand through the last of it. She was in a coma by then, and I don't know if she even realized I was there. I'd tried to get leave. Hell, I tried to resign my commission. Neither were approved. I shipped out to Okinawa two days after the funeral."

"Who took care of your daughter?"

"She came with me. She was a toddler and learned Japanese fluently."

Grimes slammed both palms on the table with an explosive force reminiscent of the split-second orders regularly issued in boot camp training. To keep the new recruits under control.

"Any more questions about my shadowed past, Agent Iverson?"

So now he'd promoted him to a field agent, at least.

"No, sir. Again, I'm sorry for your loss."

Grimes shook his head. "That was a long time ago. It's for the best I never married again. Too much trouble to bring another woman into our family and expect her to measure up, to maintain the pace I had to keep. My daughter did fine, but she didn't know any other life."

He felt compassion, although Grimes didn't strike him as the type to compromise, to meet any woman halfway. Yet the most successful military members, male or female, often had strong marriages to support them. Brad hadn't met many Navy or Marine Corps families who were screwed up and dysfunctional, the way the media often portrayed. Instead, he'd found his friends' families to be more tight-knit from going through the deployments and duty station moves together.

"Are you originally from here, General?"

"I grew up on a potato farm in Idaho. Enlisted at the tail end of Vietnam when I was seventeen and never looked back. After a tour in California, I used the GI Bill to go to college in Texas. Figured out I liked working with ground pounders, so I stayed in infantry and went on from there."

Grimes stood and carried his mug to the sink. He rinsed it then looked out the window.

"I met Amanda when I was in college. She was a year ahead of me but four years younger. A beautiful girl." He shook his head as if ridding himself of a memory too painful to entertain.

Brad's hands itched to go and pat the old dude on the back, reassure him that he'd be okay.

But he wouldn't. Couldn't.

This was a US Marine Corps General. Retired made no difference; he was a lifer and every inch

the Marine he'd always been. He never asked anyone for help or direction. It was in his DNA to
call the shots, give the orders.

Brad walked over to the sink with his mug.
Grimes turned to look at him, eyes blazing with
emotion and a begrudging respect.

"Don't be as stupid as I was, Iverson. Enjoy
whatever relationships you can while you can get
them. 'Course, you got out. It might be easier for
you now." Grimes spat the words as if they were
poison.

"Getting out isn't a bad thing. And I'm still
serving my country."

"Looks like it's doing you a lot of good, too."

They both laughed. Brad felt more at ease with
Grimes than he ever would, in all likelihood, feel
again. His internal warning system wouldn't stop
pinging, however. The same way it did before a
mission was about to go sour.

Like the one he'd worked under General
Grimes when Farid's village had been ripped
apart.

JOY FELT GUILTY being in her house getting ready
for a bath when Brad's undercover op, possibly
his life, might hang in the balance. When there
was a chance she and Brad had been manipulated by Farid.

Although her money was on a member of
Farid's extended family. Farid had been honest,

judging not only by his testimony, but also that of others.

After being assaulted by events beyond her control for the past two days, all Joy wanted was a hot soak in her claw-foot tub with a huge mug of peppermint tea. The memories of her home being virtually broken into by Brad, and then of being awakened by the "police," pitted her flight instinct against her need for comfort. She needed a retreat from the constant apprehension that had been her companion since yesterday morning.

The deep tub was one of the features that had sold the house to her, that and its private but sweeping view of Puget Sound. As water poured from the elegant brass faucet, she sat on the edge and tried to figure out how she could search for more personal information on General Grimes than would be available online.

She measured out bath salts and a scoop of dried lavender, which she'd purchased at the local lavender farm she'd come across during her house-hunting trip last year.

She could get in her car and drive straight to Emily's place in Anacortes on Fidalgo Island.

But Emily wasn't home; she was on her way to the book signing in Coupeville at the local yarn shop where they'd initially met. And Joy couldn't ask Emily for help with this. It was too dangerous, too big.

There was Dennis, but she'd already involved

him as much as she was going to. Brad was the person she really needed to talk to, but he was at General Grimes's, and he'd stay there until he called her to get him. He'd made that much clear.

She'd have to keep what she knew close for now. Nothing she hadn't done as a JAG, that was for sure. As an attorney she was expected to hold confidences.

To maintain the appearance of normalcy she'd act as if nothing was amiss and head down to Emily's book signing. At least that would show anyone watching her—if anyone *was* watching her—that she had nothing to hide and no idea where Brad was.

The scent of the lavender drifted through the bathroom, and she stepped out of her clothes, eager to sink into the hot water. The immediate warmth soothed her, and she let her mind wander.

Vaguely recalling a conversation with the general about how he'd decided to go Marine Infantry, she remembered that he'd gone to college in Texas.

That was it! Her alma mater, the US Naval Academy, was always publishing summaries of what graduates were up to in *Shipmate*, its alumni magazine. Certainly someone like General Grimes would be a person of interest to his alma mater.

She soaked until her fingers looked like prunes, then got out and made herself another cup of peppermint tea. There was still time to do a little research before the book signing.

After she opened her laptop, she entered the college name and alumni magazine.

Bingo.

Clicking on the most recent issue, she scanned it for any mention of Grimes. Nothing. She bit her fingernails. She didn't even know his class year. This was going to be a bitch.

Unless…

She typed in the title Grimes had held while in Afghanistan. The alumni website opened with the current commanding officer's bio. She clicked on *history* and found Grimes's entry. His biography was the usual droning on of all his military accomplishments, but it did mention that he'd graduated from college in 1979. She cross-referenced the year with the alumni magazine's entries and started to go through each quarterly publication, beginning with the present issue and going backward until she reached the entry she'd been hoping for.

Instead of the usual excitement she felt as she closed in on a case, anxiety tightened its hold on her.

In an article dated four years prior, two full years before she'd interviewed Grimes in Norfolk, an entry by a college alumnus from a different year highlighted the most recent activity of General Jeremiah Grimes.

"Jeremiah is as tough as ever, kicking ass as the commander in charge of the entire region. He's dodging recriminatory press coverage and doesn't seem to take anything personally, unless one of his troops gets injured or worse. We are all honored to be classmates with a true national hero."

Joy gnawed on her lip. The Grimes she'd interviewed had been intimidating and decisive. He'd also appeared bored, as if testifying on the witness stand was all in a day's work for him. He'd been patronizing at times, such as when she'd asked him the same question twice, and told Brad he should stay in the Navy as a SEAL. "Tough it out to retirement" was what he'd said.

As far as Grimes was concerned, anyone remotely connected to the Taliban or any village they occupied was suspect. But even he had grudgingly admitted that Farid's aid during the war had saved American and Afghan civilian lives.

Unfortunately, the Taliban had wanted Farid dead. So he'd befriended the American SEALs he'd met while preparing to take a college preparatory exam, the SAT, at the military base—the only safe place for a student to do so at the time.

Brad and his team had always had to be careful. Solicitations by enemy agents were widespread and could end with a dead American or allied troop. Brad had told her of a SEAL who'd made the mistake of falling in love with an Afghan interpreter, a woman later connected to the Taliban. He'd had to leave her behind during a firestorm of bullets and never heard from her again. He'd never been able to find out whether she'd made it out of the war zone alive. He couldn't, not if he wanted to remain an American and a lawful SEAL.

Grimes's testimony had been a worry for her, but in the end it had gone fine, and Brad's defense of Farid had been flawless. Farid's dream was to go to med school, and she knew he'd be the best of doctors. He was a natural protector, a rescuer. He'd witnessed the worst possible crimes by the Taliban and had wanted to do what he could to free his village and his family from their brutality. He wanted to save lives, an impulse motivated by his own experiences. She hoped his dream came true.

Grimes had never mentioned his contempt for the press to her during the trial questioning. Of course, it hadn't been relevant, so why would he? And he wasn't alone; most military leaders treated the press with caution. Today's hero could quickly become tomorrow's war criminal in the eyes of the media.

She clicked onto a page with the banner "Alumni in the News." Scanning URLs that included Op-Eds, diplomatic links, social reports and athletic achievements, she took a closer look at the last link on the page.

"Alumnus at War: Reconciling Facts with the Press" by Jeremiah Grimes.

Her initial hope that she'd found something on Grimes faded to ashes as she read a bland four-paragraph editorial by the general, describing the difference between what he saw and what the press reported. It was nothing she hadn't heard before. As a JAG she'd witnessed firsthand how reporters could take information she or the public affairs officer provided and twist it to represent what the reporters' agenda, or their network's, happened to be. This certainly didn't indicate anything incriminatory against General Grimes.

Beyond a doubt, the general was solid.

Joy looked at her computer clock and closed her laptop. She had twenty minutes to get to Coupeville for Emily's signing. The twenty-minute drive would give her enough time to construct a facade of excited exhaustion at starting her new career.

Hopefully, she'd hear from Brad before the night was over. They needed to determine if the unknown suspect, or suspects, might be from Farid's village, and if they were, what was their relation to Farid?

Walking into the midst of the crowd at Whidbey Fibers reminded Joy that she'd finally found her home. A community where her life was predictable and never frantic the way it had been with her parents or in the Navy. Entering the well-appointed space usually felt like receiving a warm hug, but tonight a low roar of conversation was punctuated by loud laughs and women's raised voices. Joy's typical calm eluded her.

The stacked wire baskets that lined the enormous back wall were filled with hanks of yarn in brilliant colors. They were an interesting contrast to the muted natural fibers for sale in old whiskey barrels on the floor. The owner, Winnie Ford, had increased her stock fourfold since Joy had started coming to the weekly knit-ins. Even new colors of her favorite selection of luxury cashmere yarn wasn't enough to snap her out of her fixation on finding out who was behind the domestic terrorists.

"Joy! How are you doing, officemate?" Serena Delgado said, walking up to her.

"I DIDN'T KNOW you were a knitter, too, Serena."

The dark-eyed beauty smiled. "I'm what I call a process knitter. I'm not good at finishing big projects. But so many of my friends come here, and Emily's been my best friend since I moved to Whidbey with my son two years ago. I've also been getting hand-knit items from local knitters into the holiday spirit baskets they make up each year down in Angelville."

"Wow. I need to take lessons from you in how to get connected in the area." For a relative newcomer to the island, Serena had certainly become embedded in the community.

"Hey, Joy!" Winnie stepped up to offer Joy a mug of mulled wine. "This is Max's secret family recipe. But if you don't want wine, there's hot cider over there, too."

"Thanks." She'd only have a sip or two since she was driving. Winnie's eyes lit up at the mere mention of her husband, Max. Winnie had what Joy hoped for one day. A man she could count on to be home each night.

Not a former SEAL turned rogue FBI agent.

She sipped the warm wine and whistled. "Wow! This is awfully strong. I'm driving, so I need to keep my bearings. I'll take the mulled cider, please." The single sip she'd taken burned the back of her throat.

Winnie smiled and exchanged her mug for a cup of cider then went to greet another group of knitters as they came into the shop.

There were far more faces than the dozen or so at their knitting group. Joy liked that she could blend in without having to engage in major conversation, but she did have to make sure she said hello to Emily.

Working her way through the crowd, she spotted Emily speaking with a tall familiar male. She walked up to them.

"Joy, I'm so glad you made it." Emily gave her

a tight hug and whispered in her ear. "You look like hell. Bad first couple of days?"

"It's only my second day and no, they've been okay. So far. Who's your friend? Didn't I see him this morning?" she asked in a low voice.

Emily pulled back, nodding.

"Joy, let me introduce you to Ben."

The tall man smiled and thrust out his hand. "Ben Franklin."

"As in 'a penny saved is a penny earned'? Sorry. You must get that a lot. Nice to meet you, Ben." She turned from him to Emily and decided that her original assessment this morning appeared to be correct.

Definite sparks flying here. The romantic kind.

"What's going on?" Emily's question caught her off guard and made her wish she'd asked Emily first.

Conscious of inquisitive eyes on her, including Ben's, Joy let out a laugh she hoped would put an end to their speculation. "Just tired. Nothing more than starting a new job and a new life. Like I said, it's been fine, but seeing the explosion from my balcony yesterday morning—that was rough." She felt like a number one slime. Using a probable attempted murder or terrorist event to gain sympathy and distract from what she was really doing. She'd reached a new low.

"Oh, honey, that's awful." Immediately, it

seemed as though all the women present had to offer their comments.

"I heard it's another one of those PTSD cases."

"Thank God they didn't blow up any planes! My husband was on the flight schedule today."

"The base is under the tightest security. I had to go to Walmart instead of the commissary for my groceries."

Joy raised her hands and tried to smile. "I know! It's been surreal these past two days, hasn't it?" Talk about an understatement.

"Please take a seat. We're about to get started." Winnie clapped her hands and gestured to the rows of folding chairs set up for the occasion. Joy marveled at her authority and her grace. The group was geared up to go on and on about the explosion, and peppering Joy with questions about how much of it she'd seen. Winnie's timing was perfect.

And of course, there was always the topic of Joy's love life. Or rather, lack thereof.

"Are there any cute guys at the law firm?"

Joy made her way to a seat, hoping to put off answering.

Serena shook her head before Joy had to. "They're all happily married. But Paul does have a single brother…"

"I'm not dating the boss's brother. I'm not dating anyone. C'mon, ladies, you know I didn't come to Whidbey to find a man."

At their collective groan, she shrugged. "Not right away, that is."

"Ladies and gentlemen!" Winnie stood at a makeshift podium. Joy noticed several new knitters, including two men, in the crowd, all identifiable by their knitting bags and the projects they worked on as they listened to Winnie.

"Emily's getting quite the following since her patterns popped up on Ravelry," Amy Miller whispered in Joy's ear, referring to a social media site for knitters and crocheters. She took the adjacent seat. Amy, whose bright blond spiral curls framed a cherubic face, was one of the other single women in the knitting group. The two of them had spent a couple of nights out in Seattle at dance clubs.

"She's worked so hard for this. I'm thrilled for her."

Amy placed her hand on Joy's arm. "How are you, really? You look wiped out. It must be hard changing careers. Or have you finally realized you're going to get bored here?" Amy's eyes reflected concern, and Joy felt a twinge of guilt.

"I'm not changing careers, not really. And like I've said a hundred times before, I'm done moving. This is where I want to be. The new job is great. I'm just having a slightly harder time adjusting to life after the Navy than I expected. And the explosion yesterday sure didn't help."

Winnie introduced Emily and thankfully put

an end to Amy's inquisition. Joy loved watching Emily share her passion and her enthusiasm for creating patterns and putting together her book.

Emily seemed so happy and content in her life, but Joy wondered if she ever felt lonely.

Maybe not with the scintillating Ben Franklin on the scene, she suspected.

Loneliness—not a stranger to Joy.

She'd never thought of herself as lonely. Growing up the child of two career diplomats, she'd appreciated the different countries and cultures they'd been posted to and made friends in each new place. Learning new languages was a challenge, and one she enjoyed. When it was time to go to college, Joy had known she wanted to make a difference in the world, but she also knew she didn't want to move as often as her family had.

Yet she'd chosen to accept a full-ride scholarship from the Navy for law school once she'd finished the academy, and had loved her years as a JAG. But she'd hit a wall. After working with Brad on Farid's case, she'd been faced with the reality that she was in her early thirties and if she hoped to settle down, have a family someday, she had to do something about it now.

The family might not happen, but she had control over the settling-down part.

If she didn't start building the life she wanted, it might not happen, either. Traveling the globe was fine for her parents; they had each other and had married young, giving them a shared history that had sustained them through the toughest tours.

She smiled as she thought of her parents. She was supposed to visit them during the holidays at their latest and probably last Foreign Service posting—Paris.

Emily finished speaking and after the applause died down, the guests stood to get in line for the book signing.

"Do you already have her book?" Amy almost spilled her drink as she leaned close to Joy.

"No, but I will tonight. I'm going to buy three and have her sign them." She'd keep one and send one to her mother and the other to her aunt, a rabid knitter.

"You can say you're *fine* all you want, Joy, but I know something's up. Call me when you're ready to talk. I'm here for you."

She accepted Amy's warm hug and tried to soak up the affection in spite of her serious case of the guilts. She couldn't tell Amy anything remotely close to the truth.

Brad was the only person who knew what kind of trouble she was courting by going out on a limb for him.

Brad.

Why, why, *why* was the only man she'd felt a strong connection to out of reach? What was it with her? The men who were emotionally available, who could be reliable, steady partners, had no sexual appeal for her.

She told herself, yet again, that she didn't want Brad *or* his crazy life.

Of course, he hadn't offered her anything.

And why was she even spending time worrying about this? She had books to get signed and work to do at home. Emily ended her remarks and because she sat in the second row, Joy was able to get her books signed in short order.

"Em, I'm so proud of you! We'll catch up next week." When Emily had signed the three copies, Joy kissed her friend and took the books to the cash register to pay for them. Winnie had her assistant ringing up the books as she put them in a colorful tote emblazoned with the knitting cooperative's logo. Whidbey Fibers had become its own empire in Puget Sound. Winnie had been a Navy wife who'd lost her first husband and married a second Navy man, Max. She'd managed to make a career for herself, while raising three beautiful girls. Winnie had it all—stability, family, a husband she obviously adored.

Don't compare.

"What was that?" Winnie tilted her head and looked at Joy.

Crap, had she spoken out loud?

"Are you okay, Joy?"

"Why does everyone keep asking me that? I'm

fine, really I am. Maybe just a little tired from starting a new job."

"Of course you are." Winnie nodded emphatically. "And let's not even talk about what happened yesterday… On a different topic, have you seen the schedule for next month? We're having the sweater class for the kimono jacket you admired on Amy last month. It's straight knitting, no seams. Think of it as a big scarf!"

Winnie handed her the tote over the crowded counter.

"I'll think about it. Thanks, Winnie." Joy took the schedule and dropped it into the bag. Winnie gave out class schedules as if they were a secret chicken noodle soup recipe. A sure cure for whatever ailed a person.

"You can sign up online or call us here."

"I'll probably do that."

It seemed too much to ask, to hope that she'd be free in a week and able to do something as lovely and simple as a knitting class. Without the constant worry over Brad's welfare and Farid's case.

Hot and tired, she had to get out of the jam-packed shop. Her agitation was so great she didn't even stop to tell Winnie that she'd progressed to more complicated patterns. The tickle in her stomach was turning into a full-fledged GERD attack. She needed quiet and space. No more thoughts about men and relationships.

As she drove out of Coupeville on the way

north, it was tempting to turn toward General Grimes's house in the woods. But her cell phone had no messages from Brad or the general. Neither did her email.

Nothing to do but go home.

CHAPTER FOURTEEN

"YOU DIDN'T NEED to drive me home, but thank you." Emily sat in Ben's small fuel-efficient car as he maneuvered across Deception Pass onto Fidalgo Island.

"It's my pleasure, and the least I could do since you wouldn't let me buy you dinner."

"I told you, no dates. We're colleagues, and we can be friends."

"That's right, friends. I know I take all my work friends out hoping they'll let me spring for a meal."

"You're not being fair, Ben."

"Tell me how you got interested in knitting." She admired the way he didn't hold grudges, the way he changed the topic as smoothly as she'd seen him care for a newborn who needed extra attention. He was the senior pediatrician at Naval Hospital Oak Harbor, and the scuttlebutt was that he was also the Navy's best. It was only a matter of time before he got transferred to a bigger base, a teaching hospital, where he'd be able to reach more patients and instruct residents.

At least, that was what Emily thought.

"I learned to knit as a child. My grandmother taught me. I picked it up again after my husband died. It gave me something to do with my hands and kept me from going crazy those first couple of years after he got sick and then died. After a while I realized it's truly a passion of mine, and I started making my own designs."

"I find it impressive that you're as accomplished at knitting as you are at nursing."

"Thank you." She was grateful for the dark interior of the car; she hated when anyone saw her blush. Her pale skin made her look like a beet when she did.

"You're taking the next left." She didn't want him to miss the awkward turnoff.

"I remember." His profile was strong, but his mouth curved into a smile and she found herself wondering just how soft those lips of his were.

Was this how she was finally going to break her decade-long mourning period?

"You're not the first man I've dated, you know."

"I didn't think I was. And we're not dating, remember?"

"I've tried to date other guys, and I've gotten as far as a few weeks, but it never worked out."

He pulled into her long drive. "I don't need your history tonight, Emily."

"It's just that a lot of people assume I'm gun-shy because my husband died when we were still newlyweds. I loved Peter, but I've done my grieving and moved on. My life is full."

Ben didn't respond as he put the car in Park and turned off the ignition. His windows were down and his moonroof open. The sound of the wind as it rustled across the grass in the fields surrounding her subdivision, the distant sound of waves hitting West Beach, the occasional *hoot* of a great horned owl—they all soothed her and helped her feel not quite as foolish as she supposed she should.

"Ben, I don't want you to think it's you. But I'm not ready—"

She stopped as he unbuckled first his belt and then hers. And reached over the console to grasp her face in his hands. His elegant masculine hands revealed all their strength and gentleness as they held tiny babies. She'd noticed those hands when she'd worked alongside him.

"Emily, all I want to do is kiss you. May I?"

She blinked and nodded, unwilling to miss out on this. Just in case...

Several minutes later Ben lifted his mouth from hers, and she was very, very grateful she'd opted for *just in case.*

"Thank you, Emily." His voice, usually so smooth and commanding at the hospital, was rougher, huskier. Sexy as all get-out.

"Thank you, Ben."

He stroked her cheek once more before he pulled back and got out of the car. Emily tried to gather her thoughts as he walked around the front of the vehicle, but there was nothing to gather.

He'd left her unable to focus on anything but her reaction to his kiss.

Her door opened and she slid out, rising to her full height, which meant she reached his shoulder.

"You don't have to walk me to the door, Ben." Really, this was getting a little silly. Unless… Did he expect to come in?

"I don't do anything I don't want to, Emily. That's something you'll figure out as we get to know each other better."

"Ben, this doesn't have to be the start of anything. I'm not expecting it to."

They were at her front door, and she slid her key in the lock. Inside, loud barking commenced.

"You have a dog?" he asked.

"Two. You?"

"Three."

"You have three dogs?"

"I rescued them from the shelter last Christmas. I couldn't take one and leave the other two." He shrugged.

"And I thought I was crazy with my two. Plus eight cats, but only three live inside."

He kissed her on the cheek. "Good night, Emily. See you in the morning."

TECHNOLOGY WAS ONE of Joy's best friends as it allowed her to keep her calendar up-to-date with the ease of one entry, whether it was via phone, laptop or tablet. Still, after years of post-graduate education, whenever she was stymied over a case she wasn't afraid to rely on more basic old-tech methods.

She sat at her kitchen table minutes after she returned from the book signing and quickly wrote down everything she knew about Farid's village from what General Grimes had testified and Brad had told her. With each mark of her pencil on the yellow legal pad, she hoped to put the memory of Brad's kisses further from her thoughts and in-crease her chances—*their* chances—of finding out who the unknown terrorist was. The GERD and her nerves were agitated because this hadn't been solved. Her reaction didn't have anything to do with Brad.

But his kisses… His lips hadn't disappointed. She put her pencil down.

It wasn't her imagination. Their physical chem-istry was as strong as it had ever been when they were unable to act on it. Brad felt it, too; that was obvious from the way he'd grabbed her and held her against the undeniable erection under his cargo pants.

There wasn't anything keeping them apart at this point—if she was willing to give up every-thing she'd worked so hard for. If he was willing to let go of his past and try again. She wasn't. He wasn't.

At least, she *hadn't* been willing to change. Those kisses certainly could've been game changers in other circumstances…

But it wasn't his kisses that compelled her to help Brad. He was an honorable man, and this was the right thing to do, would've been the right thing, even if they shared zero chemistry.

Her phone vibrated and she looked at the screen, expecting a local number.

Maria Alexander.

"Mom!"

"Hi, sweetheart. We saw CNN earlier and were concerned about what they're reporting. Was it very close to you, the explosion?"

"Not really." The less said to her mom, the better. There wasn't any sense in worrying her or her father.

"Are you sure?"

"Yes, Mom. I'm so busy with my new job and getting out of the Navy that I've barely kept up with the news." Lying to her mother topped her list of most shameful activities.

"Speaking of which, how's the new job?"

Her mother was thousands of miles away in one of Joy's favorite cities, and it sounded as though she was in the same room. That didn't seem fair, not when Joy needed her right here, beside her. She actually ached for one of her mother's hugs.

"It's fine. I'm fine. How are you?"

"Your dad and I are doing well, thanks. Now, no chitchat. It's me, honey. How are you *really*?" Her mother's flair for the dramatic, normally annoying, was oddly comforting her.

"Hanging in there. It's…complicated."

Her mother's warm chuckle brought tears to her eyes.

"When is it *not* complicated with you, darling?"

"Have I always been that difficult?"

"You're not difficult, Joy. You're just too smart for most of the men on the planet. This is about a man, right?"

"Kind of."

"So you've met someone. Well, that happened more quickly than I expected. Especially with you in the middle of nowhere."

"Mom, Whidbey isn't the middle of nowhere. Seattle is only two hours away, as is Vancouver. You and Dad will see when you come out and visit."

"We will indeed. You're still planning on coming to Paris for Christmas, aren't you?"

"Yes. I wouldn't miss it for the world. Will Tommy and Elaine be there?" She referred to her brother and sister-in-law.

"Tommy's not sure he'll be able to get leave, but they're working on it." Tommy had followed in their father's footsteps and was also a Foreign Service officer. He was a junior in the State

Department, on his second post, in Djibouti. He'd met his wife in the Peace Corps after college.

She felt a sudden pang of self-doubt. "Mom, I have to go—I've got a case I'm working on. Can I call you back in a few days?"

"Tomorrow we're going to London with the British Ambassador and his wife, but we'll be back by the weekend. We'll catch up then if that works for you. Try to call me on Skype next time."

Mom loved to use Skype; she said she felt as if she was in the same room with Joy. Joy suspected her mother wanted to see if she was really healthy and happy.

"Sure, Mom. Love you."

"Love you, too, sweetie." They ended the connection, and she fiddled with her phone. She needed to talk to Brad, to work through her notes and memory of the case with him.

The dozen or so lines of text she'd written blurred in front of her.

Her perfect life had imploded in the hours since yesterday morning.

Two hours later Joy wasn't any further with her private investigation. She stood up from the kitchen table and lifted her arms over her head. It was almost midnight, and she'd have to be up early to go into the office.

The thought of being at work exhausted her—having to pretend she had nothing on her mind but her new job, that she wasn't trying to figure out a puzzle that had life-or-death consequences.

Sleep wouldn't come easy, so she decided to get ready for bed and try to take her mind off everything. It looked as though Brad was safely entrenched at General Grimes's or elsewhere, at least for the night. Until she heard from him or found out whether Grimes remembered anything else that would help, there was nothing more she could do.

She'd never been comfortable admitting her own powerlessness.

Good old Navy training kicked in, and she went methodically through her nightly routine, taking off her makeup and brushing her teeth.

IT SEEMED DARKER around Joy's house than it had at General Grimes's. He still couldn't believe the old man had handed him the keys to his Wrangler.

"Take it and go out the back road."

"I can't put you at risk here, too, General."

"The news is reporting that they're closing the case. No one's looking for you anymore, or not publicly at any rate. You know as well as I do that my security detail told your boss you were here the minute they identified you. He won't be worried now, but you may have one angry guy on your hands. We also both know that if anyone was going to come here, asking more questions, they already would have. Just be very careful about saying anything related to Farid or his village on open comms, at least until you get your information further up the chain." For a man like General Grimes, a reporting senior would never be more than a link in the chain of command.

They'd shaken hands and Brad had promised to have the vehicle back to Grimes as soon as possible.

What the Jeep lacked in shock absorbers, it made up for in fun driving. He contented himself with letting the wind blow through the open windows as the moon played hide-and-seek with the clouds racing across the inky sky.

He'd parked the car in dense brush a mile from Joy's and hoofed it the rest of the way, careful to stay hidden from the road. He didn't give a rat's ass what the news media reported. He was already exposed by his simple action of not staying ashore through the op, and then his disruption of their attempted aircraft takedown. They knew by now that he was an undercover operative, in place to take *them* down. The people who were out to hurt innocent Americans didn't think for a minute that he was dead. And they wouldn't, not until they had his body as proof.

All the lights were out at Joy's, except for the

soft glow from an upstairs window. He leaned over the side of the house from his perch on her stone deck and figured it was the master bedroom.

Joy's bedroom.

Damn it, he wished they'd met under different circumstances. Where time didn't matter and they had nothing but long nights in front of them.

He told himself it wouldn't make any difference. He'd still be doing this kind of work. Which meant no more serious relationships. Joy deserved better—and wasn't she seeking something better by making a nice life for herself out here?

Still, a man could dream.

Just not now. He'd have to save his fantasies for after he'd wrapped up this case and Joy was nowhere near the bastards who dealt in death.

He let himself into her house with the key she'd given him; opening her door reminded him of the way he'd entered her place yesterday. It had been far too easy—and the idea of anyone else breaking in made him clench his fists. Once inside, he walked through the kitchen and up the stairs. If she was sleeping he'd leave her and settle on the couch. Whether she was awake or asleep, he needed to know she was safe.

The sounds of splashing water and a low-throated humming came out of the bathroom as he neared the door. He hated to scare her or invade her privacy.

He also hated that he couldn't interrupt her in a sexier way.

Silence from the bathroom. She'd heard something.

"Joy, it's me, Brad."

"Nice time to stop by, Ivy." As tough as her tone was, he also detected the quaver. He felt bad about scaring her. He'd brought enough darkness into her life over the past forty-eight hours. Less than that, actually.

"Grimes gave me the keys to one of his cars."

"Wait, let me come out."

"No, take your time." She needed to relax. And sleep. He could use some sleep, too. "We can talk after you're done, or even in the morning. I'll crash on your sofa." Where he could monitor her front door and the sliding glass doors in back. So she'd be out of his reach… *You don't want to behave nicely. You want to…*

"No!"

"No what?" Joy stood in front of him, wearing a thick robe. Her face was obscured in shadow; the bathroom light behind her was the only source of brightness in the entire room.

"No, as in 'no, I don't want to interrupt your routine.'"

She smelled pretty and fresh, just like the Navy lieutenant commander he'd originally met in Gitmo. No matter how starched her collars had been, her scent was never less than utterly feminine.

The woman standing there—this was the Joy he'd imagined asking for a date. Before he'd un-leashed the hounds of hell…

"This isn't my routine, Ivy. I usually brush my teeth and wash my face around nine. Then I'm asleep by ten." She was guarding herself from him. Part of her defensive posture had always been to call him "Ivy."

"Hell, I didn't know the Boat School's routine was still imprinted on you."

She smirked; Boat School was slang for the US Naval Academy.

"Not all of us are almost-PhDs."

She slipped back into the banter that had helped them lighten their load in Norfolk. They'd needed to relieve the pressure when they'd had military and political heavyweights breathing down their necks during Farid's case.

He knew how he'd dreamed of relieving that stress, and how he'd like to dispel the tension that pressed in on them now.

"Joy—"

"Let's go to the kitchen." She walked past him, into the hallway. Her mouth was set in a stubborn line, and she shoved her hands in the pockets of her robe. She wanted the same thing he did, but she'd decided it couldn't happen. And her decision was the sanest option.

"Good idea," he said.

CHAPTER FIFTEEN

TEN MINUTES LATER they had Irish coffees in front of them. The light over the stove threw long shadows and accentuated the dark smudges under her eyes. He hated being the cause of it.

"Don't you need to sleep before work tomorrow?" he asked.

"I will. The coffee is decaf. And there's only a small amount of sugar in the whipped cream. Why don't we go into the sunroom and watch the water in the moonlight?"

He nodded, pointing at her drink as he stood up. "You never struck me as a whiskey girl."

"I'm not. Unless it's mixed into this or hot chocolate in the middle of winter." They sat down on her rattan sofa with its floral pillows. Brad recognized the style from several detachments that had routed him through Hawaii.

"Did you get a lot of your furniture overseas?"

"Enough of it. Especially once I started to think about getting out and settling down."

"You don't think you'll *ever* miss the moving? Being in new locations?"

"Nope. It's hard to believe for a lifer like you, I'm sure, but I'm done with the constant change. I'll get my excitement through work. I'm especially interested in family law—that means a lot to me. And so does having a place to finally call home."

"I'm not a *lifer*, either, Joy. I got out, too. Remember?"

"You've stayed reserves, and you're still in a business that'll move you around quite a bit."

"If you're so happy to have gotten out of the Navy, why do you sound wistful about it?"

"You're hearing my exhaustion from the last two days. I'm tired, Brad. No complaining, but it's been kind of a stretch, starting a new job *and* trying to save your life."

Her tone was light, and he could tell she didn't want him to know how much of a burden his situation had placed on her.

"I'm sorry about that, Joy. I mean it." He took a large gulp from his mug, wishing he could have the whiskey full strength.

"Stop saying that. It's not your fault that some psychos decided to smuggle in a SAM. Now they might want to kill you or hurt innocent civilians."

"Not on my watch."

"Or mine." She sipped her coffee. "My knitting group was all abuzz about it."

"Your knitting group. I thought you were at a book signing."

"Yes, I mentioned it earlier. Knitting's not just for grandmas, you know."

"Go on."

"As a matter of fact, there are a number of active-duty sailors and spouses in the group. Many have graduate degrees, and one even has a doctorate. Two of us are lawyers. Two more are—wait for it—men!"

"Hey, you proved your point. I've obviously been living under a rock." He grinned then asked in a more serious tone, "What were they saying about the explosion?"

"Mostly the comments you'd expect—that they hope the NCIS and FBI get the bastards behind it. That they hope it was really an accident and the boat blew up because of faulty wiring or some other problem. That they're all happy no one's been hurt...yet. They're Navy. They know that the base, their loved ones, the aircraft they fly and ships they drive are always targets. They want the reasons for what happened and the people responsible in custody."

"What's their consensus? About who might be guilty and why."

She sipped more coffee before she answered. She squared her shoulders, and he saw her turn toward him in the dim light.

"Most of them think it was terrorist related. Some kind of a warning. It's hard not to, when it happened in the middle of a big Fleet exercise.

Navy, and military, families are more attuned to this sort of thing. I don't have to tell you that."

His jaw tightened. "They're right. These guys don't do anything without goals and real deliberation."

"No, they don't. They're not the only ones capable of purposeful action, however. We're better than they are by a long shot. They had the benefit of surprise with the SAM, that's it. You were in deep in their cell, ready to break them apart. We'll get to the bottom of it, Brad, trust me."

He did trust her. Implicitly.

He knew she trusted him, too. He wasn't sure why, and yet she'd never doubted him. When they worked on Farid's testimony she'd held her judgment in reserve until she got to know him, but she'd never treated him with anything less than respect. Nor did she consider any of the negative press about him to be true. They'd skewered him for testifying in favor of releasing a known terrorist suspect. These attacks by certain elements of the media had been anonymous, since the Navy had protected his identity, but the story got out nonetheless.

"You need to make sure you can trust me," he said. He saw her shake her head dismissively.

"Already covered this, Ivy."

"So tell me what you're thinking about all of this."

She was silent for so long that he wondered if

the Irish coffee was kicking in and she was starting to drift off. Then she moved, tucking her foot beneath her and leaning her head on the back of the sofa.

"I think General Grimes is right. This goes back to someone who's out for revenge and is using the domestic cell to do it. It might be someone Farid knew, or even his family."

"Go on."

"Grimes was there, in Afghanistan, when you were, Brad. He had every opportunity to interact with all types of village leaders and Afghan tribesmen. He saw Farid's village just like you did. Many of the villagers, if not all, hold us responsible for the atrocities the Taliban committed. It's how the bad guys maintain control over there. They blame the US and our allies." She paused. "You know that even better than I do."

"Yeah. But let me tell you, Grimes is a straight arrow. He may be a son of a bitch to work for, but he's solid. He told me more after you left. He thinks looking into the events and persons related to Farid's village is the way to go. His opinion is that it has to happen at a higher level than the FBI."

He heard her laughter in the darkened space between them and closed his eyes, savoring the sweet sound. He loved it when he made her laugh.

"Of course he did." She decided to make her

confession. "I feel guilty admitting that I checked out his background, looking for terrorist motives."

"You were being thorough. No need for guilt."

"I suppose."

"His wife died very young."

"How do you know that?"

Satisfaction warmed him. He actually had more information on Grimes than she did—a first.

"I know more than you give me credit for." He related what Grimes had shared.

"General Grimes told me why he never remarried. He had the love of his life years ago and didn't want to put another woman at risk of being tossed about by his Marine Corps career."

"More like he didn't want to risk losing someone he loved again."

"Rewrite it however you'd like to, but he's on our side. He has a daughter he raised almost single-handedly, too."

"Maybe he came to Whidbey to find love, now that he's retired. There are plenty of single women his age in this area."

"I never pegged you as a romantic, Joy."

"You've only seen my JAG side, Ivy. Besides, it's not something we ever talked about before."

"No, I suppose we didn't." They'd rarely strayed from the business at hand. Their brief forays into kidding around had been to relieve stress; that was all.

And the kisses?

"I can't believe he gave you his car."

He was really tired of talking about General Grimes. In fact, he was tired of anything related to his work. He wanted—no, needed—to know more about Joy.

"Yes, he did. His Jeep. It was generous and trusting of him."

At her silence, he turned toward her. "Enough about General Grimes. What about you, Joy? What do you do besides knit?"

"I enjoy day trips off the island. British Columbia, Seattle."

"Do you go up to Canada a lot?" Canada was only two hours from Whidbey, a straight shot to Vancouver.

"I've taken the ferry to Victoria a couple of times, and I went on a knitting-skiing retreat to Whistler last fall. Because of the early winter, we were able to ski, and there's an indoor ice-skating rink."

"I've heard Whistler's beautiful." Talking to her about anything ordinary felt indulgent and... right. Joy was the best company he'd kept in years, maybe ever.

"Yeah, it is. So you haven't been up there yet?" Was that an accusatory tone? Or did she think he was a dumb guy who didn't do anything other than work and play video games?

"I've only been in Seattle for a few months."

"And most of that time's been undercover."

"Yes. That's why I didn't call you sooner, Joy. I couldn't."

"It's okay, Brad."

She didn't elaborate, but that was just as well. The more he found out about Joy Alexander, the more he questioned his decision to remain single.

Then he remembered that anyone he showed the slightest interest in could get hurt…

JOY COULD'VE SAT in the sunroom—which she'd decided to rename the moon room—with Brad all night and into the sunrise. It felt so natural to be around him, with him, next to him. His male scent was becoming so familiar again, so appealing, she wondered how she'd live without it once he was gone.

The fact that he believed she'd be able to solve his case for him at once overwhelmed and honored her to the point of tears.

Tears she used the edge of her terry robe to wipe away, grateful for the darkness that hid her sentimentality.

Why couldn't she be more relaxed, more easygoing, and have sex with Brad to get him out of her system?

Because it would never be only sex. Not for her. Not with him.

"What's bothering you, Joy?"

"I really thought we might find something on Grimes," she said with a shrug.

"But he doesn't even have a motive."

She punched his shoulder lightly. "Gee, Ivy, you make me think you should've gone to law school instead of the Bureau."

"Hey, I'm a trained case agent. Plus, I like a good thriller novel on my days off."

"Yes, but back to motive. General Grimes has had his share of run-ins with his superiors."

"Who hasn't? And in spite of all of it, the guy made three star. Pretty impressive."

"He didn't get offered a fourth star, or command of the Corps. And he wasn't offered a shiny civilian job in DC." She mentally reviewed the press releases she'd skimmed on Grimes.

"He was probably offered a slew of high-paying civilian jobs. He turned them down. A man like Grimes doesn't care about the prestige or the money. I get that about him."

"You think because I was JAG and female that I don't get it, too? I went through plebe summer and the same kinds of training as my classmates who went Marine Corps. None of us are in the Navy or Marine Corps for the money."

"Grimes told me he wasn't interested in being a contractor. It means more to him that he can call his own shots on his own land. He couldn't have done that if he had to work around all those bigwigs in DC. At the moment, though, I wish he was in DC instead of here. He'd be safer and easier to protect than out in his cabin. He'd also be in a position to get us the answers we need more quickly."

"You have surveillance on his place."

"Yes, but how long will he agree to that? You can imagine a Marine Corps general being told what he can and can't do by a bunch of guys who could almost be his grandkids."

"Sounds like you two have a bromance going. He confides in you, gives you his car…"

"Careful, Joy."

She smiled, delighted by the low grumble of his voice.

"Anyway, when I was looking up stuff on him, I also found an old Op-Ed from the *Wall Street Journal* that described Grimes as an egomaniac who had zero tolerance for the current administration."

"He's in a big club, Joy. A lot of military don't like it when the White House or Congress isn't one hundred percent pro-defense establishment."

"I don't like how quick he was to try to pit your boss against you."

Brad's sigh revealed more than exhaustion. Revelation?

"Joy, let's drop it. We have bigger fish to fry right now. You have to admit, you're still resentful of how he treated you during the trial."

"Yes, I suppose I am. Has it occurred to you

that you might never find out who wanted to kill
you?"

"I think it's kind of obvious that it was the
cell I infiltrated. My goal is to stay alive and
pass enough information to my team to get them
rounded up before they can do any more dam-
age."

"So those guards at General's—do they know
you're undercover?"

"Not officially, no. No one knows, Joy. Only
you and my boss. And I have no doubt that Mike
knew I was still alive within seconds of us pulling up to General's A-frame."

A contemplative silence settled over them.
Joy didn't miss the fact that if they hadn't been
thrown together again, for the sake of doing the
right thing for their country, this could be a very
different time. A very different experience.

Her nipples hardened under her terry robe, and
she bit back a curse. Some professional *she* was
when she couldn't keep her body from betraying
her desire for Brad.

It'd been there since she'd met him, but their
public workplaces and the knowledge that he was
engaged, no matter how precariously, had extin-
guished her arousal.

Here they were, both supposedly free and
alone—she naked under her robe. A robe that
could hit the moon room's tiles with one tug on
her belt.

"Joy, don't."

"Don't?" He had to feel her need, despite the near-darkness; she was barely containing it.

"Don't second-guess this. We work well together. It can't, shouldn't, be more than that." She heard the rasp of his clothing, felt his weight shift on the cushion.

"That's pretty arrogant, Ivy, even for you."

Did he hear her desire in every word?

"We've been through a lot together. Emotional entanglement isn't something we want to add to the list."

"It is risky, true. Just think, you could be in the throes of the greatest sex of your life and *bam*! A sniper takes you out."

"Not funny, Joy."

It wasn't fair. Even as Brad turned her down, made sure she understood there'd never be anything physical, other than those kisses, he turned her on with the sexy growl in his voice.

"I'm not trying to be funny."

"Look, I messed up. Kissing you—it shouldn't have happened. We both know that, right?"

She stood up, needing to be anywhere but next to him on a couch in the dark. Where she could feel every move he made and his nearness increased the excruciating tension.

"Yes, you're right. Of course."

She sighed. She really, really didn't want to

make this any harder on herself. Her body seemed to have a mind of its own, but her will was stronger.

"What is it, Joy? Tell me."

"For the first time in my life I don't know what my next move is. I don't know what to tell you to do, either."

"Welcome to the club."

"I wish there was some way to get to Farid, to make sure he didn't withhold something you could use now."

"Already covered. If that information is available, it'll be collected by a US Marshal. They're the ones in charge of the WSP."

"Gee, thanks for the explanation, Ivy. I figured as much. I'm ill-prepared to help you any further, other than telling you what I read in the case files, and then on the internet. I wasn't Intel, and the attorney in me loathes going through personal information that's truly none of my business."

"Come here, Joy." His tone indicated that his thoughts were elsewhere.

"Have you heard a word I've said?"

"Come. Here."

She heard him pat the sofa cushion next to him.

"Brad…" She allowed herself to feel how exhausted she really was.

"I'm not going to kiss you. Promise." Why not?

She took two short steps and lowered herself onto the sofa. Brad reached her waist and he pulled her down beside him.

She could feel the heat of his body through her terry robe. He might not want to kiss her but it didn't matter who started it. Because *she* wanted to kiss *him*. Badly.

"Lean your head against me." He wrapped his arm around her shoulder, and she put her head on his. After a few minutes she realized he was serious—this wasn't going to be a lovemaking session.

"Brad? What exactly is this about?" Even as she tried to stir up the energy to confront him, her bones melted into his warmth. Brad's sheer strength comforted her as nothing else could.

"We're resting, Joy. Neither of us will get any sleep knowing the other one is near. We can't have sex or we'll ruin our wonderful working relationship. So let's do the friendly thing and just be quiet for a bit. Rest."

Really? Did he think she could sleep when her nerve endings tingled with awareness, and there were goose bumps on her arm where his breath blew across it? When his solid weight under her cheek made her crazy with wanting him?

She closed her eyes, knowing that sleep was impossible.

BRAD STRAIGHTENED HIS legs slowly as he woke from a wonderful power nap. He didn't want to wake Joy—she needed the rest more than he did at this point. She had to pretend everything was normal and continue with her new job.

He loved the way she was leaning against him. She'd curled her legs under her so he eased her onto his lap, where he'd placed a pillow. He didn't want her to wake up and think he was some kind of perv.

Long fingers of dawn began to streak across the sky and the sea, and he wondered if he'd ever seen such a beautiful start to the day. The reddish glow made him think of the old rhyme, "Red sky at morning, sailors take warning."

Storms seemed to be a way of life for him.

In this quiet, with a woman he cared about more than he'd ever planned to, the future seemed simple.

It was time to let go of his lifestyle and begin a new life without the encumbrances of working for the US Government as either a SEAL or an FBI agent. Time to give the younger generation a shot at these life-changing experiences. He'd outgrown the need for the constant adrenaline rush, the need to know that he was doing something that made a crucial difference to national security.

And Joy was right; he wasn't responsible for Marci's death. Her addiction had been her compulsion, and he'd been powerless over that. He hated it and would never understand it, but it was reality.

What he wasn't powerless over was moving

forward once he was free of this op. Did he want to even contemplate making a go of things with Joy? Would she be interested after he'd missed his earlier opportunities with her?

First, he had a case to close. He only hoped her heart wouldn't be permanently shut by the time he did.

AN ACHE IN her shoulder woke her up, the same shoulder she'd messed up at the academy when she was on the rowing team. She'd leaned on it as she slept in Brad's lap.

Brad's lap.

She sat up.

"Easy. Bad dream?"

As her disorientation cleared, she realized that at some point she'd fallen asleep, daylight had emerged and Brad had put a pillow on his lap for her head. She was also covered with the ivory alpaca throw she'd knitted last winter.

Which was a good thing, since she was pretty sure she would have exposed her naked bottom to Brad otherwise. Her terry robe wasn't that long.

"I was out cold."

"You needed it." His voice comforted her.

"Did you get any rest?"

"Some."

"You should've left me here and stretched out in the guest room or on the living room sofa."

"And miss that beautiful sunrise? No way. Besides, you didn't sleep much longer than I did."

As she remembered what lay ahead of her today, she sagged against the cushions. "I can't believe I have to go to work for the third day pretending that there's nothing going on in my life. That I'm not harboring a semi-fugitive."

She turned. His face was too close to hers.

"I'm leaving today, Joy."

"What?"

"I'm going. You won't have to pretend anymore. Except for not mentioning that you ever saw me."

"I don't disagree that you have to get out of here. I'm just worried that a terrorist might still be after you. Do you have a plan?"

She was pushing it, asking Brad—a former SEAL, an undercover FBI agent—if he was prepared. She couldn't help it.

"My plan's the same as it always was. To get to the bottom of this. You never did tell me what you found in the notes. Have you had a chance to go through all of them yet?"

She was relieved that they were talking about the case again. Crucial, yes, but it was also a distraction from her feelings, her craving for him. That reprieve wouldn't last, however, not as long as she stayed in this robe.

"Hold that thought. Let me go get dressed.

Grab whatever you want from the kitchen, of course. You'll still be here when I get back?"

"Yes. And, Joy? Thanks."

She all but ran into her room, grateful to escape from his nearness.

There was no escaping her desire for him, though.

CHAPTER SIXTEEN

BRAD SAT ON the sofa for a moment after Joy went to dress. He'd come so close to pulling her into his arms and picking up where their hallway kiss had left off.

He stood up and paced the sunroom. The longer he stayed here, the greater the chances that Joy would be targeted. But maybe what she said was true; whoever was after him might think he was dead—killed while taking out the SAM shooter—and had called off the search for him. There'd been no reports of any sightings of him from what he'd seen on TV and via the internet at General Grimes's. Of course Grimes had seen him, but he trusted him implicitly. The general was as solid as they came.

It was past time to call Mike.

"Want some more coffee?" Joy's soft voice interrupted his thoughts and he stopped pacing.

"Sure."

"You're pacing. What are you figuring out?"

He couldn't stop the warmth that spread through him at her observation.

"Do you remember *everything* about me?" he asked.

She'd seen him pacing several times in Norfolk, during court recesses.

"I told you, I have an excellent memory. Better than I'd like to, believe me."

He admired her figure in workout pants and some kind of fuzzy pink pullover. He'd imagined her naked countless times but more than that, he'd fantasized about her smile, her laughter, the sheer energy that had always flowed between them.

But he had to be certain—of her, of himself— before he got further involved with Joy.

He trailed her into the kitchen and leaned against the counter while she made coffee.

"I'm going to do a French press if that's okay with you. If I make another pot of drip it'll kill my stomach by the end of the day."

"Beggars can't be choosers."

Her hand paused over the canister of beans, and the light glinted off the stainless steel measuring scoop. And, he could've sworn, off the steel glinting in the depths of her gaze.

"You're hardly a beggar, Brad."

She jammed the grinder shut, and the loud whir of the blades was followed by the unmistakable scent of freshly ground coffee.

His hands reached out for her before he could think about it. He kneaded her shoulders, small and firm beneath his palms. An affectionate gesture between friends.

Except, as a rule, friendly gestures didn't make him hard.

He dropped his arms to his sides. "I'm happy with whatever you offer me, Joy." He shoved his hands into his pockets.

"Apparently not." The grinder whirred again.

"Don't tell me you want to start a relationship with someone like me, in the middle of this mess?"

"No, no, I don't. I moved here to get away from men of adventure and the constant feeling that whomever I was dating could be posted overseas at a moment's notice. I want stability in my life, not a man who's coming and going more than he can keep track of."

She pressed down on the grinder again.

"You certainly deserve that, Joy," he shouted over the blades. He meant what he said. So what if his stomach felt as if it was being crushed? He'd never be able to offer *her* what she wanted.

Not now.

"I do deserve it. Most definitely." She didn't sound so sure but he didn't call her on it.

The refrigerator light illuminated the space between them as she reached for the creamer.

"Hazelnut okay?"

"I'll take mine black. I didn't think you ate or drank anything artificial."

Back in Norfolk she'd eaten veggie wraps or salads at her desk, and appeared to snack only on healthy food. He'd hoped to take her out for a fancy meal in one of DC's best restaurants after the case was closed.

Instead, he'd had to deal with the mess from Marci's murder—the grief and the guilt, as well as the allegations—and focus on getting out of the Navy, beginning his new job.

By the time he was out of the Navy and settled in his new job with the FBI, it was too late. He couldn't track Joy down for a date for more than a year after they'd said goodbye. At least not without some serious prep work, like emails and phone calls.

You managed to find her now.

"I like to eat clean as much as possible, yes. But I have my vices, and hazelnut creamer happens to be one of them."

"Do you like Nutella, too?"

"You mean because it's hazelnut-flavored? Yes, I do. On toast. But all I have right now is peanut butter. Want some?" She pulled out a loaf of bread and popped two slices into the bright yellow toaster that sat on the counter.

"I'll pass. I will take one of those yogurts you have, though."

"Sure." She took a single-serving Greek yogurt from the fridge and fished around in her silverware drawer for a spoon, which she handed to him. She was careful to hold the handle far enough so their fingers wouldn't touch.

"It's key lime. That's the only one I buy except for plain."

"Why am I not surprised? Tart with a little bit of sweetness." Finding he was very hungry all of a sudden, he spooned a huge dollop of the yogurt into his mouth. The explosion of lime on his tongue reminded him of Joy's perfume, which had citrusy undertones.

"There are eggs if you want to make yourself some. You need your protein, I'm sure. That little container of yogurt won't tide you over until lunch...or later."

"Ah, no, thanks. The yogurt is perfect."

"But it's not enough to hold anyone for a few hours, much less a day. You could be out for a long while..."

What she didn't say, he surmised—hell, he'd lived it countless times. He could be without a decent place to stay, without fresh food, without a known end point to the day, much less the case.

"You're right. I'll take some of that bread when you're done with the toaster."

She took her toast to the table, leaving him with the toaster, the loaf of multigrain bread and a jar of peanut butter.

He'd just sat down with her when the doorbell sounded, followed by loud knocking.

She raised her eyebrows. "Expecting someone, Ivy?"

JOY OPENED HER door to a lone man on her front porch. She recognized him immediately. He was tall and a bit disheveled, but that didn't detract from his good looks. She noticed the same wary watchfulness she'd grown used to with Brad. It was the SEAL training, she'd decided, that left a man with the ability to make you feel you'd just been scrutinized and assessed for your value as a warrior.

In one quick glance.

"Joy Alexander."

"Nice to see you again, Agent Rubio." They shook hands.

He kept it official as he flipped open his badge holder and held it at eye level. "Michael Rubio, FBI Agent and Brad's immediate supervisor."

"I told you I know who you are. Come on in."

She turned and let him follow her in. There was nothing to lose at this point. If he'd brought a team of men to arrest Brad, she wouldn't be able to stop them.

But she didn't think he had. He'd come to talk to his friend.

"You have a guest, Brad."

"Mike!" Brad crossed the floor and stopped in front of his former SEAL teammate.

"Well, I'll be damned. I hoped I was wrong and I'm glad I am, but for a little while there, I was afraid you'd been blown up in a fishing boat, Iverson."

Although Mike called Brad by his last name, the closeness of their bond was palpable. Mike's joy at seeing Brad alive was reflected in the broad grin he flashed at his former SEAL teammate.

"I'm here, in one piece. Let me guess—you're taking me in?"

Mike held his hands out in front of him. "Whoa, what? No way, man, I'm here to question Joy about what she witnessed during the explosion. But since you're here, too, I may have some words for you."

"I'll bet. Do they have any resemblance to 'you're fired'?" Brad wasn't backing down. He expected the worst.

"I'd hoped and prayed you were still alive. I really thought they might've gotten you this time, Brad. Until I got the call from the agents guarding General Grimes's place. They mentioned seeing you. So as you can imagine, I'm pissed as hell at you. Why didn't you call in?"

"You know damned well why I didn't call in. I couldn't risk it. And for the record, Grimes tried to implicate you in front of Joy and me."

"He's a Marine. What do you expect?"

They laughed at the inside joke. SEALs working a mission under a Marine commander they didn't report to inevitably butted heads.

"Would you like some coffee, Agent Rubio?" Joy didn't want to watch these men go at it without more caffeine in her system. She needed to remember every word that was about to be exchanged.

"No, thanks. I have a reusable cup in the car. And it's Mike."

"If you want to get your cup, I'll put fresh coffee in it for you."

"That's okay, thanks."

Her hospitality was lost on Mike, who continued to stare at Brad. "We need to talk, man. How about coming for a ride with me?"

"That sounds like an order, *boss*."

"It is."

"We'll talk here," Brad said pointedly. He sat in one of the kitchen chairs. "You can say whatever you need to in front of Joy. She's my attorney."

Brad and his boss glared at each other like gladiators preparing for a match.

"You don't need a damned lawyer," Mike said angrily. "Jeez, I kept you undercover for too long. You're in too deep. You should've reported in, Brad."

Brad shrugged. "I thought differently. It was hard to feel safe about anything after I saw that

SAM in a boat right off the island. Right off American soil, damn it."

"You weren't the only one who was shocked by the SAM. Pieces of a SA-7 have been retrieved from the scene."

"I didn't have a choice, Mike. I couldn't let a SAM go off."

Mike Rubio sighed. "No, you couldn't. You're a hero, man. Thank God it was you out there and not a rookie."

She'd been around enough military men in her career to know that combat bonds ran deep. Mike's anger was natural, since he and Brad must have shared life-and-death situations. Worked up as Mike was, she understood that it came from his relief at finding Brad alive, mixed with anger that he hadn't found out sooner.

Brad's reaction, though—she couldn't put her finger on it. He seemed upset with Mike. As if he blamed his boss for interrupting his operation.

"Talk to me, Brad. Tell me what you saw."

"I'm not talking until you read me into whatever you know about the big bad guys behind all of this. What was I, Mike, chump for the terrorists? Was this the reason for all the fuss about 'you're the only man for the job'? Because I'm single and wouldn't be leaving a family behind? Sure, call me a hero *now*."

"That's crazy talk, Brad."

Problem was, Brad sounded awfully logical to her. Calm. Contained. Intelligent.

No wonder he was pissed at Mike.

"I'll tell you what I know." He looked at Joy. "I have a feeling you two have already figured most of it out."

BRAD FELT A sense of dread in his gut. He hardly ever felt it, only when he thought he'd screwed up a mission beyond repair, which was just about never. Or when he believed he'd been duped, which rarely happened. He hadn't felt this stunned, as if he'd been cold-cocked, since Marci's death.

After several minutes of a one-way conversation, Mike concluded by saying that an unknown, missing suspect remained at large. And that person fit Farid's profile.

"If you'd called in when you were supposed to, we might've worked this out sooner. We're more than colleagues, Brad. We go beyond that. Why didn't you call me?" Mike's sincerity was apparent in the frustration on his face.

"My cell phone was compromised."

"Bull."

Yeah, Mike knew him well.

"I wanted to solve the case first. I didn't want to call in until I had an answer for you. Now we both have the same answer. But I don't agree with you that it's Farid."

"What's rule number one, Brad?"

Brad shook his head. "No man is an island."

"Exactly. You have a whole team working on this, and they're just as capable as you are at digging for answers."

"They're not here. They weren't with me out on the water."

"Damn it, Brad! You know what I mean. Being undercover doesn't give you a pass from basic protocol."

"No, but being the op leader *did* give me an inside track. Unless you already had that, and were using me to prove your theory." Brad's eyes narrowed.

She forced herself to move from the counter to sit next to Brad at the table.

"Mike," she said. "I worked with Brad at length in Norfolk."

"I know that, Joy." It was a little unsettling to wonder how much he and the FBI knew about her, but she couldn't dwell on that.

"He trusted me to stay quiet about where he was, until I could get the notes from the court dockets on Farid's case."

"I remember that case, Joy. I was supposed to testify."

He'd been out on a mission with his SEAL team and unable to make it back. He'd submitted a written statement.

"What you're ignoring," Rubio said, pointing

at Brad, "is that there's a terrorist on the loose out there. If he isn't caught and shut down, NAS Whidbey, Port Everett and any other West Coast military facilities may get hit. I needed to know where you were so I could use you the most effectively."

"Maybe if you'd cut me in on the background of the entire operation to start with, we'd have *all* our suspects in custody by now, and spec ops would have taken out the perpetrators overseas."

Joy kept her expression as neutral as possible, but Brad's comeback shocked her. It had never occurred to her that he wouldn't have had all the information he needed to conduct his operation.

"You didn't have a need to know everything, Brad."

"Damn it, Mike, the rules are meant to be broken sometimes. Especially when one of your operatives is putting it all on the line for you."

"Calm down, Brad. You're right. I should've given you more information as the op went on. But would you rather have come in to get briefed or stayed in the field undercover?"

Brad remained silent.

"Let's go over what you remember from Monday morning."

Brad's anger seemed to emanate in waves off his body. Her hands longed to clasp his, to comfort him and let him know he wasn't alone. That she was here for him, no matter what.

It'd been barely forty-eight hours. Yet she wasn't the woman she'd been a week ago. Or two days ago.

She'd changed the minute Brad pushed open her kitchen door on Monday morning.

"You NEVER MAKE things easy for anyone, Brad."

"I don't get paid to make things easy."

Brad watched Mike's expression go from angry to apologetic. He'd seen it before, whenever they'd been out in the field and an op was about to fall apart without any explanation. He'd been the one who'd talk then-Lieutenant Mike Rubio down from the ledge, remind him that they were a team and that the entire SEAL team would work together. He used to tell Mike he didn't have to be such a damn loner. Now it was Mike talking to him as though Brad was the one about to explode.

Or implode.

"Tell me what happened." Mike's glance shifted to Joy, no longer dismissing her but still not completely trusting her. Brad clenched his fists. He didn't like the almost uncontrollable protective urges he had around Joy. He'd worked with other women and been able to treat them as part of the Navy team, no problem. But Joy... Joy was different.

You've fallen for her.

"I don't have to tell you anything." His harsh words came out more in response to the war between his heart and his head than any annoyance with Mike, but he wasn't about to back down.

"I can leave if you need me to. It's not a problem." She sat next to him, strong and steady.

"Stay, Joy."

"Will I get a biscuit if I do?"

He couldn't risk looking at her, not when he had to keep his focus on Mike.

"Can it, Joy."

"Aye, aye, sir." It was barely audible but loud enough. Even stone-faced Mike had to fight to hold back his grin—Brad saw his upper lip twitch.

"There's not a lot to tell you, Mike. I thought I was in fine with the cell suspects. They were planning to recon the area, find the best places to get on base. I was going to call in a report Sunday night. But on Sunday afternoon they arranged an impromptu meeting. All of us. Together."

"Together?" Mike's eyebrows rose, and Brad saw that his boss and former shipmate finally got it.

"Yeah. I knew they were about to do something bigger, so I hedged my bets and went to the meeting. It was late at night on the beach and their faces were covered with hats and scarves, even in the heat wave."

"Typical."

"Yes. I stayed quiet unless spoken to directly.

That's how I've always done it. One of the guys, not the lead, mentioned that they'd found the house of the person they'd been searching for. Another guy said he couldn't wait to finally tell their 'chief' that revenge for his family had been completed."

Mike nodded. "Go on."

"That's when I had my team here run down all military personnel in the area who'd served over there, as you know. About a month ago."

"And they came up with Grimes." Mike spoke quietly, his initial indignant attitude gone.

"Right. I knew Grimes would be adequately protected once I called in, and I wanted to catch these dirtbags in the act. If I'd had even the slightest idea they had serious weapons that could take down an aircraft or incapacitate the Naval Air Station's operations, I would've called for backup. Especially with the Naval exercise about to kick off."

Mike sighed and leaned back, the first sign that he was as frustrated as Brad was by what they faced.

"How did you happen to be on the water at the same time as the shooter?"

"One of the suspects said he'd have an observation boat in the water by daybreak, from the boat launch on West Beach. The head honcho of this group told me to stay on the beach and watch what happened—and take a video of it.

Somehow they'd learned about the exercise, but I don't know their source. I assume they'd been eavesdropping on sailors at the local bars. I told them I'd hunker down on West Beach, posing as a photographer. They told me the video I captured would be critical to their success. I realized then that they were planning something big. With the way terrorists use social media these days, I figured that's why my video was going to be so crucial."

Mike whistled under his breath. "Did you get any video?"

"No. I stood watch all night, and when I saw one of the suspects pull up to the boat launch with a pickup and a small fishing boat, I followed him. He never knew I was there."

Mike smiled and slapped his hand on the table, startling Joy.

"Hey, you're the man!"

Brad nodded. "I think you know the rest. I had my rifle loaded and ready. When I saw the SAM I didn't hesitate. As soon as the suspect picked it up and prepared to fire, I beat him to it. I shot at the missile first, to distract him. As soon as he'd dropped his aim toward the water, I killed him. The warhead still exploded but not in the air."

Mike rubbed his face. "You saved at least a flight crew, Brad, and you made it out alive. More good news is that we caught the terrorists you've been embedded with."

He felt Joy stiffen next to him and surreptitiously placed his hand on her thigh under the table.

"How?"

"Two were caught as they surveilled the perimeter of the Naval Air Station, and Canadian Customs apprehended the third at the border."

"Why hasn't this shown up on the news?"

"In case there are any more out there. We haven't finished our debriefs yet."

"Do you really think there are more? I never heard of any loner, and I was with these guys for six months. I think I would've heard if they had another accomplice."

Mike grunted. "Remember, they operate individually first. The fact that they came together was a huge sign that they're taking orders from a single source. I have to admit they're some of the dumber suspects we've observed."

"Still smart enough to kill innocents. And the question remains—how the hell did they get that SAM?"

"The Navy and US Customs are on it." Mike didn't have to say the CIA was involved. They all knew it and knew not to mention it.

They sat quietly, everyone except Joy, who drummed her fingers against her porcelain mug.

"I have good news, Brad. You're free to go, buddy. Once you debrief the team on the base, you're done with the op and you can report back to the office. I'd suggest you take some leave. You'll need it once you come off the adrenaline rush."

"That's it? All that work, months undercover, and Brad's free to walk out of here? He's not at any risk?" Joy's voice was incredulous, and she gripped the side of the kitchen table. He recognized the defense mechanism; he did it, too, whenever he had to stop his hands from shaking.

"Joy, it's okay." She didn't understand that closing a case was often anticlimactic.

"No, it's not okay! Please tell me the FBI has a decent debrief for this man who saved your ass by putting *his* at risk. All so he could take down what you call the terrorist 'B' team. Tell him that he's one hundred percent safe. Guarantee that he'll not be held liable for anything that happened, and that his name won't be dragged through the mud. That there still isn't some crazy out there waiting to get him."

Joy's eyes sparked with anger at Mike, and Brad would have laughed if she wasn't so serious. For his part, Mike played it cool. "Your concerns are reasonable, Joy, but it's in Brad's job description. He's better than anyone else at it, and he's certainly aware of the risks involved."

"It's okay, Joy," Brad said again. "Really." He attempted to put his hand on her arm, but she pushed her chair back and shook off his arm.

"I can see that neither of you needs my services

at this point. Brad, you know where everything is. Help yourself to whatever. I've got a new job to get to."

HE WATCHED JOY all but stomp out of the room.

"Some real interesting tension between you two, huh?"

"Go to hell, Mike."

They were back on friendly terms, which was a relief to Brad.

"I didn't know if you trusted me, Mike. Not considering how quickly it could've gone bad. I never expected the SAM."

"Stop beating yourself up. None of us saw it coming. We've always known it's a possibility, but still..." Mike stood beside him as they looked out from the sunroom over West Beach. Joy was still doing whatever last-minute prep she needed before she went to the law firm.

He wondered if that included sticking pins in an effigy of him. He could've told her more, given her more details, but he'd had good reason not to reveal everything. Sometimes the less you knew in this business, the better.

He looked back at Mike. "It did turn on a dime, but that's nothing we haven't faced before, right?"

Mike ran his hand through his hair, and Brad wanted to tease him about how much longer it was than when they'd done SEAL ops. He didn't have a leg to stand on, though, since his was inordinately long for undercover work.

"Like I told you, I was afraid I'd really lost you for a while there, Brad."

"What made you realize you hadn't?"

"I didn't think you were so stupid as to be in a boat with a SAM. NCIS sent out a report that concluded the SAM's warhead had been detonated before it launched. I put my money on your sharpshooter skills."

"Who apprehended the cell members?"

"Two guys from your team, along with several local LEA agents and officers. I had to convince them you were alive, to keep anyone from losing it when they took the cell into custody."

Brad suppressed a grin. "That's my team."

"Once we figured out that Joy Alexander lived close to where your cell phone went missing, it wasn't exactly a challenge to find you."

"Then you sent out that ragtag group of LEA posing as Oak Harbor PD to Joy's door."

Mike grinned. "She's a bulldog, Brad. They said she looked like she was gonna tear them limb from limb."

"I'll bet she did. But still, how could you be so sure she'd help me out?"

"She went out on a limb for you before, remember? And you've never talked about her. You always talk about the women you meet *unless* they mean something to you."

Brad let Mike's observation sit for a moment.

"So your time with Joy—has it brought up anything other than memories of Norfolk? And I'm not talking about the case."

"No, nothing. We're not like that, Mike." Mike would know he was lying but he said it anyway. Mike would understand that it was too touchy to talk about. "I respect her and felt I could trust her. That's why I came here. We're friends. She's on her civilian career path now."

"So are you."

"Who are you trying to kid? I don't call working for the Bureau a civvie job, and you don't, either."

"I've been thinking it's time to make some changes. Not with my job, but my personal life." Mike never spoke about his personal life. Neither of them had ever had much of one, and whenever they did, it hadn't worked out.

"Have you met someone?"

Mike shook his head. "No, no one who'd have me. Yet. When you were out there, and I thought this could be the one time you didn't come back, I realized that I don't want to wake up twenty years from now and have nothing to show for it except my job."

"It's a damn fine job."

"It is, it is. But it doesn't keep me warm at night, and it doesn't carry on my family name."

"Mike, I do believe you've taken a hit to the head."

"Brad, *you need* a hit to the head. If you let Joy get away…"

"That ship's not even going to leave the pier, buddy. It's not going to work."

They stood for a few more minutes, during which Brad heard the familiar sound of Joy's heels clicking on the hardwood floors. She didn't come into the sunroom, though. The next thing he heard was her front door opening and then closing.

She hadn't even said goodbye.

She was obviously ready to let him move on.

CHAPTER SEVENTEEN

JOY WATCHED PAUL speak to the staff and wondered how quickly he'd fire her if he knew she'd
harbored a potential fugitive this past week, and
that she'd had confidential government case files
in her possession.

"Our workload has increased exponentially
since last year, and it shows no sign of slowing
down." Paul's tone was factual, without a hint of
pride or arrogance. She really liked her new boss.

Uncomfortable with her questionable moral
standing, she turned to look out the huge picture window in the conference room. Sunlight
fell through the tall firs and created intricate patterns on the mossy ground. Whidbey was never
short on soul-restoring scenery.

How could it be only a few days ago that this
had been the long-sought conclusion of her search
for a home, a community, a place to finally settle?

Since Brad had shown up, she'd begun to question everything she'd done over the past year.
More important, what she *hadn't* done.

"Because of the increase in construction, our

real estate group is going to need extra help. I'm planning to hire two more attorneys over the next six months."

"What's the reason for the increase?" She had to at least appear to be paying attention.

Paul nodded toward her. "Glad you asked, Joy. It's the local real estate market. Between new-builds and sales, Whidbey is booming again. There are always rumors that the base could close, but for the foreseeable future, we're looking good."

Base closure.

It was a worry in hard economic times, and whenever politicians needed a way to trim the budget. If the base closed, so many other businesses would be at risk, including Paul's law firm.

"The local community would never let the Naval Air Station go without a huge fight." Serena sounded thoughtful. She'd been through a lot, first as an Army wife, then an Army widow and single mother. Now she'd found new happiness as a Navy wife. For several years, her life hadn't been easy. Maybe Joy didn't have it so bad.

"Exactly." Paul stood up.

"That's it for this morning. Everyone clear on what they need to get done before the end of the week? Remember, I don't want anyone in the office on Friday. I want you to take a long Labor

Day weekend. Come back on Tuesday ready to hit it hard."

Murmured affirmations from the staff seated around the oak table reminded Joy of all-officer meetings, AOMs, in the Navy. The difference was that here no one felt obligated to rise when Paul did, or to tell him what they thought he wanted to hear. He paid his staff—attorneys and administrative—to be honest with their opinions. She'd been fortunate, as she'd had commanding officers who were solid. They hadn't needed ego-stroking or sugar-coated reports. Of course, she'd been a JAG, and the JAG Corps was a bit different from the rest of the Navy. Their job was to keep the Navy justice system running smoothly, all in support of the operators—those who flew the aircraft and drove the ships. The men and women who were the backbone of the Navy.

She quickly called Dennis, but his voice mail picked up. "Dennis, it's Joy. I want to thank you for everything, and to tell you that the suspects have been apprehended. My person of interest is free and clear. There's nothing left to be concerned about."

Saying anything more specific in a recorded message was ill-advised, and besides, Dennis understood her well enough to know she destroyed the notes he'd given her.

Her coffee had gone cold, but she didn't want to take the time to get a fresh one. She told Dennis the case was over. *Was* it? Her chance to form any kind of relationship with Brad certainly seemed to be.

What would Helen do?

The sudden thought made her stomach flip-flop. That reaction was followed by a rush of relief.

Of course!

Her first boss had been a "mere" lieutenant commander during Joy's initial JAG tour. Helen Bolling. Unlike Joy, Helen hadn't gone to the academy, and she'd had a successful civilian legal career before she joined the Navy. She'd come into the JAG Corps hoping not only to serve but also to see the world and had ended up on the fast track to admiral. Helen had pinned on her second star two months ago.

Helen could expect to be appointed to the highest position a JAG could hold.

Yes, she could call Helen, who knew Joy better than anyone professionally—and had also become a good friend. She could be counted on to have useful insights into Joy's reluctance to believe the case was closed simply because the known members of the terrorist cell had been placed in custody.

But would she be putting her mentor and friend on the spot?

A quick internet search and a few phone calls later, Joy ascertained where Helen would be for the weekend and planned to meet her there. Helen's schedule was tight, so it was up to Joy to go to her. The long weekend Paul was giving his staff was the perfect opportunity.

She fingered the printout of the electronic airline ticket she'd just purchased. Maybe the ability to request someone's help had started when she'd had to ask Dennis to get her the case files. It wasn't so daunting, after all.

BRAD LEFT THE NCIS office at the Naval Air Station around lunchtime and drove toward Joy's office, his heart pounding.

After Mike had driven off, Brad had spent the morning with the dedicated NCIS agents and local LEAs they'd called in for his debrief. A debrief was paramount; it ensured that everyone had the same updated information about the suspects and their apprehension and what they knew about each step of their thankfully failed operation. Yet this morning had dragged like no other, and when it looked as though it might spill over into an afternoon of war stories, Brad pulled his trump card.

"I'm beat, guys. I've got to get back to my place in Seattle and to the office before close of business today. I can come back up next week or you can send me a text with anything else you think of."

All eyes were on him. The younger agents and

police officers nodded, eager to show that they understood what he'd been through.

The more seasoned vets looked down at their notepads and phones, making sure they hadn't missed anything. They knew that as soon as Brad left, this op would become one of many in his mind. The crispness of the facts and the nuances of the case would fade away.

They could miss something that might prove fatal later on, like an additional thread of the investigation they'd skipped entirely.

Still, he held the winning hand with his exhaustion plea. And they already had three of the bad guys in custody.

"How soon will the suspects be brought to trial, in your estimation?" The head of Whidbey NCIS asked the question, his gaze frank. Like Brad, he was experienced.

"This will move more quickly than other criminal cases, you know that. Terrorism charges go to the front of the judicial line." Lots of head nodding, men and women sipping coffee. Brad knew how they felt; he knew they had a new sense of purpose.

"On behalf of the FBI, I have to thank all of you for your cooperation. From everything I've heard and seen, this entire team has worked together flawlessly. Well-done."

"Thank *you* for your work, Agent Iverson." A young female NCIS agent spoke up, her gaze inquisitive. "It had to be a hardship going undercover for so many months and then hiding out these past few days."

"All part of the job. But you're welcome. Any further questions for me?"

Prayers hadn't been in his repertoire since he'd lived with Marci's addiction to drugs, but damned if he wasn't saying a silent prayer that none of them had any more questions or comments.

"No? Great." He stood up and made a point of shaking the hand of every officer present.

They'd done a good job, and he was again reminded why he'd sworn an oath to the FBI after having served for so many years as a SEAL. This was what it was about—keeping everyone safe, military, law enforcement and, of course, the public at large. Problem was, he was tired of it all. It was a slow ache in his bones, one that didn't come from the fatigue or emotions of the past few months and days.

It wasn't burnout. He'd had that, too, and come back from it more than once.

The way he felt now was an intuitive understanding that he was done with this kind of work. For whatever reason, his life's path needed to change.

You know the reason.

He had to be crazy, but since Mike had pronounced the case more or less closed, he hadn't been able to think about anyone or anything other than Joy. About what he had to do to make a fresh start with her.

As he closed the distance to her office in General Grimes's Wrangler, he told himself, *You have to do this right*.

He couldn't go to Joy and say "hey, the case is closed, let's get together." She deserved to be wooed, to be treated like the woman she was. Full of integrity. Honest. Funny. Sexy as hell. Beautiful.

"Well, son of a bitch."

Gravel spewed from under the Jeep's tires as he made an immediate U-turn and headed back to Deception Pass Bridge. Off the island, toward Seattle.

"THANKS FOR MEETING me on such short notice, Em."

They sat at the diner on Highway 20 that specialized in grilled cedar plank salmon sandwiches with its own secret roasted red pepper sauce. Sunlight warmed her back as a gentle but chilly breeze came in off the Sound. The rays made Emily's eyes seem luminous, almost angelic.

She'd proven to be an angel to Joy on numerous occasions over the past two years.

"I'm just glad I had the time off today. I'm on a three-day break, which, believe me, I need."

"What's going on?"

"Work's been insane. You know the theory that

more babies are conceived during a rough winter because people are stuck at home? Well, last year was no exception. All those cold winter nights are being celebrated in Labor and Delivery."

Joy laughed. "How many babies are you delivering?"

"Usually it's eight to ten a week, give or take. The last two weeks we've delivered thirty-two."

"Wow! Sounds intense. I'll stick to my files."

"Yes, but I get to see the happy side of it, with the start of a new life. You have to deal with the not-so-nice parts of divorce and the ensuing child custody issues."

"True, but when your job goes bad…" She didn't want to finish her comment. Naval Hospital Oak Harbor and Em had suffered a terrible loss last spring when a baby didn't make it.

"Well, that's part of my job, too. When that happens—yes, it's very, very sad."

"Too risky for me. I like to know everything's going to be okay."

"You don't look like it's all okay right now. Want to tell me what's up?"

Joy pushed her sweet potato fries around in the paper-lined basket. Even her favorite junk food wasn't enough to lift her spirits.

"I was helping a friend, a colleague I worked with in Norfolk during a tough trial two years ago. He was here taking care of some…business he had on island. He's based in Seattle." She wasn't sure how much to say about the terrorist cell; nothing was the best option, since she didn't want to reveal anything she shouldn't.

"And?"

"Well, he and I, we..."

Em waited.

Joy gave in and told her the truth.

"I think I care a lot about him. And I thought he might care about me. But now his op is over and he's gone, and I'm not sure I'll hear from him again. Just like before."

"His *op*? *Like before?*"

Briefly, Joy filled Em in on what had happened between her and Brad since Norfolk. She explained that Brad was FBI—that couldn't hurt. Joy told her everything, including her own feelings for Brad, hoping against hope that Em might help her understand, decide what to do. Help her see that Brad wasn't the man she needed. See that she had to cut her losses and move on.

When she finished, she took a deep breath and an equally big gulp of her iced tea. "So, what are you hearing me say?"

Em put her sandwich down, wiped her mouth and folded her hands in front of her.

"Joy, how old are you?"

"Um, thirty-four. But I don't see how that's relevant. Brad's the same age."

"I get the sense that you can't or don't want to share everything he's doing work-wise. That's fine. But honestly, it's the twenty-first century, and there's this new way of finding out whatever you need to know about practically anything or anyone."

"If you tell me to go to counseling, I'm going to scream."

"Nothing that complicated, Joy. You can find out where he lives—use the information you have—and just show up. You don't know why he's not reaching out, but from what you've told me, my bet is that he believes he's protecting you from something. His life, his job, maybe his crazy personality." Emily pointed a finger at Joy. "Because let's get real. You have to have some crazy in you to even *think* about being a SEAL. And he was one for how long?"

"Fifteen years?" She wasn't exactly sure. Discomfort at how little she knew about this man she'd been ready to give up everything for made her skin crawl.

"Go find him, Joy. Show up at his doorstep if you can. Rock his world. Let him know you're not going anywhere. A guy like that isn't used to a woman who's willing to be there for him through thick and thin. He's gun-shy, sweetie. That's all."

"A gun-shy former SEAL and current FBI agent?"

Emily didn't budge. "You know what I'm talking about. How many Navy guys have you dated, Joy?"

"Several dozen. It's why I don't want a relationship with one."

"*Seriously* dated, I mean. One drink during happy hour doesn't count."

Joy groaned. Emily was always so exacting in her discussions, whether the conversation was about a knitting stitch or about men.

"One or two, maybe three. There were some civilian guys in there, too."

"Let's focus on the military guys, and you've worked alongside them for as long as I have. They act one way at work, but off duty, alone, they're a different animal. Statistics show that most of them are actually introverts."

"Yeah, yeah, I took all the same personality-type tests. Supposedly I'm an introverted, touchy-feely intellect. What does that prove? Zip. Nada."

"It demonstrates that most of these guys are sensitive. They wouldn't be able to do their jobs at the level of expertise they do if they weren't."

"They're sensitive, all right. So sensitive they don't remember to call a girl for over a year."

"Aha! I knew you had a deep resentment about him. It's from when you worked together before, isn't it? What happened there, Joy?"

"Nothing. Not in the way you think or want. Yes, we share an attraction. No, it's never gotten further than a—" She stopped herself.

Emily's steady gaze made Joy clench her jaw.

"We've kissed, okay? And only recently. Nothing happened until we weren't under the jurisdiction of the Uniformed Code of Military Justice anymore."

"Spoken like a Navy JAG."

"Former. As of right now, as a matter of fact, I'm a full-fledged civilian."

"Welcome to the real world, Joy."

"Thanks."

"In this world, women go after what they want, no matter what. Well, as long as it's not hurting someone else. And you obviously want Brad. You can't sit on your hands here. Trust me, he'll thank you for it, and you'll thank me for telling you this."

"What makes you such an expert, Em? You didn't look too happy when I left you with your guy, Ben. Although he seemed very enthusiastic at your book signing."

The usually unflappable Emily turned as pink as her hoodie. "He's just someone I work with. We're…friends."

"Do you blush over all the medical professionals you work with?"

"Give it a rest. I'm not ready for anything more than a date or two."

"Your husband's been gone for over a decade, Em. It's time."

"It was time five years ago, if you ask me. The right guy hasn't shown up yet. A common occurrence for a career woman on an isolated island in Puget Sound."

"Whidbey's not that isolated. And you work on the Naval Air Station, where there have to be at least a zillion single men who'd love to get to know you."

"Maybe I don't want to get to know them. I'm happy here. Like you, I like my life just as it is."

"You've told me you want to move on. Maybe even leave the island."

"For the right reasons. A Navy guy who's going to be uprooted every other year? I'm not sure I want that lifestyle again."

Joy stayed silent. Like Serena, but in a different way, Emily had been through a horrific experience early in her marriage to a young Navy man. She'd made Whidbey her home after she'd lost her husband.

As much as Joy didn't want to see Emily leave Whidbey, she couldn't help thinking giving up a house was nothing compared to the chance to be with the man you wanted to spend your life with.

"You really care about him, don't you?"

Emily's hand paused over the soggy fries. "Yes, I suppose I do. Still, he's so persistent and…and presumptuous. Just because we get along well in the delivery room, he thinks that'll translate to the outside world—and to the bedroom."

"Has he asked you into his bedroom?"

"Not in so many words. Let's say we've had

our kisses, too." Emily looked at her watch. "I've got to go. I'm late."

"You have today off."

"I scheduled a mani-pedi and massage. Pamper-me stuff."

"So you're doing that for you?" Joy had never seen Emily with polished nails. She kept them short and clean for nursing and for knitting.

"Why not?"

"Kid yourself if you want, Em, but you're not fooling me. You've got the hots for the good doctor."

"Maybe, but you've got a lot *more* than the hots for your SEAL, Joy. You've got the makings of a life-changing relationship. Go find that man."

Emily stood up from the wooden bench, and Joy followed suit.

As she dumped the contents of her plastic basket into the trash receptacle and placed it in the pile collecting on top, she noticed a blue Jeep Wrangler speeding past. She only caught a brief glimpse of the driver, but she'd know him anywhere.

Brad. And he was driving north. Toward Deception Pass Bridge, which meant he was leaving the island.

She knew he was going back to Seattle, knew the case here was done for him. Her defenses had never let her down before, but in the flash of seeing him again, a pang of regret and longing squeezed something buried in her chest.

Her heart.

"I'M STOPPING IN at the office today, Mike. Not a new problem or anything." He spoke on the new Bureau hands-free cell phone Mike had given him before he left Joy's.

"No, you've done enough for a while. Go home, get some rest. Report back on Monday morning. You did a good job, bro."

"So did you, and my team deserves some extra perks for their hours, Mike."

"Already done. Most of them are taking the rest of the week off, too. This case has attracted attention at the highest levels. The director is going to brief POTUS in fifteen minutes."

"You need me on the line for that, Mike. What if he has more questions?"

"Then the director will answer them with the notes you provided earlier. If he needs backup, that's what I'm being paid the big bucks for. Go home."

"Right."

"And, Brad?"

"Yeah?"

"Have you decided to make it real with Joy?"

Brad swerved to avoid a pickup truck that had turned into his lane with no warning.

"Brad?"

"I'm here. Just had to dodge a bad driver. I swear I-5 gets worse every day."

"Stop avoiding the question, teammate."

"There's nothing to avoid. You know she's the JAG I had to work with to get a villager freed. I trusted her, then and now, and it was the right decision. She was a good shipmate, helped me get through the past few days. Got me to Grimes, where I got this Jeep."

"You sure she didn't do anything else for you?"

Crap. Did Mike know about the case files?

"She might have done some searching, tried to unearth some info on the previous case. You know, with…"

He didn't want to say Farid's name over an insecure line, and certainly not on a cell phone.

"Gotcha. We're checking that out, too."

"Let me do it. Let me talk to him." He'd love to be able to see Farid face-to-face again. Reassure himself that he and Joy had made the right decision all those months ago.

"You can't, you know that. We'll talk about it on Monday. It can wait until then. You still didn't answer the question, bro."

"And I'm not going to."

He disconnected in the middle of Mike's bark of laughter.

JOY HAD NEVER done anything this crazy. Driving into Seattle on a work night, when she had to be at work in the morning. The two-hour drive wasn't such a burden, but doing it twice in less than twelve hours was a bit much.

"Exit in one mile."

Her GPS told her what she knew—she was close to Brad's place. She had the address from the information she'd taken while they'd discussed the facts of the explosion. When she'd agreed to help him again.

As she eased off the highway, she entered a residential neighborhood. She wasn't all that familiar with Seattle and had imagined Brad in an apartment or condo.

Instead, her GPS directed her to a lovely craftsman-style home on a street completely lined with trees. It was obviously Brad's as General Grimes's Jeep sat in his driveway.

Butterflies whirled around in her stomach as though she'd swallowed an entire flock. Before she could change her mind, she squared her shoulders and got out of the car.

Wide steps led up to a bright red door, which she thought was a nice touch for a bachelor.

He could have had a woman's help.

She shoved the irritating image of Brad with another woman out of her mind. This was scary enough.

The door opened within seconds of her pressing the doorbell.

"Joy."

He was fresh out of the shower, his hair damp, and wearing a gray T-shirt that stretched over his broad shoulders. It emphasized the physique that had enabled him to scale West Beach as if it were a child's playground equipment.

"Hi, Brad."

"Just happened to be in the neighborhood?"

His eyes were surrounded by lines of exhaustion, but their glimmer was unmistakable. He was happy to see her.

"Something like that."

"Come on in." He stepped aside, and she caught a whiff of his soap and the clean smell of the house.

Clean wasn't the right word. The house *sparkled*. The wooden bannisters and molding gleamed; that had to be the result of hours of physical labor. The deep cherrywood offset the cream wallpaper and simple but elegant brass touches on the light fixtures and switches.

"Brad, this is beautiful."

He shrugged. "I needed something to do on my weekends."

"Are you renting or is this yours?" She walked farther into his home and ran her fingers along the wood, relishing the cool, firm feel of it. This was a pleasant change from the modern design of her house.

"I bought it. The Bureau doesn't move agents

around as much as the Navy, unless you really want to transfer."

"Was it already in decent shape or did you have a lot to do?"

"The bones were all there, but I rebuilt the walls and refinished the molding."

"That's an enormous project."

He was beside her and she wanted to turn toward him but felt suddenly shy, wondering if she'd made a mistake.

It didn't matter. She was here, and it was time to start living the life she wanted instead of hiding from what she feared.

"Like I said, my weekends were free, at least before I went undercover." His fingers were in her hair, lifting the strands as he worked his way down to her neck, massaging it.

"Was there a lot of traffic?" he asked.

"Not once I decided to come…oh! That feels so good." She leaned over to allow him access to her sore muscles.

"Let's go into the kitchen and get something to drink. Later I can give you a full massage."

"Full?" She turned to look at him.

"Yes." The same hands that had been stroking her neck were at her lower back as he pulled her against him.

His head lowered and she closed her eyes, wanting to soak up every bit of their time together.

CHAPTER EIGHTEEN

BRAD LOVED THE need in Joy's kiss, hot and wet. He wanted to devour every inch of her.

Not yet.

He pulled back, and his erection became harder at the flush on her cheeks and her dilated pupils. All from a quick neck rub and one kiss. She'd be positively glowing after a climax…

"Have you eaten dinner?" he asked.

"I grabbed a burger on the way down. I didn't want to waste any more time."

That was as close to a confession of need or want he'd ever heard from Joy. "What's making you so anxious?"

He didn't wait for her answer, but grabbed her hand and pulled her into the kitchen with him. He turned back when she stopped in her tracks.

"What?"

"This kitchen is incredible, Brad. I didn't know you were a cook, too." She gestured at the copper pots hanging on the wall.

"I like to keep my tools handy, whether it's woodworking or cooking. Hanging the pots gave me more room in the cupboards. These old homes don't have big kitchens like yours."

"It looks like you've made the most of every inch of this place."

"Yeah, well, I'll give you the big tour in a few minutes. Red or white?" He pulled out a corkscrew.

"Do you have any open?"

"Nope. I'm usually a beer guy. Your choices are limited, but I do have a couple of nice bottles of each. They're in the beverage cooler on the other side of the island. I don't have high-quality glasses, though."

"That's okay."

Watching her ass in her jeans as she walked around the butcher-block work surface was something he could get used to. *Too* used to.

"You have my favorite. Hey, it's fate."

She held up a bottle of Washington State Cabernet Sauvignon.

"I always aim to please the ladies."

It was supposed to be an offhanded comment. But in typical fashion he'd shoved his big foot in his wayward mouth, judging by the lines of wariness that were back on Joy's face.

"Joy, that's just an expression."

She blew a strand of her lovely hair off her forehead and handed him the bottle.

"It's none of my business."

He opened the wine and left the cork on the island.

"I'd like it to be your business. If you want it to be."

The island was the only thing separating them. The obvious question was—how serious were they willing to make this?

"Why don't you show me the rest of the house while the wine breathes?" He'd always respected Joy's composure and grace under pressure. It was the same thing he found himself resenting now. He wanted to tear down every last inch of the wall she kept between herself and the outside world.

"Let's start upstairs."

HE ENJOYED WATCHING her expression, her reactions to each room as he opened the doors.

"I keep the doors closed so the house stays warmer this time of year. I open them in the summer."

"I'm surprised you haven't put in central air."

"It's coming. Much as I hate the thought of it, it's a reality that our summers are getting warmer. The heat this last summer was insane."

"Yes, it was. So we both were moving into our new homes at about the same time?" She ran her fingers over the ivory and cobalt subway tiles in the smallish bathroom. "Are these original?"

"No, I wanted them in the same style, but I

couldn't bear the Pepto-Bismol pink of the originals. Plus, a lot of them were cracked."

"This is more masculine, for sure, but not too much. I like how clean and fresh it looks. Sometimes an old bathroom can make the entire house feel grungy."

"True."

"It'd be nice if this bathroom had a big tub."

"I'm a shower person. I know the claw-foot is a big thing now, but I went all out on the shower. I did have help. Mike's brother is a contractor in the city, and he took care of it."

As she looked at the large shower with glass on three sides, all he could envision was her naked body pressed up against the steamed glass, with him behind her...

"I think the wine's done breathing."

She looked surprised. His tone was rough, but damn it, he only had so much control when he was around her, and he didn't want to take her to bed until they'd had a chance to talk. Until they were clear on one thing—that they both wanted this.

"WE NEED TO TALK. About us." Joy braced herself for his response, hoping he wouldn't resist any attempt at communication that didn't involve terrorists, felons or war.

"I agree." He leaned over and poured more wine into their glasses. They'd had their first glass in his kitchen. She'd almost laughed at the way they'd danced around what she was really there for. How they looked at each other over the rim of the acrylic glasses, waiting to see what the other was going to do, to say.

"Mind if I go first?" He gave Joy her glass.

"No, not at all." Did he see her hand shake when she took the glass from him? Did he have any idea that the tremor was caused by desire?

"Obviously, you'll be staying the night. You're having a second glass of wine and since it's at least an hour since you've eaten, plus it's a two-hour drive to Whidbey—well, it's a done deal."

Despite everything, defiance rose in her throat. "Slow down, Brad."

"I'm not finished." He sipped his wine and studied the red liquid in the plastic glass. "I need to get real glasses if you're going to be here more often. But I digress."

"I'm listening."

He chuckled. "I'm sure you are. This is killing the lawyer in you, isn't it? Having to listen to me first. What I want to tell you is that there's nothing I want more than you staying the night, with me, in my bed. And you didn't ask, but I'm telling you anyway. You're the only woman who's ever been in this house with me."

"Oh."

"I don't have a long list of requirements for a relationship, Joy. I'm a simple man with a complicated job. Truth is, I've never looked for much of a relationship before. Marci was a disastrous exception."

"This isn't necessarily about a relationship, Brad. It's about a closure of sorts. And it's about exploration. Curiosity." That sounded sophisticated and no-strings-attached, didn't it?

"I'm waving the flag on that one, Joy." She knew he was referring to the bullshit flag, common Navy parlance. "You and I have shared too much for anything between us to be free and easy. If we have sex, it's going to be the start of a relationship. We're on the same page, right?"

"Yes, but—"

"Ah, the *but*. I guess it's my turn to listen."

"*But* we have choices at every stage of this, Brad. I'm not going to hold you emotionally hostage if it doesn't work out for us. We might discover that we're not compatible."

"Seriously?"

His expression of incredulity forced a laugh from her.

"The anticipation is often much more exciting than the actual, um, follow-through."

His fingers were on her cheek, her jaw, the side of her neck.

"Who hurt you, Joy? Who made you think that the *follow-through* wasn't much to write home about?"

She swallowed. "It's not any one person. I don't

have a long history of failed relationships or even a divorce. Just that my work has always proved more interesting than the effort it'd take to form a real relationship." There. Finally, she'd voiced what she'd never told anyone else. That she didn't believe any man could compare to the mental challenge and satisfaction she got from practicing law.

"I agree with you."

She knew she sounded shocked. "You do? That's, that's...wonderful?"

They both smiled, and he clinked his glass to hers. It was more of a *clunk* since the acrylic didn't have the resonance of crystal or glass, but she felt the vibration. "Joy, we each have very interesting and exciting careers. Other than fantastic sex, which almost always becomes routine, what else could measure up to our work?"

She blinked. "Right. So we agree this will be closure. We'll have no expectation of seeing each other at definite intervals, no holidays or weekends together."

"Jeez, Joy, are you sure you even want to start this?"

"Yes! I mean, yes, I'm certain." The flock of butterflies was back, and she felt fear crawl along her spine. Fear that she'd blown it and ruined any chance for her and Brad to get together at all.

Because if she didn't experience what being with Brad was like, in the most complete way, she didn't know if she'd ever have the nerve to attempt an intimate relationship with any other man.

Since she'd met Brad, there hadn't been any other man.

That wasn't something she was willing to share with him. Not yet.

Brad stared at the space in front of him as if he was working through a mission plan before its execution.

"What are you thinking now?" she asked.

After leaning over and placing his glass on the coffee table, he took her glass and did the same. His green eyes blazed with an emotion she wasn't ready to acknowledge. "I'm thinking it's time to stop talking and—what did you say earlier? Oh, yeah. Explore other means of communication. Like this."

She closed her eyes, willing him to kiss her.

"Open your eyes, Joy."

When she saw the desire in his expression, she thought she'd melt into the couch. He cupped her face before sliding his hands down to her shoulders, her waist and then back up to her breasts. He cupped them through her pullover and tank top, caressing and gently squeezing until her breath caught.

She reached up and caressed his face. His jaw was rough with stubble, contrasting with the smooth skin on his cheeks. He did his best to distract her with the play of his fingers over her breasts, but she gave as good as she got. His chest was hard, firm and entirely too heavily clothed.

Tugging his shirt out of his jeans, she reached up to lift it over his arms. Brad took advantage of her position and lifted off her top, leaving her in her tank and bra. They took turns stroking, nipping, sucking and teasing until they were both breathing in shallow gasps.

Yet only after she thought she couldn't possibly wait any longer did Brad close the gap between them and cover her mouth with his.

The kiss went from seductive to possessive as Brad's tongue dipped into her mouth.

Joy had always enjoyed kissing, but kissing Brad was elevated above any previous kiss. It was another level of intimacy she'd never experienced. As if they were talking to each other with their lips, their hands.

The cool leather of his sofa contrasted with her hot skin as he eased her back and lay above her. He supported his weight on his forearms, his hips above hers but not touching them. Was he afraid of hurting her?

She drew his hips down to hers until they were pelvis to pelvis, belly to belly. A sound that was more like a growl came from his throat, and pure female satisfaction made her senses even more aware of him.

This was what she'd longed for since they'd met.

JOY KNEW SOMEWHERE deep inside her that this was going to happen. She'd known it from the first moment he'd touched her, less than seventy-two hours ago, standing in her kitchen. She'd anticipated the feel of him since the very beginning—since that brief first glimpse in Gitmo and through the long days in Norfolk. Since the hours spent poring over his testimony and her defendant's, breathing the same air in the close confines of the tiny office, where they'd studied the classified documents. Now, no vestiges of professional demeanor remained to keep them from acting on the chemistry between them. As they continued to kiss and caress, getting closer to a point of no return, she couldn't help the fact that one part of her mind held back and tried to make sense of how she felt about Brad.

He'd always been different from other men. He didn't ogle her, nor did he pretend that the sexual tension wasn't there. While they worked together with such intensity on an extraordinary case, they'd never, in any way, addressed their attraction. The way he'd looked her in the eye as they discussed important parts of the case, the way he'd allowed her plenty of personal space—it all showed that he'd respected the need to abstain from any involvement beyond the professional.

She'd ignored her own reactions, too—at least when they were together. Back in her Virginia apartment, she'd list the reasons she didn't make a habit of getting involved with colleagues, especially Navy shipmates. Too complicated. Too much baggage on both sides, especially if the affair started downrange and then they tried to take it back stateside. That rarely worked. Sex for escape was common during times of extreme duress.

Defending a man who'd been identified as working with the Taliban, with enough evidence to send him to prison for life, had been one of those times. Because if she was wrong, if *they* were wrong, she'd have to live with the fact that she'd helped free a terrorist.

Farid *was* innocent; she'd known it from Brad's confidence, his acknowledgement that yes, Farid had looked like a ruthless terrorist on paper. But, according to Brad, Farid had saved his life and the lives of scores of other Americans.

Everything had hinged on Brad's testimony.

They'd done it. They'd set Farid free, and then all parted ways.

She'd watched Brad walk away after that last day in court. His step was sure, his khaki uniform emphasizing the superb shape he kept himself in, even when he'd probably never serve in another SEAL mission. She'd blinked back tears. They'd accomplished a feat very few others had. And she'd never be able to share it with anyone else. The details of the case had to be sealed for the next few decades.

She'd refused to admit she'd fallen for Brad. *How can you fall for someone you've never touched?* Someone who'd had a fiancée, who'd never made a single move toward her.

And besides all that, he'd been an enlisted man, a man Navy regulations had forbidden her to have a relationship with.

Yet the quiet voice inside her heart told the truth—if they'd met elsewhere, at a different time, if they'd both been free, they might've become a couple. Might, by now, have been a couple for years. Now that he stood in front of her, so close to her, she heard that small voice again.

You've been waiting for this your whole life.

She pushed against his shoulders until he sat up, giving her space to stand.

"Brad, please tell me this isn't your idea of a joke, or a quick tension reliever in the middle of… of battle." Because they were in a battle. A battle that would decide whether they were willing to even consider changing their lives.

Her heart was at risk here.

He stood and took her hands. "I'm not joking, Joy. No playing around."

His hands moved to her shoulders, and she closed her eyes as his lips touched the side of her throat. He applied a soft suction to her skin and she groaned.

"Don't stop now, Brad." She grasped his upper arms and reveled in the sheer strength under her fingertips. He hadn't let his Bureau time soften his physique. She could hardly hear his breath over her pounding heart, but she felt their chests rise and fall in unison. She'd dreamed it would be like this with him.

His hands cradled her face. "You're so beautiful."

She opened her eyes to see the intensity in his gaze.

"I've wanted you since the moment I met you. This isn't a way to get off at the end of a stressed-out op, Joy."

"I hope not."

"I know not."

He lowered his mouth to hers. And kept her waiting, wanting, ready to beg. "Brad, please."

"No more words. Feel it. Do you feel it?"

He closed the gap between them, and with this kiss ended the months and years of waiting. The knowledge that their lovemaking was near and that it was going to be better than either of them had fantasized.

They fit together with an ease usually reserved for longer relationships. The lasting kind. The kiss deepened, and he pulled her up against his erection while his hands kneaded her buttocks.

She drew back and whispered, "Let's go to your room."

"Roger that." He lifted her into his arms as if she were as light as the backpack he'd carried downrange and made his way toward the stairs at the back of the house.

"Wait—the candle."

Still holding her, he walked to the coffee table and leaned over. "Grab it," he said.

She took the votive from the table, intending to blow out the flame. It flickered between them as Brad straightened and walked back to his room. When he finally set her down next to his bed, she placed the candle on the nightstand.

"Leave it burning, Joy. I want to see you when I make love to you."

BRAD WATCHED THE flush creep over her cheeks. The hair that tumbled across her forehead rose with each breath. He wanted to brush that lock of hair away and not stop until he held her head in his hand, his tongue touching hers.

She had to say yes. It had to be mutual. Because the insanity of the past few days, the reality that he was up against a wall until the unknown terrorist was apprehended—it all spelled disaster for a new relationship. He wanted to protect any chance they had.

"Do you want this, Joy?"

No blinks, no sighs, no biting her lower lip. Just her calm, steady stare. The slight tremor that made her shoulders shake a little. If he hadn't been so close, he would've missed it.

"Hell, yes."

His hands clasped her waist the same instant her lips met his. The firmness of her physique under his hands seemed at odds with the softness of her mouth. She still had a warrior's body, still kept herself combat-ready. And it'd been over a year since she'd been on board a ship.

They'd known each other almost two years, and he'd never dreamed he'd have her in his arms without the pressure of their jobs. The prim Navy JAG she'd been gave way to a hot, volatile lover who demanded everything from him.

Everything.

"Get undressed," she told him. She pulled her hoodie off and drew her silky tank over her head in measured tugs. Her breasts were perfect, spilling out of a black lace bra.

She shimmied out of her leggings as Brad whipped off his belt, shoved his jeans down, along with his boxer briefs, and took his shirt off.

They faced each other. He, naked with a raging hard-on, and she, in that ridiculously delicate bra and matching thong.

He brushed his fingers down past her waist to the creamy skin of her buttocks. "You're still dressed." His voice sounded choked, as if he'd just emerged from sleep. But he hadn't felt more awake since the day they'd saved Farid.

"Take them off if you want to," she said.

He wanted to rip them off, but Joy deserved respect and gentleness. This was the woman of his dreams, and he wasn't going to screw this up.

He'd make it good for her.

"Turn around."

She complied and he was against her back, pressing into her and reaching around her to hold her breasts. He leaned down and while his teeth nipped at the nape of her neck, he unfastened her front bra clasp.

He felt that her shudders and trembling were more reward than the piles of gold or the ancient treasures he and his team had found during their earlier battles.

"Is that some SEAL technique?"

"Shh." He spun her around and, finally, they were skin on skin. Now he began to tremble.

She reached up and grasped his shoulders, urging him closer. He took her lips with no apology, no warning. Driven by pure need for Joy, he gave himself over to the passion he'd always known they shared.

Joy murmured as she kissed him, sucked on his bottom lip, traced around his mouth with her tongue.

"This will be over too soon if you keep doing that." He wasn't kidding. She had him at the edge, and they weren't even horizontal yet.

"We have all night, remember?"

Unable to wait any longer, he lowered them both to the bed and lay next to her, breathing in her scent, surrounding himself with her essence.

"Maybe even some time in the morning, before you have to leave for work."

"Shut up and keep kissing me, Brad."

"Yes, ma'am."

JOY HAD TREMBLED like this once before, when she'd made love with her high school sweetheart during their first break after freshman year in college. The newness, the sheer awe at the power of hormones.

Brad wasn't her first love or lover; making love with him was something far more profound than that. He was the only man who'd ever made her feel every nuance of every gesture. Each kiss deepened their connection. It wasn't some sappy pop song; it was gloriously real. This was how it was supposed to be.

He shifted over her, and she almost screamed in her need to have him inside her.

"Brad, don't make me wait any longer."

"Uh, one thing…"

"Yes, yes!" She slid out from under him as he reached for the nightstand drawer. She'd brought protection, too, but was glad she didn't have to get up and go to her purse for it.

"Here. Let me." She took the condom from his

hands and quickly put it on him. Before she could say anything else, he was inside her.

Fully.

"Oh…"

He stilled above her. "Am I too heavy?"

"Too heavy? No."

"Too, too…"

"Big? Just big enough." She moved her hips, raised her knees to allow him in farther.

Sensation after sensation rocked her as her mind tried to keep up with the sheer pleasure of being as close as she could possibly be to the man who'd haunted her dreams for the past two years.

"Come with me, Joy," he groaned. And then she stopped thinking.

Their words turned into gasps as perspiration slicked their skin. Brad's hips moved with hers, meeting her where she was.

"Don't hold back, Brad. I won't break."

She didn't have to tell him twice. With the same intensity she'd seen in him when he was working a case or an op, he brought them both to the edge of complete abandon, not allowing his own release until he heard her cry out.

Joy hung on to the feeling of complete union as long as she could. Their breathing slowed to normal and their bodies, still connected, cooled. She didn't want to let go.

With a man like Brad, you never knew what was going to happen next—and slam the ecstasy right out of you.

CHAPTER NINETEEN

BRAD SAT AT the kitchen island, determined to savor every second of this first real "morning after" with Joy.

And not pay attention to the fact that there was so much they still had to work out.

"You look like you've got the weight of the world on your shoulders," she said. He inhaled Joy's lavender scent as she placed a kiss on his lips and put a hot cup of coffee in front of him in one graceful gesture.

He pulled her close, until she was straddling his lap.

"I'd rather have *your* weight here." He kissed her thoroughly. Too thoroughly. If he didn't stop he'd have her back in bed.

And he needed to save both their jobs.

"Don't stop now. I don't have to be at work for another three hours. It only takes two hours to get to Whidbey."

"That's issue number one. Do you have to go to work today?"

"I do. It's still my first week. My boss is giving

us tomorrow off, to make this a long weekend. But I'm still the new kid on the block. I have a job to do, remember?"

"Okay, so you'll go to work." He leaned in and found himself lost in kissing her again.

"What's the other issue?" Her breath was short, and he loved the way his kiss did that to her.

He eased her off his lap. "The other issue is, when do we see each other again?"

JOY DIDN'T WANT to squelch the rosy glow of this new part of their relationship, but she needed time and space. Even if she thought everything was going to work out between her and Brad, she needed to talk to Helen.

Because of Brad.

"I've got plans for this weekend."

A brief flicker of disappointment flared in his eyes before Brad had his game face back on.

"That's fine. I need to rest, anyway, according to Mike."

"He's right, you know. You've hardly slept at all since the explosion."

As she uttered the words, it was as if the reality of the past five days finally hit her. A wave of grief blindsided her as she realized what they could so easily have lost. This time they were sharing could just as easily never have happened. If Brad hadn't followed his instincts and used his professional skills, they could both be dead.

Her eyes filled with tears and he reached over to brush one off her cheek.

"Don't, Joy. It's over. We're safe."

"Yes, but I can't help feeling…overwhelmed. I kept my feelings to myself through that whole damned trial. All those days working side by side in Norfolk—I never asked you for more. I never let you know. And now that I know you care about me, too, and that we might have a chance together—I'm not giving up."

"Joy, you've turned my life inside out since the minute I met you. But if we don't look after ourselves, there won't be anything left to make a relationship with. We can afford to take this slow."

"Nothing about last night was slow." The words were out, and she didn't regret it. They were past the point of holding their thoughts back, weren't they? Of keeping secrets?

So why won't you tell him that you're going to see Helen? To see if she can help, professionally and personally?

Brad's eyes widened, and he brought her close again. "If we're going to get you to work on time, we'll have to hurry."

When his lips met hers, she forgot about telling Brad anything.

BRAD SLEPT SOUNDLY as Joy got ready for work in his bathroom. She didn't want to wake him.

They'd made love again with the ferocity of

lovers reunited after a long separation. As if they hadn't made love three times last night. Her skin still hummed from his touch, and she smiled at the whisker burns on her neck. She'd packed a scarf with her outfit, not realizing she'd need it for subtle camouflage.

Her cell phone buzzed, and she stopped applying her makeup to see who it was.

Serena.

Will you still be late?

She'd texted Serena last night, giving her a heads-up just in case she did drive back to Oak Harbor past eight-thirty or so.

No, on time. See you soon. You're up early.:)

Besides Emily, Serena was the only person on Whidbey who knew she was off-island.

With Brad.

It was going to take some getting used to, adding him to her life. Officially and openly.

Dressed and with her overnight tote on her shoulder, she tiptoed into Brad's room and leaned over to kiss his cheek. He smiled, and his arm shot out to wrap around her thigh.

"Sure you have to go?"

"Yes. And I'm more than sure that you need to rest. I'll call you later."

"Bet you tell that to all the guys." He pulled her down for a lingering kiss before she stood up again and walked out of the room.

At the front door, she remembered she'd left her bracelets and watch on the kitchen island and went in to retrieve them. Her gaze landed on a tray with a stack of letters. Brad seemed to be as organized as she was; she, too, had a tray she kept her letters in.

They might just make this work, the two of them.

She let herself out and drove toward Whidbey, toward her new life. A life she might be able to share with Brad.

Joy read the same family court case file for the third time in half an hour. Nothing.

She finally had what she'd wanted, as recently as Monday morning. A new job, a new life. She'd made love to Brad after believing it'd never happen.

No anchors were holding her back, dragging her down, not anymore.

"Joy, you okay?" Serena asked.

"You probably think I'm crazy, don't you? I've only been here for one week, and I think you've asked me that every day."

"It sounds corny, but you remind me of myself. I was a bit lost when I came to Whidbey, and more so when I applied for work here. I thought I had it all together, all planned out, and then… I didn't."

Serena's happiness was evident as she simultaneously smiled and sent Joy a look of genuine concern.

"I'm fine. It's always a challenge, getting into a new routine. I'm not complaining. This is the nicest place I've ever worked, and I believe I can make a difference." She glanced down at her file. "But these child custody cases are a little sad, I must admit."

"You didn't do those in the Navy, did you?"

"No. I did more in the line of defending clients who'd gotten themselves in trouble, either administratively or criminally. I also helped prosecute, depending on the tour. It was usually a lot clearer who the bad guy was. In a custody case, no one's the real winner, and my heart breaks for the kids."

Serena nodded. "You speak like a mom."

Joy laughed. "Nope. I don't even have a dog. But I'd like a family someday. That's why I'm settling down here."

They both went back to their work, and Joy hoped her doubts didn't show on her face.

Her doubt at her own words. Her convictions. Because if Brad walked through the door of her office right this minute and asked her to follow him, to give up her new life, she wasn't certain what her answer would be.

Only five days ago, she was absolutely certain that putting an end to her frivolous fantasies about a Navy SEAL she'd only known professionally was for the best.

How quickly things changed.

She needed to talk to Helen—and not just about the domestic terrorists and their actions.

"GOOD MORNING, EMILY." Ben walked up to her Thursday morning as she looked over her charts in the Labor and Delivery area of the Naval Hospital.

"Hello, Dr. Franklin." She purposely kept her gaze fixed on the charts, which was pathetic. They had no laboring patients at the moment—although that wouldn't last—and only two women who were due to deliver in the next few days. It was their lowest caseload in weeks.

"Really? We're back to that?"

Her face grew hot. His voice reminded her of the way he'd sounded after he'd kissed her on Tuesday night.

"We're at work." She risked a glance at him and was rewarded by the warmth that emanated from his eyes. He smiled as he touched her arm briefly.

"Yes, we are, and we will be after we're together for good."

"Together for good, Ben? In case you haven't noticed, it's the twenty-first century and we live in the United States of America. A kiss is not a declaration of anything other than...than—"

"Than letting you know I'm interested in you. And that I've wanted to ask you out since I got stationed here over a year ago. That I was trying to see if I'm alone in my interest, which, I'm happy to remind you, I'm not."

"You're pretty sure of yourself, aren't you?"

"I'm humbled that you kissed me back the other night, Emily."

If she were fifteen years older, she'd swear she was having a hot flash. Since she wasn't, she knew it was her body's involuntary response to his attention.

"I don't know what to say, Ben." She looked around the nurses' station and was relieved that no one else was near. The other nurses and Navy Hospital Corpsmen were either on break or helping mothers preparing to take their babies home.

"Say you'll go out with me, and this time you'll let me buy you dinner. Tomorrow night."

"I don't know," she said again.

"Listen, Emily. You've been alone for a long time, and you need to have some fun of your own."

She bit her lip and wanted to laugh *and* cry, but wasn't sure which would come out.

"What?"

She couldn't tell him that she'd just given her best friend on the island the same advice she should be taking herself.

And she'd never be able to face Joy with any sense of integrity if she ran from her chance at a relationship.

"Yes."

"Yes?" He stared at her blankly before a huge grin broke across his face.

"I'll pick you up on Friday, tomorrow, at five-thirty. Dress casually."

He walked away, and as the hospital doors automatically clicked open to let him out of L&D, she wondered if she'd done the right thing.

As she turned back to her work she realized she was fingering the rings she wore on a chain around her neck. The wedding rings from her first marriage. She hadn't thought of Peter once during her conversation with Ben.

That had to be a sign.

"WHAT'S IT FEEL like to admit you've had a hot man in your house for the past week?"

Joy looked across the sofa at her friend and wondered when their Thursday night girls' nights had turned into an inquisition.

Emily went on knitting as if she'd commented on the weather instead of asking Joy about something she considered private. Sort of.

"It's…hard to say."

Emily put her needles and yarn in her lap. "You were with him last night, weren't you?"

"Yes. I took your advice."

"You must be exhausted, since you got to work on time this morning. With a two-hour drive."

"Serena told you!"

"No, not Serena. But she told Jonas, who may have mentioned it to Ben, who—" Now Emily looked like a mouse in a trap.

"Ben? You mean the man you're only *friends* with?"

Emily blushed. Beet red. "Yes."

"Emily, I've never seen you blush over anything. But since Ben's come into your life, it's all you seem to do."

"There's nothing to blush over, not…yet."

"Don't tell me there's nothing to get excited about and then reveal that you've considered a future with him in the same breath, Em."

Emily glanced up from her knitting.

"Do you have any wine?"

HALF A PIZZA LATER, Joy leaned back on her sofa and gazed up at her ceiling.

"The thing is, I miss Brad. He wasn't here more than a night or two, and it feels like he always lived here. And I felt comfortable at his place, too."

"You're so screwed, Joy. The perfect lawyer has fallen for a man with a very messy job. Have you thought about what you'll have to do with this whole new life you've planned for yourself?"

"That would be getting ahead of ourselves. Brad and I agreed we were keeping it simple."

"So when will you see him again?"

"Not too soon. I'm flying out tomorrow for an overnight in Texas."

"Texas? What's in Texas? Wait—don't tell me you have to let some other guy off the hook first!"

"No, no. I'm too controlling to bother with a long-distance relationship, remember? No, I'm going out there to see a friend of mine. We worked together and she's been a mentor to me. I have to run some…stuff by her, and I didn't want to do it over the phone."

"Maybe it's a good idea for you to get out of here, even if it's only overnight. This has been a crazy week, and it's not over yet. You were all set to have the perfect life with the perfect new job and—no pun intended—it all blew up in your face on Monday morning."

"Yes, it's a mess." A bigger one than Emily realized. Joy loved her but didn't want to share all her observations. She couldn't. Not until she saw Helen and got the validation she needed.

CHAPTER TWENTY

SUMMER'S END WAS nowhere in sight in San Antonio, Texas. Joy's blouse stuck to her skin, and sweat rolled down her forehead. Couples ambled by along the River Walk as she tried her best to people-watch from her seat at the outdoor café. Helen was due here any minute, but waiting for her felt more like a lifetime than an hour as she sipped the best iced tea she'd had in years.

Iced tea was a Southern secret, she'd learned during many permanent and temporary tours of duty, TDYs, south of the Mason-Dixon Line. The San Antonio version included a huge wedge of lime instead of the more customary lemon.

A couple holding hands, not paying attention to where they were going, halted when the man nudged Joy's table, moving the wrought-iron top into her belly.

"Oof."

"Sorry!" The woman giggled and tugged her man away, oblivious to Joy's discomfort.

Joy didn't care; she was focused on a different,

more potent and intangible punch to her gut. Her memories of Brad.

She wished he was here. That *they* were the couple strolling along the River Walk—without any demons chasing them. No enemy and no mission to control where their relationship might go.

Returning to their hotel room whenever they wanted…

Stop it.

"Joy!"

"Admiral." She rose, and since Helen was also in civilian clothes, gave her a hug. Helen squeezed Joy back, whispering in her ear.

"It's so good to see you. But you've got me worried, Joy."

Joy pulled back. "I know, and I'm sorry for chasing you down like this. I couldn't talk on the phone."

Helen's gray eyes narrowed, and Joy knew that lunch was going to be intense. She had one chance, one conversation to convince Helen to do some digging for her. For Brad.

No matter. She needed a friend she could count on, at any cost.

And Brad needed her.

AFTER TWO LARGE plates of delicious tortillas and carne asada, Helen wiped her mouth with her napkin and leaned back.

"I never pegged you as an outlier, Joy."

Oh, crap. Here it comes. Helen was about to lay down the law and blast Joy for her attempts to help Brad out by digging up old case files.

"I know. I'm certainly not playing by the rules the Navy taught me, or legal school, either. But you were always big on staying the course, following my intuition. Above all, you've taught me to do what's right, regardless of the consequences."

"And that's what you think you're doing, breaking every Navy regulation, federal, military and local law, lying to your new employer?"

Helen Bolling looked every inch the Navy admiral, even in her casual blouse and linen skirt. She was the one woman, besides her mother, Joy would never want to disappoint or worse, betray.

In that moment the truth with a capital *T* shone clear to her in the bright Texas sun, which glinted off the narrow San Antonio River as it passed by them like a slow smile.

"I'm doing what's right, I'm sure of it."

Helen regarded her closely.

"It's more than that, Helen." She called her friend by her first name when they were in private, but always remained aware that Helen was an admiral. "I'm afraid the bad guys are very close to making their big move, but the red tape at the higher levels of government means catching them in time will be too difficult."

"This might be a terrible, deadly mistake, Joy.

Do you realize how emotionally involved you are? Are you doing this as some kind of misguided attempt to show Brad how much you care?"

"It isn't only about Brad. It's about making sure I've done my duty. That I haven't missed anything I should've handled while I was still in uniform."

"Well, that was going to be my next point. You aren't in uniform any longer, and it's not your war to wage. Don't you think General Grimes and most other officers sometimes wish they could go back in time to tie up loose ends? No operation is ever perfect. The same goes for legal cases."

"Maybe, but there's nothing wrong with doing a little cleanup."

"I met Jerry years ago. Didn't you say he helped Brad out, gave him his car?"

Hearing Helen refer to General Grimes as "Jerry" was a bit unsettling. She knew him?

"Yes, he did. Do you know him well?" Joy fiddled with the lime in her iced tea. Grimes *had* been generous.

Helen's gaze was steady. This was why Joy had taken the time to come here. She needed Helen's strength and wisdom.

"I worked with the man for months on the most important case of my career, right after 9-11. Nothing passed between us during the case. He was still hung up on his deceased wife and was raising his daughter at the time. And I was too busy with my career to make any effort at a relationship." Helen's eyes misted. "It's funny how quickly life goes by, how soon a career is over. Then we're all faced with ourselves." She blinked back the tears and cleared her throat.

Joy wasn't the only one who had feelings for a man she'd worked with during an intense case.

"Tell me, Joy. The FBI agent, the former SEAL—how deeply are you involved with him?"

Joy looked Helen in the eye with no hesitation. "I'm drowning."

She braced herself for one of the tongue-lashings Helen was famous for. Helen had taken her to task more than once during that first tour, and each time Joy had sworn she'd felt every caustic word as a physical blow. Helen was the Navy's best lawyer because she'd earned it, case by case, command by command.

Helen laughed. "Good girl."

Shock jolted Joy, and she clasped and unclasped her hands under the table. "What?"

Helen grinned. "Honey, it's clear to me that this Brad is more than just a colleague or former shipmate you're willing to go the distance for. We all stick our necks out for our shipmates, more than once in a career. But what you're facing here, it's a once-in-a-lifetime experience. You get that, right?"

"Yes."

"A woman will fight to the death for her children and for the man she loves."

"Whoa, Helen, I'm not talking about *love* here."

"You might not be talking about it, sweetie, but you're living it. Admit that much to yourself, if to no one else."

Joy rolled her sweating glass of iced tea on her cheeks. They were as hot as if Helen had slapped her.

Because she had. Helen had verbally slapped the truth into her.

She loved Brad.

The groan that came from her throat surprised her and made Helen smirk.

"You haven't come to terms with it yet, I take it?"

Joy shook her head. "Not…completely."

Helen leaned back and signaled the waiter, who immediately came over to the table.

"Two margaritas on ice, with extra shots in each."

"You took a cab, right?"

Joy laughed. "From the airport, yes. But I have a room in the same hotel as you. I can walk back."

"Good. Don't want you driving after we get done. When do you fly back?"

"Zero-dark-thirty tomorrow."

Helen gave a low whistle.

"That's my girl. Not wasting any time. Okay, let's get to work."

HELEN SAT ON the sofa in her hotel room, where she'd invited Joy after lunch. She listened as Joy told her everything she could recall about the case.

Helen nodded. "Farid heard and knew more than he said during the trial, I'm certain. But that doesn't make him a criminal, Joy. If he's the man you believe him to be, he only stayed quiet to save more lives."

Tears stung her eyes. "What he stayed quiet about could've killed Brad. It still could, if some crazy mastermind is behind all this."

"You can go forward with a clear conscience, knowing you did all you could to help. And I agree that there's someone bigger behind this, or the domestic terrorists wouldn't have been able to smuggle in a SAM."

"So you don't think I'm crazy." Exhaustion tickled her eyelids and weighed on her chest.

"No, I've never thought you had *crazy* in you, Joy. You're a bit of a control freak, I'll grant you that. That's why you're such a great lawyer. The JAG Corps is less without you."

"So now you're making me feel guilty over my resignation?"

"You know I'm not."

She leaned her head against the back of the settee. "I could end up incriminating Brad and General Grimes, if Farid has information that

Brad and General Grimes were aware of at the time, too."

"That's unlikely."

"You don't have any connections in the Witness Security Program, do you?"

Helen shook her head.

"I've worked with them on some cases, of course, but a mere mortal like me can't pick up the phone and find out where a protected witness is."

"Damn."

"You were hoping to get to Farid, get him to tell you what he might have left out of his testimony?"

"Yes."

"You're not going to like this, Joy, but none of it's your concern any longer. Even if I could get the Intel you want. You were a JAG, for God's sake. Not intelligence! You need to forget about the Norfolk trials. They're over."

Helen's words burst through Joy's denial, and her hopes sank like the fishing boat in the explosion on Monday morning. Had it really been less than a week?

"But I have to make sure—"

"Stop being such a damned perfectionist. You've got to accept that you did your best at the time, Joy. No remorse, no regret. You're not responsible for anything the terrorists have or haven't done, just like you're not responsible for any testimony Farid didn't give. You had a client to represent. You did it flawlessly. Farid's safe in WSP, and Brad's just broken apart an ugly domestic cell that may or may not have a connection to the bad guys from Farid's village."

Helen was right; she was always right. More important, Joy respected her and needed her counsel. But...

"I'll never be able to live with myself if I walk away now and something awful happens later."

"What's your worst fear?"

"I'm afraid—" She stopped. Her first thought, her instant reply, scared the hell out of her.

"Joy?"

"I was going to say I'm afraid that another SAM will reach its target on our soil. That *should* be my biggest fear."

"But?"

"My biggest worry is...Brad. I'm afraid an unnamed terrorist is still trying to get him for what his SEAL team accomplished during the war."

Helen nodded. "Now you're talking. That's a valid, if rather inflated, fear."

"I just wish I'd had the foresight during the case to see this as a possibility in the future."

"My colleagues who were there to see you work said that your handling of the case was exemplary."

Joy ignored the praise, although praise was

something Helen didn't dish out randomly or excessively.

"I was trained by the best—you. I'm not fishing for compliments. I'm trying to keep Brad alive. God, I don't know what to think anymore, Helen."

Her inner turmoil muddied everything. So this was what caring more about someone than herself or her career actually meant. That none of it mattered the way it used to, the way she expected.

Only one thing mattered—that Brad was safe and alive.

"You've got excellent instincts, Joy. Let's go with them on this, and I'll see if I can connect with some of my contacts, see what I can stir up, within reason. In the meantime, I suggest you go sit in the hotel spa and use the time to chill out. You look like you could use it."

Joy stood up. She didn't think anything except nailing whoever had that SAM shipped to the US was going to ease her agitation. But far be it from her to argue with Helen.

"That sounds good."

SITTING IN THE spa's thermal room, where rainforest sounds and soft music echoed about the cavernous space, filled with plants Joy had never seen before, Joy tried to let go of her racing thoughts.

Perspiration dripped from every pore, and she wiped her face with the thick, soft terry towel to no avail; the sweat was pouring out of her and wasn't going to stop as long as she sat here. That was the point of a spa, wasn't it? To detoxify?

She'd tried to call Brad but had been switched directly to his voice mail. He'd given her his number and had texted her several times since she'd left his place yesterday morning. She hadn't answered, because she didn't trust herself not to spill the beans on what she was trying to accomplish. Now *he* was incommunicado.

He'd likely gone in to work and would get back to her later.

She hated feeling so needy but in only five days, it seemed, that was what she'd become. Needy. For Brad.

No, it was more than five days. It was almost two years of feeling emotionally attached to the man.

Is this what real love feels like?

No matter how long she sat in the spa she wasn't going to find the answer to that here.

BACK IN HELEN'S room two hours later, as they sipped iced tea with lime from fancy hotel glasses, Helen's phone chimed, indicating she had a message. Her eyes widened, and a smile lit her face as she read it.

"Bingo, Joy. We've got a lucky break."

Hope surged, and Joy tried to quell it. If the result was disappointing, it wouldn't be just a lost case.

It was Brad's life and at this point hers, too.

"What do you know, Helen?"

"Have you ever read the unclassified accounts of the Taliban's reach?"

"A few, but it's not my usual area of interest." Not until this past week.

After a few quick taps on her phone, Helen looked back up. "We'll read it together."

"How are you getting this information?"

Helen winked.

"I told you that you should've stayed in and come to work for me in DC. This job has a lot of extra perks, the biggest being the sources I can draw from when needed." Helen ran her fingers through her silver strands, the chic bob falling perfectly back into place.

"But you can't get to Farid."

"No, that's reserved for Assistants to God, of which I'm not one."

They both laughed.

Joy's phone vibrated, and she opened the email file from Helen.

She read through the file Helen had sent. It was a declassified report that illustrated in detail the ties that bound several different Taliban leaders, and how their partnership with al Qaeda allowed their reach to be global. Eerily so.

"Holy crap, Helen! Any one of these organizations could be responsible for bringing in the SAM."

"Mmm." Helen was reading, too. "I'll bet your friend Brad and his team will find out who it is in a more exact fashion."

"Meaning?"

"The FBI is constantly tracking all of this, in real time and at a very classified level. Even if Brad doesn't know, someone in the Bureau probably does."

They sat quietly for the next few minutes, both reading. Joy found so many unexpected tangents, which she tried to follow.

Helen gasped.

"What? You're obviously farther along than I am."

"Skip to page 3, para 4."

Dread settled in Joy's heart.

"'A Taliban leader vowed to seek revenge and sought aid from local al Qaeda leaders,'" Helen read aloud, her leopard-print reading glasses perched on her nose.

She raised her head. "You're right to be concerned, Joy. And you may remember hearing references to this as you interviewed Farid, Brad and General Grimes. Did Mike Rubio's statement give you anything?"

"No. I've already gone over all their statements a dozen times in the last two days." She was afraid to ask Helen her next question.

"There's nothing I can do, is there? It's in the hands of people in much higher places than us."

Helen took off her glasses and closed her eyes for a moment. Joy had missed this—Helen's meditative approach to even the most heinous discoveries, the most violent cases.

When she opened her eyes, the familiar depth of conviction shone from them. It both soothed and terrified Joy. Helen never held anything back.

Helen's words were always precise, her perceptions nothing less than reliable. But it was her body language that reassured Joy. "You agree with me. There's a serious risk here, isn't there—to national security. And to Brad…"

"We've worked on too many cases together. You can read me too well." Helen offered a half smile before she went back to the file.

"But it's true, Helen. You do agree with me."

"I don't disagree with you. And deep down, yes, I think you're on to something sinister here. The question is, what are the chances you'll be able to get enough evidence together to help Brad before the FBI solves it? Let's say this goes all the way, and you can actually name a suspect. Great. Now what does the US Government have? Chances are, this person has changed his name several times since he knew Farid, and witnessed Brad's team in action."

Joy ignored her knee-jerk disappointment. She knew Helen, and she knew her friend was only trying to save her from unnecessary angst.

"You're the one who told me that justice never comes easily, Helen. Not in these kinds of situations. If it's within my power to bring justice…"

"It's not. You're risking your new position. Your civilian law credentials will go up in smoke if you're wrong. And even if you're not, you're trying to do something you don't have the legal right to."

"I'm willing to take that chance." As she uttered those words, a huge weight lifted. She felt as though she was floating instead of sitting on a utilitarian sofa in Helen's hotel room.

She was willing to risk it all—for justice.

For Brad.

"You've always been a risk-taker when it counted, Joy. I regret on a professional level that I told you it was okay to resign your commission. Of course it was, and it was the right thing for you to do personally, but the JAG Corps is less without you."

"You also told me you understood why I had to get out and that you wished you had the courage to do the same."

Helen sent her a level gaze. "I did, didn't I?"

"Yes. Speaking of which, how's *your* love life?"

"It sucks."

Helen stopped talking and stared out the window at the vista of San Antonio. Joy saw her chest rise and fall as she took a deep breath before turning to face her again.

"You could do everything right, Joy. Finally free Brad and Farid from the threat of a rogue terrorist."

"And?"

"And you could still wind up alone, get disbarred—or worse, get yourself and those who matter most to you killed."

CHAPTER TWENTY-ONE

BRAD FELT LIKE a slouch for not going in to the office Friday morning, but Mike was right; he'd done enough work for all of them over the past several months. He felt relief—and some pride— at having taken down a terrorist cell, no matter how small in the relative scheme of things. Now he sat on his sofa with his coffee, watching one of his favorite guy flicks—adventure and may- hem all the way.

A knock at the door had him alert and forget- ting his vow to relax as he muted the television. He waited. He wasn't expecting anyone and—

Joy. It had to be Joy. Maybe she'd taken the day off, after all. They'd talked at length last night and she'd said she'd be out of town on some business this weekend. That she'd fill him in later.

He walked to the door as the second knock came simultaneously with the doorbell.

Out of habit, he looked through the side frosted windows that framed the door—and froze.

The shape on his porch wasn't female, and it definitely wasn't Joy.

He checked the peephole he'd installed when he renovated the front entrance. He hadn't wanted to put in a camera, not at his home. This was his one respite from anything work related.

Maybe he'd made a mistake.

He cracked open the door.

"Hi, Mr. Brad. It's me, Farid."

"I know who you are. What are you doing here?" Brad scanned the street for signs of anyone else. "How did you find me?"

Farid shrugged. "Google. You forgot to make sure your real estate purchase wasn't put up."

Crap.

"Get in."

Brad locked the door behind them and turned to face the man he'd fought to set free from a life in prison. The man who'd saved his life and the lives of his SEAL team.

He knew Farid wasn't here on a social visit. People in the Witness Security Program made contact with former acquaintances at the risk of their own lives.

"What's this about?"

Farid looked tired but otherwise much healthier, much more alive than he had in Virginia. But lines of worry or stress streaked across his face, and Brad's stomach tensed in warning.

"I saw the news and I had to come and tell you. I know the authorities think they have everyone, but there's still someone who's not going to stop until you and General Grimes are dead."

"Spit it out, Farid."

"My name's Ricardo now. And it's someone from my village who was able to come here as a refugee. That person—I don't know exactly who—is connected to a man from my village. Hasan. And Hasan is trying to stir up trouble and wants to recruit homegrown terrorists here. He's a very bad man, Brad."

His plans to make a life with Joy collapsed.

"Why are they after me and General Grimes?"

"As far as Hasan's concerned, you're the enemy. Like me. One of us. You saved me, Mr. Brad. Without Miss Alexander's help and your testimony, I'd still be in Gitmo."

"It's Brad. Just Brad."

"Brad. I didn't tell Miss Alexander all I knew about him. I was afraid he'd find out and hurt my family before you got them here. And it didn't have anything to do with the case. Not at the time…"

"What exactly happened to make this one man so focused on me and General Grimes?"

Farid's dark eyes filled with anger, hatred, warning. "It wasn't because of the general even though he thinks it was. But some of the Taliban went crazy one night after your team had gone through our village. I witnessed them hurting the women in the village. I had to save my sisters and mother, so I did that by hiding them. But I couldn't protect all the women. In the morning, the story was that your SEAL team did the crimes. It's the propaganda the Taliban spreads against America and your allies."

Brad sank onto his stairs. "How do you know that, Farid?"

"I heard Hasan say that. I was still in the village. He vowed payback for the women who were hurt and the men who died. He's a zealot and couldn't accept that his own countrymen would do that. He let the Taliban convince him it was the Americans."

"You're talking about a very dangerous kind of operation, Farid. You say he's bringing terrorist acts to American soil?"

Farid nodded. "Yes. That is why I've come forward. When I saw the reports about Whidbey Island on television, I knew you had to be involved in the case somehow, because it's so close to where you live now, and the way it happened is pure Hasan. If who he has working for him here knows where you are, and it might be more than one person, they'll come for you. If you have a family, they'll try to hurt them, too."

Brad felt the blood drain from his face.

"Hell, Farid." His actions of the past week might have taken Hasan's thug right to Joy.

"That's why I came, Brad. I couldn't bear to see Hasan hurt one more person. I saw the names

of the men they arrested on Whidbey. One is originally from my village. He immigrated here as
a young boy. His sisters, his mother—they were
all raped by the Taliban, but like I said, he thinks
it was Americans who came in the dark of night.
His family vowed revenge."

Thoughts raced through Brad's mind. He focused in on the cell members talking about re-
taliation. Only one of them had appeared to be of
Afghan descent, but he spoke with no accent and
said he'd been in the States for ten years.

"I've got to make some calls. You're coming
into the office with me."

"Yes."

THEY WALKED INTO the Bureau office after Farid
had gone through almost an hour of extra security. Brad had already checked him over for a
weapon; after everything he'd been through in
the past few days he wasn't about to risk finding
out that Farid was a bad guy, no matter how improbable that was. He'd been wrong before. Not
often, but nothing was foolproof.

Brad's team eyed him as he walked by their
cubicles. This wasn't the time for the celebratory
high fives they'd exchange later.

There was more business to tend to first.

Mike was waiting in his office. He stood when
Brad and Farid entered.

"I thought I told you to take some time off."

"Yeah, well, think again."

"Farid." Mike stuck out his hand. Farid shook it firmly and with a confidence he hadn't had since before he'd left his native land. Apparently, the Witness Security Program had given him a good life.

"I'm sorry to meet you again under these circumstances." Farid spoke as if what he'd told Brad was concrete evidence.

"Hell, Farid, I'm sorry you're risking your life by coming out of WSP."

"Other lives are at stake. They will be until Hasan and his agents come to justice. Until my village learns the truth."

"Sit down, Farid." Mike didn't even look at Brad. He didn't have to. They were of one mind at this point in their careers.

"Fill me in on what you've said to Brad." Farid's story was the same one he'd told Brad, but he spoke with even more passion now. He believed in what he was saying, and the sickening free-fall sensation in Brad's stomach convinced him it was the truth.

"I know it was wrong to not say anything during the trial. But it wasn't asked of me, and once General Grimes was called in to testify on my behalf, I didn't want to risk letting him keep me behind bars. I know he never wanted me out." Farid looked at Brad, and his gratitude was clear, despite the immediate concern.

"Mike, we need to get someone to go after Hasan in-country."

Mike pinched the top of his nose and took a deep breath. "That sounds good, in theory. But what do we have besides Farid's testimony?" He looked at Farid. "Do you have other family members, other villagers, who'd be willing to testify against him?"

"No."

"That makes it a little tough from our end."

"You caught three here so far?" Farid—Ricardo—asked. "That's what the news said. But those three won't know Hasan personally. They might not even know *about* him. There has to be a go-between. There are always more of them, waiting for their call to action."

"Yes, you're right, and yes, we've arrested three." Mike left out the part about Brad taking out the fourth, the man who'd been in the act of launching the SAM. "If I have my say, they're going to jail for the rest of their lives for attempted terrorism, conspiracy to commit terrorism and threatening a United States Military officer."

"That's not Farid's concern, Mike."

"Farid, I need a minute with Brad. Do you mind waiting outside?"

Mike rose and escorted Farid to the reception area, where his administrative assistant offered him coffee and water.

Once back in the office, Mike shut the door and turned to Brad. "How the hell did he find you?"

"He said it was on Google. Through the real estate company."

"Son of a bitch, Brad. That was pretty damn careless."

Brad stayed silent. "Look," Mike went on. "We don't have anything on this Hasan character yet, so whatever Farid saw or knows, it's moot. It'd only be slander at this point." Mike sat back at his desk.

"Farid's a thoughtful dude, Mike. He hasn't risked his life by stepping out of WSP on a whim."

"I know."

"What about the sleeper agent we haven't ID'd yet?"

"I have a feeling he—and any accomplices he might still have—will be striking soon, one way or another. We'll get them, Brad, of that I'm certain. I just don't want to lose anyone in the process."

"I'm worried I've led them to Joy."

Mike nodded. "So am I. She's gone until tomorrow. Why don't you head out to Whidbey in the morning and meet a tech team there? Get her house swept before she gets back?"

"I'd feel better if we got a security detail on her now." She'd finally admitted in her last text that she was going to meet an old JAG friend in San Antonio.

"Already ahead of you, man."

THE NEXT MORNING, Brad let himself in Joy's side door just as he had less than a week ago, when he'd scaled the side of West Beach. He motioned for the two techs he'd brought with him to follow.

Mike's suggestion that they sweep Joy's house had given Brad pause. Mike had confirmed Brad's deepest fear. That Joy would get hurt, or worse.

"Looks like someone beat us to it." Agent Susie Blackthorne stood next to him, with Agent Tim Parker a step behind.

Brad schooled himself to stay calm and detached as he took in the disaster that used to be Joy's home. The kitchen where he'd kissed her had every drawer pulled out, the contents dumped on the floor in a pile of spice jars, smashed pantry contents and cooking utensils.

Tim whistled long and slow. "Any idea what they were after?"

Brad shook his head. "My guess is that it wasn't the same thing you're here for. Why don't you make your sweep while I look around? We'll call in the Island County sheriff when we're done."

He was stepping outside protocol, since a routine break-in was within the jurisdiction of the local authorities, either Oak Harbor PD or the sheriff. But he felt that taking some leeway was justified, because this was personal, and anyone who was after Joy would have to go through him first.

As he pulled his phone out of his pocket to call Mike, he walked gingerly around the house, not wanting to disturb any evidence. Not that he expected to find any.

"Rubio."

"Mike, it's Brad. I'm at Joy's and she's had a rough break-in. The whole place has been turned upside down. How much you want to bet it's our guy?"

"Where's Joy now?"

Brad checked his watch. "In the air. She's due to land at Sea Tac in two hours."

"I want you to get out of her place. Find whatever you can in the next ten minutes, and then get the hell out, Brad. Come back to the office. If this is our sleeper, we're going to need a team to go in and get him. No cowboy stuff, man."

Brad couldn't stop the grunt of laughter. *Cowboy stuff* was what they used to say if someone on their SEAL team was trying to be a hero. A team was a cohesive unit, no heroes allowed.

"Got it."

"I mean it, Brad. If you don't call me back in fifteen and tell me you're on the road, I'm going to write your ass up. You'll help her more by keeping her out of there and safe at your place for now."

"You're right." He disconnected then went into the living room and stopped at the table where Joy kept her house phone and a notepad. Several pages had been torn off and left crumpled next to the phone or on the floor. That wasn't Joy; she was a neat freak. He looked at the pad but didn't see any indentations. Not wanting to waste time, he scooped up all the notes and shoved them in his pockets, along with the pad. The local LEAs didn't need to catch wind of anything Joy was looking up. "Make it quick, folks. We're out of here in five minutes."

HELEN'S WORDS ECHOED in Joy's ears as she drove south on Highway 5 out of Sea Tac. She had the radio on full blast, trying to burn off some stress by singing along to Kelly Clarkson, Shania Twain and Miranda Lambert on the local country station.

Her phone rang and she saw on her dashboard's Bluetooth that it was Brad. She turned down Shania's "You're Still the One," and greeted him.

"Hey, stranger."

"Joy, where are you?"

"Heading home. I'll be there in about ninety minutes."

"Turn around."

"What?" She saw the exit sign for the Kingston Ferry. "I'm too close to home, Brad."

"Where exactly, Joy?"

"I just passed the exit for the Kingston Ferry. Why?"

"Listen to me, Joy. Go to my house."

"Oh, I get it. You miss me that much?"

"No, no. I mean, yes, of course I do. But I'm not at home. You're in danger if you go to your place. I just left and I'm on my way back to Seattle. I was at your place Joy, and…it's been ransacked."

"What?" No. Not now. Not when she was more in need than ever of her quiet respite from the world.

"Look, Joy, I don't want to have a long conversation about this on the phone. Just go to my place and let yourself in. I'll be there in a little over an hour. There'll be a security detail around my house."

"But—"

"You remember where the key is, right?"

"Yes, but I have some things to tell you, Brad."

"We'll compare notes when we meet up. Turn. Around. Now."

"I am, I am."

"Talk to you there." Brad ended the connection.

She put her blinker on for the next exit and tried to remember the way to Brad's without her GPS. It kept her from getting upset over his harsh tone, even if he had good reason to be worried.

"I CAN'T BELIEVE you actually listened to me." Mike stood at his desk, the notes Brad had collected in a neat pile. "I'll have an agent look at these and see if there's anything we can get out of 'em."

"You heard the techies found two bugs, didn't you?"

"Yeah, but they could've been put there by the same person who did the break-in, to see when she got home. It doesn't mean anyone heard your earlier conversations."

Chills went down Brad's spine, followed by a shot of adrenaline that made his hands shake. Mike looked him over, not missing any of his tells.

"Thanks for doing what I asked, Brad. You're too close to this whole situation. We have to take Hasan's agent down right or he's going to slither out of our hands."

"I know. Do you think he's smuggled in more SAMs?"

Mike shrugged. "I have no idea. If he's as twisted as I suspect he is, anything's possible. He may have lured the cell members you caught to the Northwest just so he could play cat-and-mouse with them."

"That's pure evil."

"It is, and not your concern. Take Farid back to your place, and keep him and Joy there until we get the last suspect in custody."

"Will do." He moved to grab the door handle.

"Brad?"

"Yeah?"

"It's okay to care this much for someone, you know. Healthy, in fact."

"Go to hell, man."

Mike's laughter chased him out of the office.

"I'M SORRY YOU have to babysit me, Brad." Farid sat in the passenger seat of Brad's minivan as they drove through downtown Seattle.

"No problem. Anyway, it's your lucky day. You'll get to see Joy. She'll be waiting for us."

He felt a burning anxiety to get home. He trusted Joy to be there; it wasn't that. He just needed to hold her and see for himself that she was in one piece. Hearing her voice on the phone had helped calm his nerves earlier, but the effect had worn off. After walking into her place and seeing that some rat bastard had torn the place apart.

"Your boss, Mike, he said there's enough to put Hasan's puppets away for a long while."

"Yes, hopefully. We still have to capture this last one. But it's not as straight a shot to the witness stand as we might think."

"So I've learned from watching the American television."

Brad eased them onto the highway. Good. Only thirteen more minutes, and they'd be at his place. Why was the dump truck in front of him so slow?

"You settling in okay where you are, Farid?"

He threw a quick glance at his passenger as he passed the truck on the right side.

Eleven more minutes.

The Afghan smiled, the first real sign of anything other than grim determination that he'd seen in the man, except for when he'd been pronounced "not guilty."

"At first it was very hard to be away from my family and to be dropped into the middle of American life. But now it's not so bad. And my name is Ricardo and I have a job at a big grocery store. I let my neighbors assume I'm Latino. Although I suppose that will have to change. I'll probably have to move again, won't I?"

Brad grunted. "Yeah, you've pretty much outed yourself by coming here, man."

"It's worth it if I've saved your life, and now Commander Alexander's. I had no idea she was involved as much as she is."

"She wasn't. She's just a bystander, really." She wouldn't have been involved if he hadn't dragged her into it.

He needed her.

Nine more minutes and he'd see Joy.

Had he just called the woman who'd turned his world inside out a *bystander*?

Sure. An innocent bystander he'd dragged into his case. An innocent bystander now in a terrorist's sights?

Who was he kidding? He couldn't ask Joy to

join him in his crazy lifestyle. It wasn't something he could give up, not completely. Once he knew she was safe, and their suspect was in custody, he'd have to make the break. Because unless Hasan was immobilized, taken out, he would continue to send in representatives of one type or another. Brad would always be hunted, as would anyone close to him.

That was what he'd learned true love was—sacrifice, regardless of the personal cost.

His phone rang and he grabbed it. "Iverson."

"Brad, it's Mike. Where are you?"

Mike's voice sounded too much like his had when he'd spoken to Joy an hour or so earlier.

"Getting ready to pull onto my street."

"Stop. Wait until backup gets there."

"What?" he asked incredulously. "Why?"

"I figured out what the suspect got off Joy's notepad. Your address, and where your key's hidden. You must've told her and she wrote it down. The imprint is still on some of the pages that were torn off.

"You're saying—"

"We think the suspect is at your place. Joy's already there. She's not answering her phone, Brad. We've located her at your place via her cell phone. I've got agents and Seattle PD on the way. Let them handle it. No cowboys."

Brad disconnected. Mike wouldn't get blamed for anything he didn't say to Brad.

Not handle it?

If he found one hair out of place on Joy's head, he was going to make their suspect wish he'd picked a different victim. A different person to take out his sick, misguided anger on.

JOY PARKED HER car in Brad's driveway and decided to come back later for her overnight bag. She didn't know how much time she had before he showed up, and she wanted to have a hot pot of coffee waiting for him.

She also wanted to freshen up, if possible.

She didn't notice any overt security agents but trusted they were in place.

Swinging her purse strap over her shoulder, she walked around the side of the clapboard house, straight back to the red cedar gate. She unlatched it with one tug and stepped onto the soft grass of Brad's yard. They hadn't gotten this far when he'd given her the house tour, but she easily located the broken piece of pottery where he'd hidden the key. He'd told her it was under the garden bench in the far corner of the yard.

As she bent to turn over the homemade hide-a-key, she breathed in the scent of roses and made a mental note to see where they were planted.

There wasn't a key under the pot, though, just moist earth. She got down on her knees and felt through the dirt and grass.

The sound of footsteps reached her ears at

the same moment she felt a cold object against her throat, and she was hauled to her feet by her jacket collar. A strong arm was wrapped around her shoulders but she couldn't think past the metal pressed against her skin.

A knife. Someone had a knife to her throat.

"Looking for this?"

The female voice rasped in her ear as she held Brad's house key in front of Joy's eyes.

CHAPTER TWENTY-TWO

THE WOMAN SHOVED her into Brad's kitchen and sat her on one of the island bar stools. Shorter than Joy, the woman was dressed in black and wore a black ski mask. Her eyes were dark holes devoid of any emotion.

Emotion could be manipulated. What Joy saw struck the freezing knife of fear into her heart. This woman was intent on one thing.

Revenge.

She thought she might have an escape when the woman pocketed the knife, but she pulled out a .45 mm pistol and aimed it at her.

"Don't worry. I'm not going to blow your brains out yet. Not until your lover shows up." The woman spoke with no discernible accent.

"Who are you? What's your name?"

"Shut up or I shoot."

"Go ahead, but it won't make a difference. You're going to prison for the rest of your life." This had to be the missing suspect. The one person with ties to the overseas terrorists.

The most dangerous one.

"Nobody has anything on me. They don't suspect a woman. It's Sameen, by the way."

There was no doubt she intended to kill her or she'd have never given Joy her name.

Sameen. Joy didn't recognize it from any of the case testimony.

Joy felt numb inside and she shivered, yet sweat dripped down her back and down her neck, between her breasts.

It was because of the adrenaline. Brad had told her that managing adrenaline was a big part of doing military spec ops and undercover ops for the Bureau. So she had to try to manage her adrenaline and not go into shock.

Keep her wits about her. Try to reason with this woman.

"I know why you hate Americans, Sameen." she began. "Why you want me and Brad dead. Why you went after Grimes. It *was* you, wasn't it? I'd hate anyone I thought had hurt my family, too."

Sameen's grip on her pistol faltered, and for a second Joy saw a light in her eyes that confirmed she'd hit the source of her hatred. Her anguish.

Anger quickly replaced it, and her sinister bearing was back in place.

"You don't know the half of it."

"I know that your village, your family, maybe even you, were attacked and the women raped. I know they told you it was the Americans. But it wasn't. It was the Taliban the Americans had defeated that day. The few of them who remained, it was their warning—*owwww!*"

She gasped as the barrel of the weapon slammed against her temple. Stars flashed in her eyes, and a sudden wave of intense nausea swamped her.

You never told Brad you love him.

"Shut your trap, bitch." Sameen's breath was hot on Joy's face, and her eyes almost reptilian in their lack of empathy. She radiated anger but with a calmness that was more shocking than the knife that had been at her throat or the gun now aimed between her eyes.

"It wasn't me or my sisters. It was the boy I was supposed to marry. He was killed defending our village from the Americans. Then I was forced to come here. I was only seventeen."

She lowered the pistol to the kitchen island, but still clutched the handle. Ready to fire.

As she fought against throwing up, Joy did a mental check of her status. Still breathing. Dry jeans—she hadn't wet her pants, but she wouldn't feel bad about it if she did. This was definitely a wet-your-pants situation. The grimmest she'd ever been in. It'd be easy to think there was no hope. That she was going to die.

Except Brad. The thought of being able to tell him how she felt lit a spark of warmth deep in her cold, shivering body.

"I can see why you might believe it was our fault, especially since that's what you were told. But the Americans didn't raid your village to hurt civilians. They saved hundreds of lives that day. It was war—and if your friend was fighting for the Taliban, he knew the risks."

"Shut up! You know nothing of my people. Of what we've sacrificed."

"You're an intelligent woman, Sameen. You understand that killing me or another innocent civilian won't bring anyone back to life. It won't solve anything."

"Don't give me your American propaganda." Her mouth barely moved, and she spoke as if in a trance. Joy had dealt with a few psychiatrically challenged clients in her JAG career, but none had seemed so…unreachable. As if she'd been pro-grammed to carry out this plan of revenge and would stop at nothing to achieve her desired goal.

Had killing Brad, Farid, General Grimes, been her goal all this time? If she'd believed the Tali-ban's lies, yes.

Joy had to stay alive long enough to warn Brad. If this terrorist killed her first, Brad would be a sitting duck when he came home.

"Tell me about your family."

Sameen blinked. "I have no family. They were either killed in the war or decided to stay there. They wouldn't come with my aunt and me when we were offered refugee status here. My aunt died two years ago."

Joy stayed silent.

"I didn't understand why they wouldn't take the chance to live among you so we could get our justice one day," the woman said. "I took my opportunity. I even went to university. I lost my accent by the time I was done with freshman year."

A ghost of the young girl she must've been floated across her eyes. Joy looked at her hand. Still on the pistol. At least the weapon was on the island and not pointed directly at her. But a flick of her wrist, a tug on the trigger…

No. You're going to live so you can tell Brad you love him.

"I met another boy, though, at university. He hated your government as much as I did."

"And you recruited him on to your team."

"Him and two others, yes. And your Brad never knew I was behind the whole thing. That I'd followed him after he left the Navy. After Farid had betrayed all of us by going to your government's officials. He made me leave my country."

"STAY HERE WITH the doors locked. Do not get out of this car until I come back for you." Brad parked in an empty spot six houses down from his, out of view of his place. If someone *was* in there with Joy, that person would be on the lookout for Brad or other Bureau folks to show up.

Whoever it was would want to make a big production of harming her.

A vise seemed to tighten around his lungs, and his stomach threatened to heave. Of all the situations he'd been in worldwide, this one was the worst. He'd never reacted this intensely before. Never cared this much.

He silently willed his training to kick in, giving him the blessed detachment he needed to save Joy.

A hand on his forearm. He shook it off.

"I think Miss Joy's in trouble. Let me help you."

"I don't have time to argue with you, Farid. One of Hasan's bastards might have her at my place, and we can't wait for the backup team. I'm going in now."

"But I heard Mr. Mike tell you not to go in on your own."

"I can't lose her."

He took his revolver out of his glove compartment, holstered it and got out of the car. He was running along the hard concrete sidewalk before he heard the Jeep locks click shut.

Farid was a big boy who'd have to take care of himself while Brad was away. At this point all he saw in his mind's eye was Joy.

"THAT MUST HAVE been horrible for you." If she kept the woman talking, built empathy, she'd stand a chance.

"Horrible? For me?" The woman looked over Joy's shoulder as if she was watching a movie. Seeing pictures of her life through the distorted lens of the pain she'd suffered.

"How about the horror for my family? For my villagers, my country?" she asked.

"There are better ways to mete out justice. First, you have to know that the Taliban lied to you." It took all her strength to stay calm and not try to run. Escaping a bullet wasn't one of her talents.

"You think *you're* the truth teller, don't you?"

"No, but I'll do whatever it takes to get *real* justice."

She waved the pistol wildly, and Joy wondered what the odds were of being hit if she inadvertently pulled the trigger while her arm was flailing.

"You and Iverson—he's not a good FBI agent. He couldn't even handle an undercover mission in his own country."

Spittle flew out of her mouth, and Joy sat still as the drops landed on her cheeks. Fear of being shot kept her from wiping the disgusting specks off her face.

"Agent Iverson is an American," Joy said. "Yet he risked his life to protect Americans and Afghans alike—from the Taliban and al Qaeda. He went in and arrested the men who'd hurt your family."

Those dark eyes were on her. A flicker of hope, belief perhaps?

Sameen shook her head.

"No. You'd like to think that, I'm sure. Helps you sleep at night. But that scum Farid you set free from prison had your lover boy under his spell the whole time. They were in it together!"

"Farid never wanted anyone in his village to suffer. That's why he was on the right side. And they didn't know one another before the Special Forces went in to get the Taliban out of your village."

"You lie! Farid was a traitor to our people!" Her captor's eyes were bouncing all over the place, her body rigid with determination. "Our fight started long before America was even its own country. You have no way of understanding."

Please keep talking.

Joy snuck a glance at the microwave clock to her right. How much longer until Brad got here?

What if he stopped at his office first?

"Please explain it to me. What do you expect to gain by this?"

"I will gain justice for what happened to me and my family. I went through what no girl should ever have to! And I will do what Hasan needs done here."

She gave Joy a hard shove as she let go of her neck, tipping her over the stool and onto the kitchen floor. A dull crack, followed by a sharp pain told Joy she had at least one fractured rib.

Darkness edged around her vision, and she forced herself to breathe, despite the pain. She had to stay present. Ready to help Brad.

"Get up!" The woman kicked her in the back, and an entire galaxy of stars danced across Joy's line of sight. Getting on her knees took all the stamina she had left, but she managed. Once on all fours, she actually felt the searing pain lessen a bit.

The woman's booted feet were next to her thighs, and Joy knew that if she didn't keep moving as Sameen had ordered, she'd get kicked in the kidneys again. "I said get up."

Joy looked over her right shoulder and saw the gun in Sameen's hand as she leaned against the stove. Sameen raised her left leg to kick again, and this time Joy went for broke.

Using an old fitness class move known as the "fire hydrant," she kicked at Sameen's left knee with her right leg using all the power she could muster. A split second later she heard the crunch of bones as Sameen cried out in pain. A surge of satisfaction rose in Joy.

Until she heard the ring of a gunshot and felt a crushing weight.

She couldn't breathe.

BRAD SAW THEM through the blinds he'd installed on his back kitchen door. He couldn't see much of the suspect, only her black pants and jacket—and flashes of light reflecting from the barrel of her revolver. She was built like a woman but he hadn't known for sure until he'd heard her voice through the door.

His primal inclinations fought a full-on battle with his training, and Mike's admonition not to *go cowboy*. While he didn't plan to wait for the team to show up if he didn't have to, he couldn't go charging or even sneaking in there. Not when a terrorist had a loaded gun pointed at Joy.

The suspect was a trained killer.

Joy was watching the suspect with her lawyerly expression, lips moving. Her voice was a soft murmur; he couldn't make out any words. He knew she was taking in every detail of the criminal's actions. An immediate image of her head blown open by a bullet almost had him losing it, and he had to forcibly keep his hands on the door frame.

The scene playing out in front of him changed in an instant as he saw the suspect lean over, obscuring his view of Joy. The next instant, the woman was on the other side of the island, out of his sight. Joy was gone.

"Get up!"

At the woman's harsh yell, he quietly turned the handle on the door and prayed it had been left unlocked.

It didn't budge.

He couldn't do this quietly, after all. He could take the time to put his key in the lock, or he could take the quickest action.

Please, Joy, get up. Hold on, sweetheart.

"Get up!"

On the second command, he braced himself and lunged at the door, just as a gunshot rang through the kitchen.

HE ENTERED A scene of utter chaos. The woman, a figure dressed all in black, was splayed across Joy, her breath coming in short gasps of obvious pain. Across the kitchen in the entry hall stood Farid, holding his upper arm. Blood stained his white shirt, the mark expanding.

"Get off her!" Brad dove toward the suspect.

"Brad, wait! She has a knife," Farid yelled.

Only as Brad landed near the two women, ready to grab the suspect and drag her off Joy, did he see the steel tip that she held against Joy's neck. Joy was facedown, unconscious. Not dead, he hoped.

He prayed.

He couldn't lose her. He loved her.

"FBI. Get the hell off her, now!"

"Back off or I'll slit her throat. I should've done it sooner." The terrorist panted out the words. The gun was out of sight. She must have dropped it on the way down. It had obviously misfired, and then she'd drawn her knife.

Brad hated knives. With a bullet there was always a chance of its missing the mark or being stopped by Kevlar.

Not a blade. A blade went right where you stuck it. And the woman had her blade under Joy's neck, against her jugular.

"It's me you want, not her."

"Call your team off if you want to talk to me." Her eyes burned with hatred.

Team?

He looked around. Farid was gone from the hallway and there was no team here yet.

She hadn't seen Farid; when she'd heard his voice, she'd probably thought he was one of the agents.

"Back off, guys!" he shouted as if there were a dozen agents in the living room. All the while he was trying to find evidence that Joy was still alive. Her face was so pale, and she hadn't moved. There was no blood around her, and judging from Farid's bleeding arm, the shot he'd heard had gone wild and hit him, not Joy.

But this criminal had had Joy alone for at least twenty, maybe even thirty minutes. What had she done to her?

"They're gone," he said. "We can talk."

He silently willed the terrorist to get off Joy, to let him see her breathe. To be certain she didn't have any other injuries.

Instead, the suspect grunted.

"What's to talk about? You're one of them. She's going to die, and it's all your fault." She enunciated her words with great effort, her breathing labored. Brad couldn't tell how she'd been injured, though.

"You don't have to do this. Maybe you and I can cut a deal."

"You're just desperate. You know you'll be dead next. I want to make you suffer before you die."

"You're already in a heap of trouble. I can help you get through this. You have information we need. Give me the knife and we'll talk."

"Get down here, closer." Her voice was harder to hear. She was weakening, or pretending to.

Brad bent over, keeping a safe enough distance so that he could take her out with his pistol if he had to without risking injury to Joy.

"Leave your pistol on the floor. I want to see your bare hands."

Fear, pure and lethal, flooded Brad's awareness. Without his weapon, she could kill Joy with one flick of her wrist.

He placed the gun on the floor and showed her his bare hands.

"Closer. I need to see your face."

Brad leaned in. "Why? What do you want?"

"I want to see your face when I cut the life out of her."

"No!" Brad reached for her wrist at the same

time a gunshot sounded. Her hand went slack under Brad's.

Brad looked up into Farid's steady gaze.

"I saw her drop the pistol when Joy kicked her in the knee. While you were talking to her, I picked it up."

A soft moan directed Brad's attention back to Joy. Her eyes were open, and she seemed to be in a lot of pain.

But alive.

Thank God, Joy was alive.

"WE NEED YOU to give us room, sir."

The past half hour had been a combination horror show and medical drama as the Bureau team stormed in seconds after Farid had taken out Sameen, along with the EMTs who examined and now ministered to Joy. For a third time, the burly one told Brad to get out of the room.

"I'm not going anywhere."

Joy's eyes were filled with tears as she looked at him. He wasn't sure how cognizant she was. Could she be in shock? There was dried blood on her neck and the front of her shirt, which the EMTs had cut open to reveal her pale skin and bruising under her bra line.

"Go." She said the word from behind her oxygen mask, but Brad refused to budge.

A heavy hand on his shoulder squeezed until he looked up.

"Mike."

"I need to talk to you, Brad. She's going to be okay—just a broken rib or two."

"And a punctured lung." He'd hung on every word the EMTs had said when they called in to the hospital. He hated seeing her struggle to breathe.

"Nothing life-threatening. Let them do their work."

Mike all but dragged him from the area where the EMTs worked and led him into the living room. The front door was wide-open as another EMT, flanked by FBI agents, wheeled out Sameen on a gurney. She'd been shot by Farid but not lethally. He'd hit her shoulder.

"I was too late," Brad muttered. "She almost got her."

"You were just in time. Any sooner and you might have agitated her—she might've killed Joy then and there. Later, and yeah, it would've been too late. But she wanted you to see her suffer, you know. Wanted you to go through what she'd been through. It's how she thought she'd get some kind of sick closure."

"Was she involved with the cell I was in?"

"Yes, the analysts have confirmed that she helped the suspect you knew as Snake bring the other two into the cell. She's the one who has the connection to Hasan. We knew there was at least one more, if not several, so the pieces have come together now that we have her."

"She almost killed her, Mike," he said again. "Joy, she didn't, she—"

"Take it easy, buddy. Sit down." Mike motioned toward the grass.

"I'm not sitting down."

Mike pushed his shoulders until Brad was on his ass under the large oak tree in front of his house. Mike sat next to him, and they both leaned against the tree as if they were talking about the Mariners and not how close they'd come to losing Joy.

"Joy's going to be all right. We have Sameen in custody—she'll give us the answers we need about Hasan." He paused. "Farid handled things well in there. It's worked out, Brad. Stop beating yourself up."

"Easy for you to say." He ran his hand over his head, his face. His skin was on fire, and he felt an indescribable urge to run, jump or pound his fist into the tree. Or do it all at the same time.

"Joy won't blame you for this."

"She should."

"No, she shouldn't, and she won't. She knew what she was dealing with. She had one of her heavy-hitting JAG friends do some research."

"How do you know?"

"I got a call from some higher-ups this morning. Navy Admiral Helen Bolling called in the information she'd figured out when Joy went to visit her. Joy couldn't shake the feeling that the people controlling the cell were about to call the sleepers into action. Joy feared they were after you and Grimes personally."

"She never told me. And you said nothing when I saw you earlier!"

"She was protecting you. She knew you'd go looking for Sameen if you knew."

"Do you think anything would've made a difference with Sameen if we'd made the connection sooner?"

Mike sat there quietly for several minutes, mulling over Brad's question. Brad thought of all the other times the two of them had hashed out missions together, pieced together the *who*s, the *why*s, the *when*s. Sometimes you didn't walk away with a clear answer.

"I spoke with one of the profilers earlier. Sameen's upbringing in a war-torn part of the world shaped who she is. It was only a matter of time before she snapped. Thanks to Hasan, she'd known who you were for quite a while. She'd already tracked you here, and the fact that you showed up in that cell as her boyfriend's new recruit was a sign to her. She was intent on making you suffer and taking you out. And then when she realized you'd disrupted the SAM shoot-down of US aircraft, she was incensed."

"How have you pieced all of this together?"

Mike pulled at a blade of grass. "The other suspects have revealed a lot since we took them into custody. And her boyfriend—he's a spineless piece of shit. That's why she could manipulate him so easily."

"She's caught, but Hasan's still out there."

"He is, and by this time next week I hope to hear that he's been disabled."

They shared another quiet moment. The terrorist behind what could have been the first anti-aircraft missile attack by terrorists in the United States would be captured by spec ops, most likely a SEAL team. They knew the danger involved.

"What a mess." While he cared deeply about justice for all concerned, his focus didn't veer far from one woman. Joy.

"Have you told her how you feel yet, Brad?"

"I can't."

Mike turned to face him. He looked startled—as startled as Brad felt—that he hadn't told his boss to go screw himself instead of answering so candidly.

Emotions weren't their usual topic of conversation.

"What do you mean you can't?"

"It's not fair to her. She never asked for this, and look what getting involved with me got her. If it's not Hasan, it could be another bad guy we pissed off during our time downrange or in some FBI undercover op. It never ends."

"You're not God. Stop playing the part. If you'd wrapped up your undercover op the old-fashioned way, with little fanfare and all three suspects quietly arrested, would you have thought you'd dragged her into anything?"

"No, but I wouldn't have gotten this involved with her, either."

"Oh, really? What *would* you have done? Gone out for a few drinks, dinner, a couple nights in the sack?"

Brad stared at his friend. "It was never going to be casual with her." His heart already knew that; it was his brain that had trouble catching up.

"They don't call you an FBI agent for nothing." Mike laughed, and Brad started to laugh then stopped himself.

"Screw you, Mike."

CHAPTER TWENTY-THREE

IT TOOK TWO hours on Monday morning for Joy to be discharged from the hospital in Seattle, where she'd been since Saturday afternoon. But she was finally able to put the horrors of the past week behind her. She smiled at Emily and Ben, who'd come to take her back to Whidbey. Joy let Emily ease her into the car, and held her breath as her friend buckled her seat belt.

"Thanks, Em."

"No problem, sweetie. Just happy to have you out of there and in one piece."

"Ready?" Ben sat in the driver's seat of the large luxury SUV, with Joy beside him.

"We're ready." Emily answered from the seat behind Ben's.

"I feel like a third wheel here, folks. Not to mention an invalid." She was thrilled for Emily that Ben was turning out to be more than just another man who tried to date her, but not completely comfortable around the two of them yet. She still felt hurt that she'd heard nothing from

Brad since he'd held her hand on Saturday until the EMTs came.

"You'll never be anything but our friend, Joy." Emily spoke with sincerity, and Joy didn't miss that she'd said *our*.

She'd expected Brad to come and see her. A huge bouquet of red roses had been delivered, unsigned. She assumed they were from him, but was she just kidding herself? Emily had insisted on putting the roses in the backseat for the ride back to Whidbey, and the car smelled like a florist shop. They sat next to a huge stuffed bulldog wearing a US Marine Corps outfit, a get-well gift from General Grimes.

Within minutes it was clear that Ben wasn't driving toward Whidbey. He was, in fact, maneuvering his large vehicle through the streets near Brad's neighborhood.

"Where are we going?"

"The best place in the world for you."

She turned to look at Em, and a sharp pain sliced through her left side. "Ouch!"

"Shhh. Stay calm, Joy. No need to get upset. You'll mess up that rib, and you don't want your lung crapping out on you again."

"It. Didn't. Crap. Out." She had to take a breath between each word, and a shallow one at that. A fractured rib and collapsed lung were a small price to pay for her life. Still, they were quite sore.

Believing her chance with Brad had come and gone, she was annoyed that they were bringing her to his place.

What the heck was this all about, anyway?

"Em's right. You're the lawyer here, and we're the medical professionals. Trust us when we tell you we're doing the best possible thing for you."

She couldn't find the words for a polite retort and besides, it hurt like hell to talk.

She'd save it for Brad, because they'd just turned onto his street. If they were going to stop at his place, she'd have some things to say to him, all right.

"MR. BRAD, DO you think she'll like the soup?"

Farid stirred the big pot of mystery stew he'd insisted on making for Joy's return. Brad had to rely on Emily and Ben to get the medical lowdown on her recuperation needs. He'd wanted to give her space, and to give himself time.

When you were going to make such a big change in your life, there was no sense in rushing it.

"It smells good, Farid. What's in it that's supposed to be so good?"

"Special spices that will help sweat out the sickness."

"She doesn't have a sickness, pal, just a broken rib and a sore lung."

"This will help, believe me."

"Whatever you say."

He pulled out sparkling juice for Joy, since her painkillers weren't going to mix well with alcohol, and real bubbly for the rest of them. Hopefully, they'd have something to celebrate this afternoon.

Nervous as a teen on his first date, he checked the front window for the umpteenth time. The black Lexus SUV turning into his driveway had to belong to Ben, Emily's boyfriend.

Sure enough, a tall man got out on the driver's side and opened the door for a smaller woman he assumed was Emily. She gave Ben a quick kiss on the mouth before she walked around the car to open the front passenger door and help Joy out. The brief glimpse he caught of Joy's face made his stomach drop with worry. She was pale and looked stressed.

Pain. She was in major pain. Because of him.

He opened the front door, forcing himself not to march down the steps and haul her into his arms. It would hurt her too much, anyway.

"Hi, Brad!" Emily was all smiles, and Ben stepped forward.

"Ben Franklin."

"Brad Iverson." They shook hands.

"Thanks for bringing her home."

"We wouldn't have let anyone else do it." Emily kept her hand under Joy's forearm for balance. Joy remained silent, her focus on his front porch steps.

"Can I help?" He held out his hand to Joy.

It felt as though it'd been years since he'd stared into her beautiful eyes. At her beautiful face. Her beautiful mouth.

"What's wrong? Are my battle wounds that bad?" She grasped his hand, and he noticed that her words were clear but slow. He'd had his share of cracked ribs and knew the kind of pain she was in.

"You're beautiful."

"I'm not feeling beautiful." She started to smile at him but then faltered, as if remembering something. Anger sparked in her eyes, and his Joy was back.

"Where have you been these last few days?"

"I had some things to take care of. To get ready."

"Ready for what?"

"Trust me."

He knew she was a private person, knew that her friends and Farid were watching.

What the hell.

He leaned over and kissed her full on the lips. He refused to lift his mouth from hers until he got a satisfactory response.

THEY ALL REMAINED at the dining room table, much to Joy's relief, as sitting in a firmer chair gave her more support. The thought of sinking into Brad's sofa was appealing, but getting out of it, not so much.

"I still can't believe you risked coming out of protection to warn Brad, Farid."

"It was the least I could do. You both saved my life. When I saw the names of the suspects they arrested, I knew they were related to Hasan somehow, and that they'd try to find Brad. I was really worried when I saw it was near where you live. I found you on Facebook, but never tried to friend you."

"Well, thank you. I'm so sorry you're going to have to start all over again."

"It's not so bad. I'm requesting that my girl-friend join me."

"You have a girlfriend?"

"I'm hoping she'll be my wife someday. And I owe it to you and Mr. Brad. And even to General Grimes. He wasn't happy you two got me free, but his testimony didn't hurt me."

"I wouldn't have let it." Her chest muscles ached, and she realized she was getting too worked up.

"Do you need to rest?" Brad's hand was on hers, his eyes full of what she'd always dreamed she'd see there—concern, caring and maybe more.

"I'm fine. I'm sure we'll be leaving soon."

She caught Emily shooting Ben a knowing look and laughed.

"Now what do you have up your sleeves, Emily?"

Emily coughed. "It's really not our place to say."

"So you've tossed me the ball, eh?" Brad smiled at Em, and Joy felt her heart squeeze with happiness. Her best friend and the man she loved had met, and they liked each other.

"Joy, I need your full attention. After this, I promise you'll get some rest."

"You mean go home."

"That's just it. You'll recuperate here. You *are* home. I mean, I want you to think of this as your home. As well as your place on Whidbey Island, of course."

"Okaaaaay." What was he getting at?

"Only one week together—even if it felt like a year—might not be enough time for you to know whether what we have is going to last. It's more than enough time for me, however, and I'm willing to wait, Joy. For as long as it takes you to decide that I'm the one for you. Because I've already decided. It's been in my heart since I met you. I love you, and I want to spend the rest of my life with you."

"Brad, I don't think this is the place for this conversation." The words were automatic as she tried to fully absorb what he was saying. What he was promising her.

"I'm not finished."

He stood up and walked to the threshold between the dining room and kitchen.

"I wanted to show you something that would prove my commitment to a long-term relationship. I could tell you I'm leaving the Bureau, which I have."

"You have?" Her voice squeaked.

"I could tell you I'm looking for a place on Whidbey to have my own office. I'm opening a private investigative service for the Whidbey, Fidalgo and Camano Island area."

"You are?"

"I could tell you I've already made Emily and Ben promise they'll be at our wedding."

"You—*what*?"

"But I think the best symbol of commitment from a man like me is something alive."

He disappeared into the kitchen, and she heard the back door open and close. He returned moments later, Farid at his side and a puppy in his arms.

"You got a dog?"

"No, Joy, *we* got a dog. Meet Virginia."

He walked over to her and gingerly put the puppy in her lap, carefully keeping his hands on the squirming pile of golden fur.

"Hi, Virginia." She looked up at Brad. "Come here, you."

It was her turn to put him on the spot the way he'd done to her with his kiss on the front porch. She ignored the pain and wrapped her arm around his neck, pulling him down.

"I believe you, Brad. I believe *in* you. And I believe in *us*—and Virginia."

She kissed him until Emily, Ben and Farid broke out in applause. He waited until *she'd* ended the kiss, which she liked very much. She smiled up at him and knew she'd come home.

"Will you stay with me, Joy?"

"Forever."

* * * * *

Joy and Brad invite you to enjoy the casserole they made at Joy's house...

Joy's Mac and Gruyere for Brad

Ingredients:

½ lb. whole-wheat elbow pasta
¼ c. MELT® (butter substitute)
¼ c. whole wheat flour
2 c. 1% milk
2 tsp. mustard powder
½ tsp. ground pepper
6 oz. sharp cheddar, shredded/grated
6 oz. Gruyere, shredded/grated
Panko bread crumbs for topping, if desired
1 lb. lean organic ground beef/turkey/chicken
(optional)

Directions:

Preheat oven to 350° F.

Brown meat in a saucepan (cook in a teaspoon of olive oil if you need to for very lean meat). Set aside.

Prepare noodles as directed on package, boiling until cooked al dente. Drain and set aside.

To make the sauce, melt the MELT over low heat, add flour and stir/whisk briskly until smooth. Slowly stir in milk, avoiding clumps. Add mustard powder and pepper. Heat until sauce quietly bubbles. Remove from heat and add cheeses, stirring until smooth and creamy.

Stir pasta and meat into the sauce until pasta is coated. Pour into an 8" square baking dish or 2 quart casserole. Top with ¼ cup of panko crumbs if desired.

Bake for 25–30 minutes, until golden brown.

LARGER-PRINT BOOKS!
GET 2 FREE LARGER-PRINT NOVELS PLUS
2 FREE GIFTS!

HARLEQUIN®

super romance®

More Story...More Romance

HSRLP15

LARGER-PRINT BOOKS!
GET 2 FREE LARGER-PRINT NOVELS PLUS
2 FREE GIFTS!

HARLEQUIN®

Romance

From the Heart, For the Heart

YES! Please send me 2 FREE LARGER-PRINT Harlequin® Romance novels and my 2 FREE gifts (gifts are worth about $10). After receiving them, if I don't wish to receive any more books, I can return the shipping statement marked "cancel." If I don't cancel, I will receive 4 brand-new novels every month and be billed just $5.09 per book in the U.S. or $5.49 per book in Canada. That's a savings of at least 15% off the cover price! It's quite a bargain! Shipping and handling is just 50¢ per book in the U.S. and 75¢ per book in Canada.* I understand that accepting the 2 free books and gifts places me under no obligation to buy anything. I can always return a shipment and cancel at any time. Even if I never buy another book, the two free books and gifts are mine to keep forever.

119/319 HDN GHWC

Name	(PLEASE PRINT)

Address	Apt. #

City	State/Prov.	Zip/Postal Code

Signature (if under 18, a parent or guardian must sign)

Mail to the **Reader Service:**
IN U.S.A.: P.O. Box 1867, Buffalo, NY 14240-1867
IN CANADA: P.O. Box 609, Fort Erie, Ontario L2A 5X3
Want to try two free books from another line?
Call 1-800-873-8635 or visit www.ReaderService.com.

* Terms and prices subject to change without notice. Prices do not include applicable taxes. Sales tax applicable in N.Y. Canadian residents will be charged applicable taxes. Offer not valid in Quebec. This offer is limited to one order per household. Not valid for current subscribers to Harlequin Romance Larger-Print books. All orders subject to credit approval. Credit or debit balances in a customer's account(s) may be offset by any other outstanding balance owed by or to the customer. Please allow 4 to 6 weeks for delivery. Offer available while quantities last.

Your Privacy—The Reader Service is committed to protecting your privacy. Our Privacy Policy is available online at www.ReaderService.com or upon request from the Reader Service.

We make a portion of our mailing list available to reputable third parties that offer products we believe may interest you. If you prefer that we not exchange your name with third parties, or if you wish to clarify or modify your communication preferences, please visit us at www.ReaderService.com/consumerschoice or write to us at Reader Service Preference Service, P.O. Box 9062, Buffalo, NY 14240-9062. Include your complete name and address.